SIXKILLER,

EIGHT

TO

SIXKILLER, U.S. MARSHAL:
EIGHT HOURS TO DIE

William W. Johnstone
with J. A. Johnstone

PINNACLE BOOKS
Kensington Publishing Corp.
www.kensingtonbooks.com

PINNACLE BOOKS are published by

Kensington Publishing Corp.
119 West 40th Street
New York, NY 10018

PUBLISHER'S NOTE
Following the death of William W. Johnstone, the Johnstone family is working with a carefully selected writer to organize and complete Mr. Johnstone's outlines and many unfinished manuscripts to create additional novels in all of his series like The Last Gunfighter, Mountain Man, and Eagles, among others. This novel was inspired by Mr. Johnstone's superb storytelling.

All Kensington titles, imprints, and distributed lines are available at special quantity discounts for bulk purchases for sales promotions, premiums, fund-raising, educational, or institutional use. Special book excerpts or customized printings can also be created to fit specific needs. For details, write or phone the office of the Kensington special sales manager: Kensington Publishing Corp., 119 West 40th Street, New York, NY 10018, attn: Special Sales Department; phone 1-800-221-2647.

ISBN-13: 978-0-7860-2903-7
ISBN-10: 0-7860-2903-X

First printing: December 2012

10 9 8 7 6 5 4 3 2 1

Printed in the United States of America

Chapter One

A telegram was waiting for Deputy United States Marshal John Henry Sixkiller when he got to El Paso. It was from his boss, Judge Isaac Parker in Fort Smith, Arkansas.

John Henry was on his way back to Arkansas from an assignment in the western part of New Mexico Territory. Before leading his horse, Iron Heart, into a stable car and boarding the Southern Pacific train in Lordsburg, he had wired Judge Parker to let the judge know that he was on his way home.

Parker must have immediately sent his telegram to the railroad station in El Paso, along with a request that when the train John Henry was on arrived, someone there should find the deputy marshal and pass along the message.

The porter who brought the telegram came along the aisle of the passenger car where John

Henry sat, calling, "Lookin' for John Henry Sixkiller! John Henry Sixkiller!"

"I'm Sixkiller," John Henry said as he stood up from the bench seat. He was in the first of the passenger cars, which had saved the red-jacketed porter from having to search all of them. "Is something wrong?"

"No, sir, just got a wire for you."

The uniformed man held out a yellow telegraph flimsy. John Henry took it and gave the porter a half dollar. Then he sat down, thumbed back his hat, and unfolded the message to read it.

URGENT YOU MEET WITH LEW WALLACE
GOVERNOR NMT IN SANTA FE STOP RENDER
ALL DUE ASSISTANCE WALLACE REQUESTS
STOP PARKER.

You couldn't get much plainer than that, John Henry thought.

The porter was still standing there, probably in the hope of getting another half dollar if John Henry wanted to send a reply, which was indeed the case.

First, though, John Henry asked, "When's the next train leaving for Santa Fe?"

The porter took out his watch and checked it.

"'Bout an hour and a half from now," he replied as he snapped the timepiece closed. "You need a ticket on it, sir?"

"I do. And I need to send a reply to this wire, as well."

"The Western Union office is on the other side of the depot lobby. If you'd like, I can get the ticket while you send your telegram, Mr. Sixkiller."

John Henry nodded and gave the man money for the ticket. He reached down to pick up his carpetbag.

"I've got a horse in the stable car, too, along with my saddle and rifle. They'll need to go on the train bound for Santa Fe."

"I'll take care of it."

John Henry gave the porter an extra dollar this time. He left the train and headed through the lobby toward the Western Union window.

When he got there he picked up a telegraph form and a stub of pencil and printed his reply to Parker, which was a simple one:

UNDERSTOOD STOP WILL COMPLY STOP
SIXKILLER.

By the time he'd sent the message, the porter was there with his ticket for the train to Santa Fe, which appropriately enough would be an Atchison, Topeka, & Santa Fe train.

"I'll have your things brought to you here," the porter said. "You can wait in the lobby. Your horse will be tied up just outside."

"I'm obliged," John Henry told him.

He sat down on one of the hard benches to wait.

It was a shame he hadn't gotten that telegram a few minutes earlier, he thought. His traveling companion from Lordsburg, Miss Sophie Clearwater, had already left the train, saying that she planned to stay here in El Paso for a few days on business.

If John Henry had known he was going to have more than an hour to kill, he might have tried to prevail on Sophie to linger and keep him company until he left for Santa Fe. The time would have passed more pleasantly with her around, that was for sure, he told himself with a sigh.

But there was nothing that could be done about it now. He had said his good-byes to Sophie, and that was that. Someone had left a newspaper on the bench, so John Henry picked it up and began leafing through it instead.

He hadn't been looking at the paper for long when three young men came into the depot from the street entrance. They were dressed like cowboys, and the well-worn saddles they carried on their shoulders were further evidence that was their profession.

John Henry barely glanced at them when they came in, and that was only because they were talking loudly among themselves and laughing. Even though it was the middle of the afternoon, they seemed to have been drinking.

He would have ignored them as they walked on past the bench where he sat, if not for the fact that one of the men stopped short and the other two then followed suit. All three of them set their saddles on the floor at their feet.

The one who had stopped first stared at John Henry for a moment and then said, "Look at that, boys. Unless I miss my guess, that there's an Injun in white man's duds."

John Henry heard the words but pretended to ignore them. He didn't want any trouble. These cowhands could say whatever they wanted to as long as they moved on.

"You sure about that, Wiley?" one of the other young men asked. "He don't really look like an Injun to me."

"You ever see anybody with red skin like that who wasn't?"

The third man laughed and said, "Yeah, me when I was blistered by the sun."

"And I think his eyes are blue, too," the second cowboy put in.

"That don't mean nothin' except that he's a stinkin' breed," Wiley insisted. He moved a step closer to John Henry and went on, "Hey, mister. You a stinkin' breed? Your mama get carried off by some Comanche or Apache buck?"

John Henry sighed. The young cowboy called Wiley was drunk, stubborn, and obnoxious . . . a bad combination. John Henry folded the newspaper in fourths longwise, set it in his lap, and said, "I'm half Cherokee, and I don't appreciate your comments. I'd take it kindly if you wouldn't say anything else about my mother."

"Cherokee, eh?" Wiley said. "Hell, from what I've heard they ain't even real Injuns. Of course, they ain't white, neither. I don't know what that makes you, mister. Some sort of mongrel dog, I reckon."

Wiley's companions must have gotten the idea that harassing this calm, powerfully built, gun-toting stranger probably wasn't a very smart thing to do. One of them tugged at his friend's arm and said, "Come on, Wiley, we got a train to catch."

Wiley pulled free with a violent shrug.

"Hell with that," he snapped. "Did you hear the way this redskin talked to me? Like he thought he was better than me? I ain't gonna stand for that!"

John Henry thought about pushing back the lapel of his coat to reveal the badge pinned to his shirt. He had concealed his true identity as a federal lawman for much of his just-concluded assignment, but there was no reason for him to do so here in El Paso. Usually the sight of a tin star would make even a drunk think twice about raising a ruckus.

Before he could do that, however, Wiley kicked at the sole of John Henry's boot and said, "Get up on your feet, you son of a bitch. You're wearin' a gun like a white man, so we'll settle this like white men! I'm callin' you out!"

"Wiley, you damned fool—" one of his companions began.

John Henry stood up, still holding the folded newspaper in his left hand.

"Mister, please don't kill him," the other young cowhand pleaded. "He's just drunker'n a skunk."

"I know that," John Henry said. "You should take him somewhere and let him sober up."

"Damn your red hide!" Wiley howled, drawing the attention of everybody in the lobby now. "Stop talkin' about me like I ain't here!"

He clawed at the butt of the revolver holstered at his hip.

Chapter Two

John Henry took a quick step forward and whipped the newspaper across Wiley's face. The blow didn't do any real damage, but it stung and took the young cowboy by surprise. Blinking, he stepped back.

That gave John Henry room to swing a hard punch with his right hand. His fist connected solidly with Wiley's jaw and jerked his head to the side. Wiley staggered back a step.

John Henry tossed the paper onto the bench behind him and bored in, hooking a left to Wiley's stomach, then hitting him with another right to the jaw.

That was enough to make Wiley's knees unhinge. He fell on them, then pitched forward to land facedown on the depot floor.

Instinct made John Henry glance toward the other two young men. They might have tried to steer their friend away from the fight, but now that the ruckus had started, their rough code of honor forced them to back Wiley's play. They came at John Henry from both sides, their fists swinging.

He ducked a punch from the closest of the young cowboys, grabbed the front of the man's shirt, and swung him around so that he crashed into the third puncher. Their feet got tangled up with each other and they went down, sprawling on the floor close to their unconscious pard.

As the two men struggled to get up, John Henry stepped back and rested his right hand on the butt of his Colt. He used his left to pull back his coat as he said, "Better just let it go, fellas. There's been no real harm done so far, and I'd like to keep it that way."

Their eyes got wide when they saw the badge. One of them said, "Good Lord, Phil, he's a lawman!"

The other puncher groaned.

"You ain't gonna arrest us and throw us in jail, are you, Sheriff?" he asked. "We got ridin' jobs waitin' for us at Sierra Blanca, and we sure do need 'em."

"I reckon a sore jaw's punishment enough for your pard," John Henry said with a faint smile. "And I'm not a sheriff, I'm a deputy U.S. marshal. The last time I checked, being young and obnoxious wasn't a federal offense, so we'll just let it go at that."

As a matter of fact, in terms of years he wasn't that much older than the three cowhands. But he had seen and done a lot in his time as a lawman, first as a member of the Cherokee Lighthorse, then as chief sheriff of the Cherokee Nation, and now as a federal deputy. That sort of life sometimes made a man older than his years.

The two cowhands climbed to their feet and picked up Wiley, who was starting to come around. They held him between them as he moaned and shook his head groggily.

"We're sure obliged to you for not arrestin' us," one of the men said.

"Don't worry about it," John Henry told them. "Just go on and catch your train. And maybe don't drink quite so much the next time you're in a saloon."

"You can count on that, Marshal," the other cowboy promised.

They helped Wiley from the lobby onto the platform. John Henry sat down and picked up the newspaper again. He was aware that a number of people in the station were looking at him and obviously trying not to stare. The fight had been a short one, but the way he'd handled the three cowboys had been impressive.

A couple of uniformed policemen wearing black-billed caps came into the train station from the street. They moved briskly, like they were there on business, and John Henry wasn't surprised when they spoke to a ticket clerk and then came across the lobby toward him.

"Stand up, mister," one of the policemen said when they reached John Henry.

Telling himself to be patient, he laid the newspaper aside again and stood up, making sure his coat was open enough that they could see his badge. They noticed it right away, and he saw the change that came over them when they did.

"Sorry to bother you, Marshal. We got a report that somebody was brawlin' in here, and it's our job to keep the peace."

"Of course it is," John Henry agreed. "You can see for yourself, though, the fight's over. It never really amounted to much."

"You were the *hombre* who was attacked?"

"It was just a misunderstanding," John Henry said.

"We can arrest the fellas who jumped you," the other policeman said.

John Henry shook his head.

"There's no need for that. No harm was done. I'd just as soon let the matter end."

"Well, if you're sure . . ."

"I'm certain," John Henry said. "I'm just waiting for a train."

"Where are you bound for, if you don't mind my askin'?"

"Santa Fe." John Henry didn't mention that he was supposed to see the governor once he got there.

"Beautiful town."

"So I've heard. I'm looking forward to seeing it."

And he was mighty curious why Governor Lew Wallace wanted to see him, too.

Santa Fe was indeed pretty, nestled as it was in the foothills of the Sangre de Cristo Mountains. Rugged, snowcapped peaks loomed in the distance, and the sky was one of the bluest blues John Henry had ever seen.

Santa Fe was also an old, old town, and that air of antiquity clung to many of the adobe buildings lining the narrow, crooked streets. John Henry had saddled Iron Heart when he left the train, and now he rode along looking for the Palace of the Governors, where the territorial government was headquartered. One of the ticket clerks at the train station had given him directions to the place.

In the meantime, he enjoyed the colorful, bustling scene. The streets were busy and crowded with people of all ages, shapes, colors, and sizes. Although New Mexico Territory was now part of the United States, it had spent a long time under Spanish rule and then had been a part of Mexico until only a few decades earlier. Most of the faces John Henry saw were brown, and most of the voices he heard spoke in rapid-fire Spanish. He understood some of it, but not much.

Mixed in with the descendants of the town's original settlers was a sizable percentage of whites, many of them dressed like businessmen. Ever since the opening of the Santa Fe Trail while this was still part of Mexico, trade had been the most important part of life in this settlement. There was still a steady flow of goods back and forth, but most of it was shipped by rail now, rather than in long wagon trains.

John Henry found the Palace of the Governors without much trouble, although navigating the labyrinth of streets was kind of a challenge. The Palace was a long, low, sprawling adobe building with a covered gallery along its front and a number of different doors. John Henry dismounted, looped Iron Heart's reins around one of the hitch racks, and went to the nearest door. It opened into a wide lobby.

A few minutes of being passed from functionary to functionary brought him to Governor Lew Wallace's office. The governor had quite a reputation as a general in the Union Army during the Civil War. John Henry had fought on the other side during that conflict, as many of the Cherokee had, but he bore no grudges now toward the North and the men who had served the Union.

A smoothly handsome, expensively dressed man stood up from a chair in the governor's outer office and extended a hand to John Henry.

"Marshal Sixkiller?"

"That's right," John Henry said as he gripped the man's hand for a moment. "And you are . . . ?"

"Filipe Montoya, one of the governor's aides. I'm told that you're here on official business?"

"I suppose. I don't really know much about it, Señor Montoya. I got a telegram from my boss asking me to come here and meet with the governor."

"You would think that I'd be aware of this, as closely as I work with Governor Wallace on territorial matters." Montoya seemed a little put out by the fact that he hadn't been informed of John Henry's visit until now, but he forced a smile and went on. "Ah well, I suppose I'll find out soon enough, if this is something the governor needs my assistance on. Please, come this way."

Montoya ushered John Henry over to a massive wooden door and knocked on it. When a voice called from the other side of the door and told them to come in, Montoya opened it and held out a hand to indicate that John Henry should go first.

"This is Marshal Sixkiller, Governor," Montoya said as he and John Henry entered Wallace's private office.

Wallace sat at a large desk with a window behind him that looked out across the plaza on which the Palace was located. He had a pen in his hand and was writing on a piece of paper. Without looking up from what he was doing, he said, "I'll be with you in just a moment, Marshal." As an afterthought, he added, "That'll be all, Filipe."

"Yes, sir," Montoya said, and again he sounded slightly annoyed. John Henry figured he was one of those bureaucratic types who felt like he had to be kept up to date on everything that was going on.

Without being asked, John Henry hung his hat on a hat tree to one side of the door. Wallace finished his writing and put his pen back in its holder. He picked up the sheet of paper, blew on it to help dry the ink, and set it on a fairly thick stack of similar pages. He stood up and came around the desk.

"Sorry to keep you waiting, Marshal," he said as he shook hands with John Henry. "I'm writing a novel, you see, and I feared losing my train of thought if I failed to complete that paragraph before setting it aside."

"Well, Governor, I never wrote anything except a few assignments for school, but I can understand how that might happen, I suppose. What's your book about?"

John Henry knew that Judge Parker hadn't sent him here to discuss literature with Wallace, but it never hurt to take an interest in the things that were important to other folks.

"It's set during the early days of Christianity," Wallace said as he waved John Henry into a comfortable-looking leather chair in front of the desk. "The leading character is a young man named Judah Ben-Hur."

"Sounds interesting," John Henry said as he settled down into the chair, which was as comfortable as it looked.

Wallace smiled. He was a distinguished gentleman, as befitted his military service and his current position as territorial governor. He had a shock of graying hair, a full mustache, and a pointed beard. There was an air of command about him, also appropriate given his background.

"I won't bore you with reading any passages," he said dryly. "Instead I'll get down to business. I contacted Judge Parker because I need a man for a special mission, and it's known far and wide that the deputies who serve under him are, for the most part, extraordinary lawmen."

"We try to do our job," John Henry said.

"It's also important that the man selected for this task not be well known in New Mexico Territory. Judge Parker replied to me that you were already in the vicinity, and you fit that requirement. Are you up to taking on another assignment so soon, Marshal Sixkiller?"

"Judge Parker told me to do whatever I can for you, Governor," John Henry said. "So I reckon I'm at your service."

Wallace grew more solemn and shook his head.

"Three men have already died trying to carry out this mission, Marshal," he said. "I ordered many men to their deaths when I served in the army. That was a necessary evil. These days, I find that it sticks in my craw more than it used to. I won't order you to take this job . . . but I'll admit that I'm in need of your help."

"Why don't you tell me what it's all about?" John Henry suggested.

"Have you ever heard of a town called Chico?"

John Henry thought about the question for a moment, then shook his head.

"No, sir, I don't believe I have."

"It's a couple of days' ride northwest of here, on the other side of the Rio Grande at the edge of the San Juan Mountains. It's located in an area where there are a number of fine ranches, along with a bit of logging and mining. Because of that, Chico was quite a thriving settlement."

John Henry had caught an important distinction in what the governor said. He leaned forward in his chair, frowned slightly, and said, "Was?"

Wallace nodded and said, "Yes. Trouble has descended on Chico and threatens its long-term existence. A man named Dav, Samuel Dav, managed to get himself elected sheriff."

"That's an unusual name."

"Dav is an unusual man," Wallace said. "He's some sort of foreigner, from what I'm told. A Gypsy, perhaps, I'm not sure. But one thing I *am* certain of is that Dav is an outlaw."

"I thought you said he was the sheriff in Chico," John Henry commented.

"He is, but that doesn't make him any less of a villain."

John Henry nodded. He understood now. He had run into a few crooked lawmen in his time, one of them pretty recently. As a man who carried a badge himself, he felt a special anger for anyone who abused that trust.

"I reckon the people of Chico didn't realize what sort of man Dav was until after they put him in office."

"That's right," Wallace said with a nod. "He immediately brought in a small army of deputies, all of them as ruthless and gun-handy as he is, and completely took over the town. He forced the town council to levy special law enforcement taxes that went directly into his own pocket."

"That's the same thing as protection money," John Henry said.

The governor nodded and said, "That's right. In addition, he began charging people to use the town's public well, and he turned the road through a nearby pass into a toll road. The local ranchers have to use that road to get their cattle out to the railroad, but Dav's deputies blocked it off and demanded payment before the herds were allowed to pass."

"Sounds like he's determined to loot as much as he can from those folks."

"And that doesn't even begin to touch on the more personal outrages being committed by Dav and his men." Wallace's mouth was a grim line under the mustache. "No woman is safe on the streets after dark. Any man who speaks up against Dav's brutal tyranny is subject to a savage beating . . . or he just simply disappears in the night. Those people are living in terror, Marshal Sixkiller."

"How do you know about all this?" John Henry

asked. "If Dav is up to such no good, you'd think that he'd keep a tight lid on the place."

"That's exactly what's happened over the past few months. Dav has clamped down tighter and tighter. The first few months after he took office, though, he wasn't as diligent about keeping anyone from getting in or out of Chico. Several of the local leaders managed to send letters to me explaining what was going on and asking for help. One, the editor of the local newspaper, even came to Santa Fe and paid me a visit. I suggested that he shouldn't go back, but he insisted that he had to." Wallace shook his head. "There's no telling what happened to him. Dav may have killed him by now. Things could be even worse than what I've told you. Considerably worse, in fact. Samuel Dav is running Chico like it's a feudal kingdom, Marshal, and he's the lord and master of all he surveys."

"Sounds like somebody needs to take him down a peg," John Henry said.

"I've tried. I've sent in three men, specially appointed investigators, tough men, each and every one of them." Wallace paused. "They've all disappeared as if they'd fallen down the deepest, darkest mine shaft you can imagine. I can't help but believe that they're all dead."

John Henry leaned back in the chair and cocked his right ankle on his left knee.

"Sounds to me like you need to send in the army," he said. "Or at least a big posse of lawmen."

"I don't have that many men to spare right now," Wallace said. "Trouble's heating up down in Lincoln County. It may turn into an outright war down there. I can't put out both of those brush fires at once. And as for the army, this is a civil, criminal matter, not a military one. I'm not going to declare martial law except as a last resort. Besides, if Dav is as vicious and ruthless as I've been told, if the army showed up he might hold the entire town hostage and start killing off the citizens. A standoff like that could turn into a wholesale slaughter."

"So you thought you'd send in one more man first," John Henry mused. "Even though you've lost three so far doing that."

Wallace's face flushed with anger.

"You can see why I said I wouldn't order you to accept this assignment, Marshal," he snapped. "There's a great deal of danger involved. Not only that, but it's somewhat out of the normal range of cases handled by federal officers. New Mexico is still a territory, though, not a state, so I think I can justify federal involvement."

"I'm not worried about jurisdiction," John Henry said. "I was thinking more along the lines of how I would keep Dav from just killing me like he probably killed those other men you sent in."

"I can't tell you that," Wallace said. "All I can do is ask if you'd be willing to give it a try. I don't really know what's going on in Chico right now, Marshal, but I'd be willing to wager that it's pretty bad for the citizens."

John Henry nodded and said, "So would I. That's why I'm going to take you up on it, Governor."

"You'll go to Chico and try to put a stop to Dav's reign of terror?"

"I'll give it my best shot," John Henry said.

And judging from everything Governor Wallace had told him, that was just what it would take.

Hot lead, and plenty of it.

Chapter Three

The mountains around Chico reminded Samuel Dav a little of home. It was true that the San Juans were taller and more rugged than the Carpathians, but the way their darkly wooded slopes cupped the valleys was similar. Chico was much larger and impressive than the tiny villages of his homeland, however. And certainly more profitable . . . for a man willing to take whatever he wanted.

Right now Dav wanted the woman named Lucinda Hammond, and he certainly was willing to do whatever it took to get her.

Of course, he could march into her fine home, put a gun to her head, and force her to do what he wanted, he thought as he leaned against one of the posts holding up the awning over the boardwalk in front of the sheriff's office. He could march up to the street to that mansion he was looking at now and claim his rights.

But that wouldn't be nearly as satisfying as if *she*

came to *him* and begged for it, he thought. Begged him to take her and make her his woman. He just had to be patient and give her a little more time.

After all, it had only been less than two weeks since he had killed her husband.

Footsteps sounded on the boardwalk to Dav's right. He turned his head lazily to see who was approaching him. The citizens of Chico were so thoroughly cowed that he didn't think the new-comer could represent a threat, and he saw that he was right about that. It was one of his deputies, Carl Miller.

The two men were a study in contrasts: Dav tall, whipcord lean, and dark, with a narrow mustache above his cruel mouth, while Miller was short and stocky with a sunburned face and curly fair hair spilling out from under his thumbed-back hat. The men were similar enough in other ways, though, most notably their capacity for ruthless violence.

"The old fella over at the bakery is givin' trouble again, Sam," Miller reported.

"Call me Sheriff," Dav said. "You know better than that."

"Oh yeah, sorry." Miller grinned broadly. "I forget sometimes that we're legal now."

"And as for the baker, you know how to deal with a problem like that."

Miller scratched his heavy jaw and said, "Yeah, but I sort of hate to shoot him. He bakes just about the best bread I ever did taste. Anyway, he said he wanted to talk to you."

"All right, I suppose I can put the fear of God into him." Dav cast one last glance toward the Hammond mansion at the other end of town as he turned to follow Miller toward the bakery.

"More like the fear of the devil," the stocky deputy said with a chuckle. "Some of these ignorant yokels seem to think you're Beelzebub his own self."

Dav smiled and said, "How do you know I'm not?"

Miller chuckled again, but it had a slightly uneasier sound to it this time.

"Don't be funnin' with me that way, Sheriff," the deputy said. "My ma always told me the devil would get me if I didn't straighten up and behave myself."

"And yet you're still here," Dav said mockingly as he clapped a hand on his lieutenant's shoulder. "You make the mistake of believing that there are such things as good and evil in the world, my friend. In reality, there are only those who get what they want . . . and those who don't."

"Yeah, I reckon you're right about that," Miller said.

They had reached Heinsdorf's Bakery. Wilhelm Heinsdorf was a fat, middle-aged German who, like Miller said, was a fine baker. But no matter how good his bread and cakes were, he couldn't be allowed to stand up to the law, Dav thought. The idea put a sardonic smile on his face.

A little bell over the door jingled when Dav opened it and strode in with Miller close behind him. A couple of female customers stood at the counter. They took one look over their shoulders at the lawmen and then scurried out of the building, leaving the loaves of bread they had purchased behind them. They ignored Heinsdorf as he called out to them.

"Don't worry, Dutchy," Dav told the baker. "They can come back for what they bought later."

Heinsdorf reached below the counter. Dav rested his hand on his gun butt, confident in his speed. Even if Heinsdorf brought out a weapon, Dav could draw and fire before the German had a chance to use it.

It was not a shotgun or a revolver Heinsdorf reached for, however. When his hand came up from behind the counter, his pudgy fingers clutched a silver crucifix.

He thrust the cross toward Dav and said in a trembling voice, "Stay back! I don't know how a foul creature like you manages to walk in the daylight, but this will protect me! I know what you are!"

Dav stared at the baker in surprise for a few seconds, then a laugh burst from him.

"You old fool!" he said. "You think I'm some monster from your Old World superstititions?"

"I . . . I know where you come from," Heinsdorf quavered. "You may be a descendant of Vlad himself!"

"Idiot," Dav muttered. He stepped closer to the counter and reached out toward the baker. "If I were truly what you think I am, would I be able to do this?"

He closed his hand around the crucifix and ripped it out of Heinsdorf's hand. Heinsdorf cried out and took a stumbling step backward.

Dav held up the cross, displaying it for Heinsdorf to see.

"Look!" he commanded. "Nothing. It means nothing to me. You really are ignorant, Heinsdorf. I'm a flesh-and-blood man, that's all."

And Lucinda Hammond would soon find out just how flesh and blood he really was, Dav thought fleetingly as he tossed the crucifix aside. It clattered to the floor.

Heinsdorf's eyes followed the cross, so he wasn't watching Dav at that moment. As slow as he was, he wouldn't have had a chance to escape anyway. Dav lunged forward, grabbed Heinsdorf's apron and the front of his shirt, and dragged the startled baker onto the counter.

Heinsdorf let out a frightened yelp and struggled to get away, but Dav's fist cracked across his face, stunning him. Dav was stronger than he looked with his lean frame. He dragged Heinsdorf the rest of the way across the counter and let him fall heavily to the floor.

Dav drew back his leg and lashed out with a vicious kick. The toe of his boot sank deep into Heinsdorf's ample gut and brought another cry of pain from the baker.

"You think the law enforcement tax is too much,

is that it?" Dav asked through clenched teeth. "You don't want to pay to keep things like *this* from happening?"

As he asked the question he kicked Heinsdorf again, this time in the side. The impact was enough to break a rib, even through the layers of fat on Heinsdorf's body. Dav heard the bone give with a sharp *snap*. Heinsdorf screamed.

"I'm tired of you people plotting against me and spreading lies about me," Dav went on. He drew his gun.

"Please, no!" Heinsdorf cried as he held up his wildly shaking hands toward Dav, as if that would protect him from a bullet. "Please don't kill me!"

Dav didn't have any intention of killing Heinsdorf. That would just take money out of his pocket.

Instead he leaned down and smashed the Colt across Heinsdorf's face. The sight raked a bloody furrow in the baker's cheek. Crimson dripped down from it as Heinsdorf sobbed.

Dav straightened and pouched his iron.

"There," he said with some satisfaction. "That ought to teach you a lesson. From now on you'll cooperate with us when we try to help you, won't you?"

"Y-yes," Heinsdorf said. His voice was muffled because he had pressed both hands to his injured face. "I . . . I won't give you any more trouble, Sheriff."

"Now that's what I like to hear." Dav jerked his head at Miller. "Come on, Carl."

Miller reached out toward one of the loaves of bread sitting on the counter.

"What do you think you're doing?" Dav asked sharply from the doorway.

"I just thought—" Miller began.

"I know what you thought. Leave that there. We're not thieves, Carl. If you want some of Herr Heinsdorf's bread, you'll have to pay for it like everybody else."

"Uh . . . yeah, sure, boss."

From where he lay huddled on the floor, Heinsdorf said, "*Nein, nein* . . . take the bread, Deputy Miller, please. It . . . it is my gift to you."

"Well, in that case . . ." Dav said. He motioned for Miller to pick up the bread. "I'm glad to see that you've come to your senses, Wilhelm. You don't think I'm a monster at all anymore, do you?"

"*Nein,*" Heinsdorf whispered.

As the two lawmen left the bakery, Heinsdorf took one hand away from his bleeding face and reached over to where his crucifix lay on the floor, where Dav had thrown it. He brought it to him, held it close.

Samuel Dav might not be the sort of monster Heinsdorf had believed him to be, but that didn't mean he wasn't the unholiest creature ever to set foot in the settlement of Chico.

Chapter Four

Lucinda Hammond stood at the window of her second-floor bedroom. Her left eye was closed, and her right eye squinted over the barrel of the rifle she held pressed firmly to her shoulder.

She saw the door of the bakery open. Samuel Dav stepped out onto the boardwalk, followed by one of his toadying deputies. Lucinda settled the rifle's sights on Dav's chest.

All she had to do was press the trigger to bring his evil existence to an end.

Or she might miss, she thought. Her late husband, Milton, had taught her how to use a rifle, but she was far from an expert shot. At a range of four blocks, her aim wouldn't have to be off by much to make the bullet miss the sheriff.

Then Dav would probably figure out where the shot had come from, march up here, and kill her for daring to even attempt such a thing. Who in

Chico would try to stop him? No one, that's who, and Lucinda knew it quite well.

With a sigh, she lowered the rifle. It was getting heavy anyway, she told herself.

She turned away from the window, leaned the rifle in a corner of the luxuriously appointed bedroom. As she did so, she saw herself in the mirror above the dressing table.

Her thick blond hair was tangled, not having known a brush or a comb for several days. Her face still retained a considerable vestige of her beauty, but her eyes were sunken and hollow from lack of sleep, and lines of grief and strain had appeared around her mouth. She hadn't gotten dressed in days, either. A silk robe twisted around her was her only garment.

She looked away from her reflection, but that just made her gaze fall on the framed photograph that sat on the dressing table. It had been made on the day of her and Milton's fifth wedding anniversary. A traveling photographer had come to Chico, with his wagon packed full of arcane equipment, and they had hired him to make their portrait.

They had posed for it downstairs in the parlor, Milton sitting in one of the chairs with his legs crossed, Lucinda standing just behind and to the side of him with one hand resting on his shoulder. She had wanted to smile—it was a happy occasion, after all—but the photographer had insisted the portrait would look better and more dignified if they wore solemn expressions.

Lucinda tore her gaze away from the photograph. The sight of her handsome husband with his curling mustaches was a bitter reminder of what she had lost. Even now, after almost two weeks, the memories of their last moments together were as fresh and painful as if they had occurred only moments earlier.

The insistent hammering of a fist on the front door made Lucinda gasp as she looked up from the needlework in her lap. She was sitting in the parlor with Milton after supper. The housekeeper and the cook had already left for the day, so there was no one to answer the summons except one of them.

Lucinda set the needlework aside and started to rise from the divan.

"No, you stay here," Milton said as he got up from his chair. He waved her back. "I'll get it."

"Milton . . ." She had to stop and swallow before she could go on. "Be careful."

"I'm not afraid of those cheap crooks," he said, and she knew he was telling the truth. He wasn't afraid. But he ought to be, Lucinda thought. She had seen the way Samuel Dav looked at her. She had seen the coldness in his eyes, too. They were as hard and inhuman as the eyes of a snake.

Milton walked from the parlor into the foyer. Despite

what he had told her, Lucinda got up from the divan and took a few steps after him, so she could see. As she watched, Milton opened the door.

"I thought it might be you," he said to whomever stood outside.

"Aren't you going to ask me in?" Sheriff Dav's mocking voice asked. "I thought you folks were big on hospitality."

Milton didn't issue an invitation, but he stepped back so that the sheriff could come in. Dav glanced over through the arched entrance to the parlor, spotted her, and used his left hand to take off his hat. He gave her a nod and said, "Good evening, Mrs. Hammond."

His polite façade didn't fool anyone. His eyes were anything but courteous as they looked her over from head to foot, lingering boldly on the curves of her bosom and her hips. He smiled, but the expression reminded her of a predator licking its chops.

He didn't try to hide his lecherous examination of her from Milton, either. Face flushing with anger, Milton asked, "What do you want, Sheriff?"

Dav took his eyes away from Lucinda with obvious reluctance.

"I hear you've been doing some talking around town," he said. "You've been trying to stir up trouble, Mr. Hammond."

"I'm trying to look out for the best interests of the community," Milton snapped.

"I can understand that, what with you being the richest man in town. You feel like you've got a responsibility to these folks."

"That's exactly how I feel," Milton said. "A responsibility to protect them from the likes of you."

"I'd remind you that I'm the legally elected sheriff of Chico County."

"I'm not even so sure about that."

Dav nodded slowly and said, "Yeah, I heard that you've been spreading rumors. You've been saying that my supporters rounded up folks and forced them to vote for me."

"Only if paying them to vote for you didn't work," Milton said. "And there were more votes cast than there are legal voters in the county. It's like everyone buried in the cemetery cast a ballot for you, Sheriff!"

"None of that has been proven." Dav clapped his hat back on his head and stepped closer to Milton. "I want you to stop lying about me, Hammond. It's against the law."

"What law?" Milton demanded. "I don't know of any law against speaking the truth."

"My law," Dav said coldly. The two men's angry faces were only inches apart now. "And you'd better not forget it."

"Get out of my house," Milton ordered. "Get out right now!"

"You can't throw me out. I'm the sheriff."

"We'll just see about that!"

Lucinda realized that her husband was about to lose his temper. He was in the prime of life and a good-sized man. He hadn't always been wealthy, either. He had started out as a bullwhacker before establishing his own freight line and expanding into other businesses, and he knew what hard work was. He was no stranger to a fight.

She cried, "Milton, no!" as he lifted his hands. He ignored her and planted both of them against Dav's chest. He gave the sheriff a hard shove that sent him staggering back a couple of steps, almost out the still-open door.

Dav caught his balance. His face twisted savagely as his hand flickered toward the gun on his hip. Lucinda threw herself forward, but she was too late. Dav drew the revolver, raised it, and fired in less than the blink of an eye. The burst of flame that exploded from the muzzle almost touched Milton's vest. Milton jerked backward.

"Noooo!" Lucinda screamed.

Milton clapped both hands to his chest and reeled from side to side. He twisted around toward Lucinda, and she saw the bright red blood welling out over his fingers. As his eyes widened in pain and shock, his mouth opened and closed a couple of times, but no words came out.

"No!" she cried. "Milton!"

He gasped and fell to his knees. She sprang toward him, went down to the rug to throw her arms around him. He sagged against her. Some incoherent sounds came from his throat. She tried to get to the wound and felt the warm wetness of his blood on her hands.

He collapsed on a twisting fall to the side, leaving her on her knees above him. She screamed his name twice more as hot tears rolled down her cheeks. She grabbed him and shook him as if that would jar the light of life back into his eyes, but they continued to stare sightlessly.

She looked up and saw Dav standing there calmly just inside the doorway, the gun still in his hand, a wisp of smoke curling from the barrel.

"Now that's a real shame," he said, "but you saw it for yourself, Mrs. Hammond. Your husband attacked me. Attacked the law. And I just defended myself."

She wasn't sure where the vile words that spilled from her mouth came from. Later she didn't even remember exactly what she'd said. But Samuel Dav just seemed mildly amused by it all. He let her hysterical outburst run out, then said, "I'll tell the undertaker there's some work up here for him." He slid his gun back into its holster and shook his head. "It's never a good idea to oppose the law."

With that he turned away and left the house. Behind him, Lucinda fell across her husband's bloody body as gut-wrenching sobs shook her.

She was all cried out now. Tears were a waste of time. Her soul was a cold, dried-up husk, and the only thing that still aroused any real feelings inside her was the sight of Samuel Dav. All she had to do was see him, and she was filled with hate and revulsion.

But she was afraid of him, too, not so much for what he might do to her but for the rest of the town. She believed that if anything ever set him off, ever pushed him over the edge into the sort of killing frenzy that she sensed lurking within him, then Chico's Main Street might well run red with blood. Milton wouldn't have wanted that. He wouldn't have wanted his own death avenged so badly that the whole town might die.

Lucinda wasn't going to forget, though. Sooner

or later her time would come. She lifted her hands now and studied them. Even though she had long since scrubbed her husband's blood from them, she still seemed to see the red stains on her skin.

And she knew that someday she would see real blood on her hands again . . . the blood of Samuel Dav.

Chapter Five

After spending so much time cooped up in train cars and stables over the past ten days, Iron Heart was more than happy to get out and stretch his legs. When they left Santa Fe heading northwest toward Chico, John Henry gave the horse his head and let Iron Heart run.

Finally, though, John Henry pulled back on the reins and slowed his loyal mount to a walk. He didn't want Iron Heart to get too carried away and hurt himself.

John Henry carried enough supplies in his saddlebags for a three-day trip, even though Governor Wallace had told him the ride to Chico would take only two days. When you were out on the trail, you never knew when something might happen to delay you. John Henry believed in being prepared for emergencies.

That was why his saddlebags also carried several boxes of .44-40 cartridges that would fit both his

Colt revolver and his Winchester. And why the Bowie knife in a sheath strapped to his other hip was razor-sharp.

When he reached the Rio Grande, he had to backtrack a short distance to the south to reach the nearest place that had a ferry. Governor Wallace had warned him about that, so he knew what to expect.

When he reached the small settlement where the ferry was located, he was waiting at the landing, standing there and holding Iron Heart's reins, when shots suddenly sounded somewhere nearby. John Henry swiveled around, his hand going to his Colt as he searched for the source of the shots.

A man came running out of an adobe cantina about fifty yards away. He paused just outside the open door to turn around and fire twice more into the building.

John Henry didn't know what was going on, but clearly the *hombre* wasn't up to any good. He dropped the reins, knowing that the well-trained Iron Heart would stay ground-hitched for a while, and started toward the gunman. He drew his revolver and shouted, "Hold it!"

The man jerked around toward him and fired. John Henry dived behind a wagon that was parked in front of a small general store. He didn't want to kill anybody without knowing exactly what was behind the violence, but he wasn't going to stand by and let somebody throw lead at him, either. He figured he could wing the gunman and then ask questions.

As he eased up, intending to take a shot over the back of the wagon, he heard a woman's scream. That made things more urgent. He ran forward, around the wagon, and as he reached the open again he saw that the gunman had grabbed a young *señorita* in a peasant blouse and long skirt.

The man's left arm was around the girl's neck while his right hand held his gun to her head. She couldn't let out a sound now because of the gunman's choking grip on her throat, but her eyes were wide with terror.

"Everybody back off!" the gunman yelled in a harsh voice. "Back off or I'll blow this bitch's brains out!"

"Take it easy, mister," John Henry called to him. "You don't want to make this any worse than it already is."

The gunman laughed and tightened his grip on the girl even more.

"They can only hang me once, so I don't reckon it can get any worse than it already is," he said.

John Henry approached the man slowly but steadily. He said, "There's no need for an innocent person to die, no matter what happens to you or me, *amigo*."

"That's where you're wrong," the gunman flared back at him. "There aren't any innocent people. And I'm damn sure not your *amigo*!"

John Henry got a better look at the gunman now.

Despite the fact that the man wore a wide-brimmed, high-crowned sombrero, he appeared to be white. In this hot, sunny country, a lot of people wore hats like that no matter what their ancestry, John Henry had noticed.

The man's hard-planed face sported several days' worth of beard stubble. His eyes held a haunted look. John Henry knew a man on the dodge when he saw one; he had come face-to-face with plenty of them during his career as a lawman.

So this hardcase had drifted into the settlement, gone into the cantina, gotten into some sort of shooting scrape, and now just wanted to escape. John Henry could understand that, but as a lawman he couldn't allow it to happen. He sure couldn't allow anybody else to be hurt if he could prevent it.

"Why don't you just let the girl go, drop that gun, and we'll talk about this," he suggested.

The gunman sneered at him.

"You sound like a damn lawman," he spat. "I don't have anything to say to you blasted star packers except you should all go to hell."

"I imagine it's pretty crowded, the way folks are just downright mean to each other."

"Don't start preaching at me," the gunman snapped. "Throw your gun away and back off. This little *señorita* and me are getting on a horse and riding out of here, and if anybody tries to stop me, she dies."

"If she dies," John Henry said softly, "then I don't have any reason not to kill you."

The gunman's lips peeled back from his teeth in a grimace, and John Henry realized he had made a mistake.

"You know what?" the man said. "Maybe that'd be best all the way around."

His finger started to whiten on the gun's trigger.

John Henry moved as fast as he ever had in his life. He had closed to within twenty feet of the gunman and the hostage. His gun came up and roared as it bucked against his palm.

The gunman had already started to squeeze the trigger. John Henry couldn't get off a shot fast enough to stop that. Nobody on earth could.

But his bullet slammed into the cylinder of the gunman's Colt just as the hammer fell. It drove the gun backward and smashed the mechanism so that the hammer missed the firing pin of the bullet in the chamber. The gun didn't go off.

Instead the slug's impact transformed it into a missile that crashed into the gunman's jaw. The stunning force of the blow jarred loose his grip on the hostage. The girl broke free and fled as the gunman staggered back a step.

John Henry was hopeful now of taking the man alive since he'd disarmed him, but that turned out not to be the case. The gunman used his left hand to jerk another pistol from behind his belt, a weapon John Henry hadn't been aware of until now because the hostage's body had blocked his view of it. Howling incoherent curses because his jaw was probably broken, the man snapped a shot from that second gun at John Henry.

As the bullet ripped past his ear, John Henry knew he couldn't take any more chances. He fired twice and sent both rounds into the gunman's chest. The man went backward like he'd been slapped by a giant hand. His gun slipped from his fingers and sailed through the air to thud into the dust of the street.

The gunman thudded into the dust as well, landing on his back with his arms outstretched. His back arched. Blood bubbled from his mouth and ran down over his chin. He sagged back to the ground as his muscles went limp.

John Henry knew death when he saw it, too.

But even though he was convinced the gunman was no longer a threat, he kept his gun trained on the man as he approached. He didn't holster the Colt until he saw the lifeless, staring eyes in the hard-bitten face.

The girl who had been taken hostage was several yards away, being comforted by a couple of older women. John Henry went over to them, touched a finger to the brim of his hat, and said, "*Señoras*, is the *señorita* all right?"

"*Sí, señor*," one of the women replied with a nod. "Thanks to you."

Several men emerged from the cantina where the earlier shooting had taken place and hurried toward John Henry. Some of them wore town clothes while the others were dressed like farmers.

One of the townies took his hat off and said, "Mister, we can't thank you enough. You've done us a big favor."

"I just didn't want to see anybody else get hurt," John Henry said. "What happened in the cantina?"

"Cobb was drunk. He made a grab for one of the women, and the man the gal was with took exception to that. He told Cobb to leave them alone, and Cobb yanked out his gun and went to shooting."

John Henry inclined his head toward the dead man and said, "I take it that's Cobb?"

"Yeah." The townsman rubbed the back of his neck. "And I got to tell you, I didn't really think anybody could take him down the way you did, mister."

Several more of the men muttered their agreement with that sentiment.

"He's a well-known badman around here, is that it?" John Henry asked.

"That's right. He's pulled some holdups and killed four men in gunfights, that I know of. I've heard that he's gunned down more than that in other places. He drifts through every few months and we all hold our breath until he's gone." The man shook his head. "Looks like we won't have to worry about that anymore."

"Did he run with a gang?"

The townsman shook his head and said, "No, he was a real lone wolf, never wanted much to do with anybody. So you don't have to worry about any pards of his coming after you to even the score, mister."

"What's his first name?" John Henry asked. An idea was starting to form in the back of his mind.

"Uh, John, I think." The townie looked around at his friends. "Is that it?"

Several of the men nodded, and one of them said, "Yeah, John Cobb. Doesn't sound as bad as he really was, does it?"

So he and the dead gunfighter shared a first name, John Henry thought. They shared more than that as well. Although their faces looked nothing alike, they were roughly the same size and had the same sort of thick black hair.

That raised some interesting possibilities. John Henry had been wondering how he would approach the job in Chico, and now he had at least the beginnings of a plan of action.

"How about the man who traded shots with Cobb in the cantina?" he asked. "Was he killed?"

The man who had done most of the talking shook his head.

"No, he was lucky. Got a bullet through the arm and a graze on his side, but he'll live, I expect."

"I'm glad to hear that," John Henry said. "I'd like to ask a favor of you folks."

"Whatever it is, you name it, mister. We're all mighty glad we won't have to walk on eggshells around that *loco* son of a gun anymore."

So far, John Henry hadn't revealed his identity

as a deputy U.S. marshal. Now he moved his coat so the citizens could see his badge.

"What I'd like for you to do is plant this fella, leave his grave unmarked for now, and don't say anything else about it. Can you do that?"

"Why, I . . . I reckon we can," the townie said. He was obviously puzzled, but he looked around at the other settlers and went on, "We can do that, can't we, folks?"

"We'll keep it to ourselves, Marshal," one of the other men promised. "But why's that so important?"

"I can't tell you right now, but if I pass through this way again, I'll explain then."

"What about the reward?" the first man asked. "There's bound to be a reward for a gunhawk like Cobb."

John Henry shook his head and said, "I'm not interested in any reward. Later on I'll let the authorities know what happened and tell them to send the money to the town. Fair enough?"

"More than fair," the man said, and a chorus of agreement came from the others.

John Henry saw that the ferry was back on this side of the river.

"I've got to go," he told the settlers. "I'm obliged to you for your help."

"You've got that backward, Marshal . . . but we'll take it."

John Henry smiled at the young woman who'd been taken hostage and tugged on the brim of his hat. She stared at him in obvious hero worship, which he ignored as he walked back to take hold of Iron Heart's reins and lead the horse onto the ferry.

"I thought I heard some shootin' a few minutes ago," the grizzled old ferryman commented. "What happened?"

"A fella got what was coming to him, I reckon," John Henry said.

And he would have to wait and see how well that worked out for him.

Chapter Six

From the little riverside settlement, the easiest route was to follow the valley north to the point where the Rio Chama flowed into the Rio Grande. The smaller stream flowed down from the San Juan Mountains, and John Henry knew from studying a map in Wallace's office that if he headed upstream, that path eventually would bring him to Chico.

This was beautiful country, John Henry thought as he rode along. The area down in the southwestern part of the territory where he had been recently had an appeal of its own, but it was more rugged and arid than this region. The slopes here were covered with tall green pines, and the meadows were carpeted with thick grass and decorated by wildflowers. Getting to see this was almost worth getting shot at, John Henry told himself.

Almost.

Since he had gotten a fairly late start from Santa

Fe, he wound up spending two nights on the trail. The days were warm, but at these elevations the nights got pretty chilly before morning. John Henry's bedroll kept the cold from settling into his bones, and in the mornings a fire felt really good. The smell of coffee brewing mixed with the tang of pine in the cool air and woke up all of John Henry's senses.

By midday, John Henry figured he was approaching Chico. The Rio Chama still bubbled along beside him. The road turned away from it, though, as the river twisted off to the right and entered a deep gorge that cut through a sharp-edged ridge up ahead. John Henry spotted a notch in that ridge and wasn't surprised when the road led to it. The pass was the easiest way through or over the natural barrier formed by the ridge.

He recalled what Governor Wallace had told him about Sheriff Dav closing off a pass near Chico and forcing the local ranchers to pay a toll if they wanted to use the road to drive their cattle to market. John Henry had a hunch he was looking at that very pass. He would know soon, he thought as he sent Iron Heart trotting toward it.

As he approached the pass, his eyes intently scanned the ridge and the surrounding landscape, searching for any stray glints of sunlight that might indicate concealed riflemen. He didn't see anything out of the ordinary . . . but that didn't mean the men weren't there.

John Henry was close enough now to see that a gate made of heavy timbers had been set up inside the pass. As rocky as the ground was, whoever had built the gate must have used dynamite to blast out holes for the support posts, which were as thick and sturdy-looking as the trunks of young trees. A herd of stampeding cattle might be able to knock down the gate, but the stock would pile up against it first and a great many of the animals would probably be injured or killed. No cattleman worth his salt would want to do that.

At the moment, the gate was open. John Henry supposed that was because the men posted at the pass could see a long distance in both directions. If someone was coming that they wanted to stop, they would have plenty of time to swing the gate closed and secure it.

They must not have considered a lone man riding toward Chico to be a threat, because they didn't close the gate as John Henry rode into the pass. Two men, however, did stand up from the rocks where they were sitting and saunter into the middle of the road. They wore six-guns and carried rifles, and they looked hard-bitten enough that most folks wouldn't want to cross them.

One of the men lifted a hand in a signal for John Henry to stop. John Henry hauled back on Iron Heart's reins.

"Howdy," he said with a pleasant nod to the guards. "Did I take a wrong turn back there somewhere? I thought this was a public road."

"Parts of it are," one of the gunmen answered, "but this stretch through the pass is a toll road."

John Henry frowned and said, "Really? I never heard of such a thing."

"Well, you have now," the other guard snapped. "You can either pay the toll, or you can turn around and go back where you came from."

"How much is it?"

The momentary hesitation on the part of both guards told John Henry that there wasn't a set price. Sheriff Dav probably allowed his men to charge whatever they thought they could get away with, depending on who wanted to go through the pass.

After a few seconds, one of them said, "Five dollars."

"Five dollars?" John Henry repeated. "Sort of a steep toll, isn't it?"

"If you don't like it, you can—"

"I know," John Henry broke in. "Turn around and go back where I came from, right?"

"Damn right," the second guard said with a curt nod.

"Well, I don't particularly want to do that, so . . ."

John Henry fished a five-dollar gold piece out of his pocket, looked at it as if he were sorry to see it go, and then flipped it toward one of the gunmen. The man had been holding his rifle in both hands, ready to use it if necessary, but he took his right hand off the weapon and reached up to catch the spinning coin.

The second guard watched the gold piece as if mesmerized, just as John Henry expected. Both men had taken the attention away from him for a second, and that was plenty long enough for what he did next.

He palmed his Colt from its holster, leveled it at the two men, and as the first guard caught the coin, John Henry said, "Now, let's talk about how much I'll charge not to blow holes in both of you fellas."

Chapter Seven

Both guards thought about making a play; John Henry could tell that by the look in their eyes.

But he had the drop on them, and they could probably tell that he was a man who knew how to handle a gun. They settled for glaring at him, and one of them said, "You're gonna be mighty sorry you did that, mister."

"You know, I don't think so," John Henry said easily. "Anyway, I was thinking five dollars would be a pretty good price, and it just so happens one of you is holding a five-dollar gold piece. That's five bucks *each*, though, so the other one's going to have to pony up."

"I swear, I'm gonna kill you," the second guard threatened harshly.

"Over a measly sawbuck?" John Henry shook his head. "I would've thought your hide was worth more than that to you, *amigo*."

"I'm not your damn *amigo*!"

"I'm starting to think nobody is," John Henry said with a sigh. He motioned with the barrel of his Colt. "Toss those Winchesters over here."

"What if it damages them?"

"Then toss them *carefully*. I swear, fellas, you're making me do all the thinking here."

The guards threw their rifles to the ground near Iron Heart.

"Now unbuckle the gun belts, let 'em fall, and back away from them."

With obvious reluctance, they followed that order.

"Where are your horses?" John Henry asked.

"Tied up on the other side of the pass," one of the men replied.

The other one glared at him and demanded, "Why the hell did you tell him that?"

"Well, they're in plain sight. He would've seen 'em as soon as he rode on through."

"Maybe, maybe not. The sheriff's not gonna like it that you cooperated with this peckerwood."

"I ain't the only one! You threw away your guns, too."

John Henry said, "Hold on a minute. You said something about a sheriff. You boys aren't lawmen, are you?"

The angrier of the two guards sneered at him and declared, "We damned sure are! We're both legally appointed deputies, and you're gonna be in a lot of trouble for throwin' down on us, mister.

We'll see you behind bars for this. Maybe even strung up!"

"I didn't know that putting a couple of two-bit crooks in their place was a hanging offense around here, even if they are deputies," John Henry said. "And for that matter, what are deputies doing collecting a toll on a road that's supposed to be public?"

"That just shows how much you know," the guard said. "If Sheriff Sam Dav says this is a toll road, then it's a toll road, by God!"

"You'll excuse me if I don't take your word for it," John Henry told them. "Now, one more thing . . . Shuck those boots."

They stared at him in disbelief.

"You want us to take our boots off?"

"I can say it in Cherokee, if you didn't understand English."

Muttering curses, the men sat down and pulled their boots off. When they had done that, John Henry made them back away even farther. They winced with every step they took as the rocks that littered the floor of the pass poked their feet through their socks.

Keeping the guards covered with the Colt, he swung down easily from the saddle and collected the boots, gun belts, and rifles. He hung the belts on his saddle horn and put the boots in an empty sack he took from one of his saddlebags. He tied that to the saddle horn along with the rifles, using some twine he carried with him.

"How far is it to the nearest town?" John Henry asked as if he didn't already know.

"Chico's about two miles on the other side of this pass," one of the men answered in a surly voice.

"Well, then, I'll leave your guns and boots with your horses in Chico," John Henry said.

"You're gonna make us walk in? In sock feet?"

"Unless you'd rather spend the rest of your life up here," John Henry said.

"I ain't gonna forget this, mister. No way in hell."

The implied threat clearly didn't bother John Henry. He mounted again and nudged Iron Heart into a walk.

"I'll be seeing you boys," he said with a smile.

"You sure will. You can count on that."

"Blast it, Harry," the second guard said. "Don't rile up the son of a bitch even more!"

With his gun hand resting on his thigh as he held the Colt, John Henry rode past the two men. The pass was only about fifty yards from one end to the other, so it didn't take him long to emerge from it. He immediately spotted two horses tied in a grove of pine trees. Without getting down from the saddle, he untied the reins and led the animals out onto the road.

The two guards had followed him, still walking gingerly on the rough ground. They stood at the mouth of the pass. John Henry grinned, waved with his gun hand, and turned Iron Heart down the slope.

A second later, he heard two things that gave him pause.

One was laughter coming from the guards.

The other was hoofbeats pounding up the trail toward him.

John Henry reined in. The road twisted in front of him, turning to wind its way down into the valley on the other side of the ridge. From up here he could see the pine-covered mountain slopes looming on the far side of the valley, and between here and there he could make out the distant cluster of buildings that formed Chico. Riders were coming from that direction, and a few seconds later they swept around the curve in the road and came into sight.

Four men, and somehow John Henry knew without being told that they were more of Sheriff Dav's deputies.

One of the guards he had disarmed and set afoot whooped in triumph.

"Now you're in for it, you dirty skunk!"

John Henry glanced around. The pines were thick on both sides of the trail. He could have left the guards' horses and taken off into the trees on Iron Heart, but he wouldn't be able to get up any speed. Not only that, but no doubt these men knew the area a lot better than he did. He'd never been here before, so he didn't know what he'd be getting into.

Besides, the half-formed plan in his head called for him to confront Dav's men sooner or later. He might as well get started on that here and now, he thought.

He waited as the four men rode closer. They had spotted him, too; he could tell that by the way they slowed down and approached him warily. A couple of the men drew rifles from saddle sheaths.

One man edged out in front of the others. When he was about twenty feet from John Henry, he stopped and lifted his hand in a signal for the others to do likewise. When they had, he walked his horse a few feet closer.

"Howdy," he said. "You look like you're armed for bear."

The man was stocky and powerful looking, with a heavy jaw and brown hair. A badge was pinned to the old buckskin shirt he wore. For all John Henry knew, this was Sheriff Samuel Dav. He hadn't been given a description of the crooked lawman.

"You mean all these guns?" he asked. "They don't all belong to me. Some of them belong to those two fellas up there." He jerked a thumb over his shoulder toward the pass. "The same goes for these horses."

"So that would make you a horse thief, as well as a regular robber."

John Henry shook his head and said, "I didn't steal anything. I was just borrowing a few things from them."

"Many a man's been strung up for *borrowin'* a horse," the spokesman for the newcomers said.

"Yes, but I was going to return these as soon as I

got to town. I had a little disagreement with those two fellas up in the pass, and I didn't want them coming after me and trying to bushwhack me."

"What sort of disagreement?"

"I didn't want to pay a toll to ride over what's supposed to be a free public road," John Henry said.

"Not anymore," the man snapped. "Not that part of it. The road through the pass is now a toll road, by order of Sheriff Sam Dav."

"That would be you?"

"Me?" The man laughed. "Not hardly. I'm one of the sheriff's deputies. Carl Miller. Who might you be, other than the fella who made a bad mistake by crossin' the law?"

"People keep telling me I've made a mistake, but so far I don't see any evidence of it."

"I asked for your name," Miller asked, impatience giving an edge to his voice.

"It's John Cobb," John Henry drawled.

Miller stiffened in the saddle, and the other three men, who also wore deputy badges, glanced at each other. Clearly, the name meant something to them.

John Henry hoped that none of them had been acquainted with the real John Cobb, or else his masquerade would evaporate quicker than the morning dew.

In his last assignment he had concealed his true identity as a federal officer and allowed people to draw the erroneous conclusion that he was a gunfighter and outlaw. He had used his real name, though. This was different. This was the first time he had deliberately posed as someone else. He hoped the ruse would work.

"I've heard of this fella Cobb," Miller said. "He's supposed to be a pretty bad *hombre*."

John Henry shrugged.

"Sometimes I feel like looking for trouble. But I never feel like running away from it."

"Well, you ran right into it this time," Miller said. He nodded toward the road behind John Henry. "I don't think Price and Hoffman are happy with you."

The two guards from the pass had been descending the slope while John Henry talked to Miller. They came up to the group of riders now, cussing because their feet hurt and out of breath from hurrying.

"Shoot the son of a bitch, Carl," the angrier of the two demanded. "He held us up, stole our horses and our gear!"

"There are two of you and one of him," Miller said dryly. "How'd he manage to do that, Hoffman?"

The man's face turned a mottled red with anger and embarrassment.

"He's tricky," Hoffman said. "He fooled us into thinkin' that he was gonna pay the toll, then threw down on us."

John Henry said, "And as I recall, you never did give me back that five-dollar piece, so technically I think I *did* pay the toll." He grinned at Miller. "See? I'm just a law-abiding citizen, whether I mean to be or not."

"Stealing horses and guns isn't law-abiding," Miller pointed out.

"Borrowing," John Henry said. "I told you, I was just borrowing them as a precaution."

"Damn it!" Hoffman burst out. "Somebody gimme a gun! I'll shoot him just to shut him up, if for no other reason!"

"Take it easy," Miller ordered. All six of these men were deputies, but Miller obviously held some sort of authority. He went on to John Henry, "You can't disrespect the law the way you done without payin' a price for it, mister. You'll come on into town with us, and the sheriff will decide what to do with you."

"Don't you mean a judge?" John Henry asked.

Several of the men chuckled. Miller said, "Oh, there's a judge in Chico, all right, but it's Sheriff Dav who makes the only decisions that matter. Toss your guns down."

John Henry didn't make a move to obey the order. Instead he asked quietly, "What if I don't?"

"Then we'll kill you," Miller said as if that were the most obvious thing in the world. "You may have a rep as a gunman, Cobb, but there are four of us and one of you. Pretty bad odds, if you ask me."

"Pretty bad," John Henry agreed, "but not bad enough to keep me from putting a bullet in your gizzard before any of those others can stop me."

Miller's mouth tightened.

"You have any other suggestions?" he asked.

"Sure," John Henry answered instantly. "Like I told you, I actually did pay the toll, so you don't have any cause to arrest me for that. And it's these two I had the problem with, so why don't you let me settle it with them?"

"Now you're talkin'," Hoffman said. "Let me have my guns back, and I'll settle things, all right."

Miller said, "Don't be a damned fool. You're a good man, Hoffman, but you're not a gunslick. Cobb is. He'd likely kill you, and then the sheriff would be on my ass for lettin' you get killed." Miller rubbed at his heavy jaw and frowned in thought. "I got a better idea. Hash this out without guns."

A grin spread across Hoffman's face as his hands clenched into hamlike fists.

"That sounds good to me," he said.

"Two against one," John Henry said. "That's not exactly a fair fight, either."

"It's as fair as you're gonna get," Miller told him. "Take it or leave it, Cobb. But if you leave it, there'll be gunplay. Unless you want to surrender and come along peacefully to town with us."

"I don't think so," John Henry said. "But how I do know you won't just shoot me if I turn over my guns?"

"You'll have to take my word for it. But I'd like to see you tangle with Hoffman and Price. I'm not too happy with 'em for lettin' you get the drop on them in the first place. So that's one reason for you to believe me."

"That's as good as any, I suppose." John Henry untied the sack from the saddle horn and tossed it to Price. "You boys will want your boots back."

While the two guards took their boots out of the sack and pulled them on, Miller told John Henry, "Get down off that horse and unbuckle your gun belt."

John Henry did what the deputy said. He didn't want to risk a shoot-out with these crooked lawmen. Not because he was afraid of dying, but because if they did manage to kill him, his assignment for Governor Lew Wallace would come to an abrupt end before he was able to do any good. He was willing to risk a bare-knuckles fight with Hoffman and Price if it gave him a chance to stay on the job longer.

John Henry took off his gun belt and hung it on the saddle horn with the others. He hung his hat on the horn as well, then took off his coat, folded it, and slipped it into his saddlebags. He looked at Miller and asked, "Are there any kind of rules to this fight?"

Miller grinned and said, "What do you think?"

The words were barely out of Miller's mouth when one of the men tackled John Henry from behind.

Chapter Eight

The impact sent John Henry staggering forward. He struggled to keep his balance but failed as his attacker continued to drive against him. He lost his footing and crashed to the hard-packed dirt of the road. The other man's weight came down on him with stunning force that drove the air from his lungs.

The man—John Henry didn't know which one it was, but he would have bet on Hoffman—grabbed his hair and jerked his head up. Even though he was dazed, he knew the man intended to smash his face into the ground, so he shot his right elbow back as hard as he could into the pit of his opponent's stomach.

John Henry smelled the man's foul breath as it gusted from his mouth. The man's grip on his hair came loose. John Henry writhed and twisted and bucked his body off the ground, throwing the attacker away from him.

John Henry rolled the other way, and as he came up he saw that the man who'd tackled him was indeed Hoffman. Hoffman wasn't the only one John Henry had to worry about. Price charged him, too, swinging a punch at his head before John Henry could get set. The only thing John Henry could do was jerk his head to the side.

Price's fist grazed his ear. It was a glancing blow, painful but lacking the power to do any real damage.

The punch served to distract John Henry, though, and delay his response, and that gave Hoffman time to scramble up and launch another attack. He waded in and hammered a punch to John Henry's ribs on the left side. John Henry grunted under the impact and swung a backhand with his left that caught Hoffman on the jaw. Knowing that he was taking a chance, he pivoted, turning his back on Price, and threw a looping right that landed on the same spot on Hoffman's jaw. Hoffman dropped.

As satisfying as that was, John Henry paid the price for it. Price grabbed him from behind in a bear hug, pinning his arms to his sides. A few feet away, Hoffman climbed to his feet with an expression of murderous fury on his face.

The other deputies had been calling out encouragement to their friends during the fight. Now Miller whooped and shouted, "Go get him, Hoffman!"

Hoffman didn't need any urging. He charged

at John Henry, obviously intent on beating him severely while Price hung on to him.

That straight-ahead rush didn't pan out the way Hoffman must have thought it would. John Henry threw his weight backward, lifted both feet, drew his legs back, and then lashed out with them. The double-barreled kick landed in the middle of Hoffman's chest and flung him backward in a wild, out-of-control spill.

At the same time, the force of the collision sent Price toppling backward as well, in the opposite direction. When he hit the ground, that jarred loose his grip on John Henry, who took advantage of the opportunity to smash an elbow under Price's chin. John Henry rolled free again.

As he came to his feet this time, he saw that Price was still down, evidently stunned. Hoffman was trying to get up, but he seemed to be having trouble catching his breath. John Henry knew his kick might have broken some of the deputy's ribs.

"Better stay down," he advised. "You don't want to—"

He was about to say that Hoffman didn't want to hurt himself even more by continuing the fracas, but Hoffman didn't give him the chance to finish. Bellowing in rage, Hoffman used his anger as fuel to drive him back to his feet. He came at John Henry again, swinging wildly.

John Henry ducked under the roundhouse punches and lifted an uppercut that landed with smashing force on Hoffman's chin. Hoffman's head went back so far on his neck it seemed like his spine must be about to crack. His eyes rolled up in their sockets. He managed to paw at the air with a couple of final, futile blows, but then he crashed to earth, out cold.

John Henry stepped back and turned toward Price, who was still on the ground. The second deputy lifted a hand toward him, palm out.

"That . . . that's enough," Price said. "No more, mister. No more."

John Henry was glad to hear that. He was running out of steam himself.

He still had Miller and the other three deputies to contend with. As he turned toward them, he wondered how long he could stand up against them. Not long, more than likely, but he would give a good account of himself for as long as he could.

A couple of the men looked angry that he had defeated Hoffman and Price, but Miller was grinning as he leaned forward in his saddle and rested his hands on the horn. He lifted a hand to motion the others back.

"Take it easy," he told them, and once again John Henry could tell that Miller was accustomed to being in command. "It was a fair fight."

"But, Carl," one of the deputies objected, "he stole their horses and guns!"

"Borrowed them," Miller said, still grinning. "You heard what Cobb said, and I reckon we can give him the benefit of the doubt. Anybody who can brawl like that deserves it, as far as I'm concerned."

John Henry nodded, wiped the back of his left hand across his mouth, and said, "I'm obliged to you for that, Deputy. I've had about enough trouble for one day."

"Oh, I didn't say you were out of trouble. That'll be up to the sheriff." Miller drew his gun and pointed it at John Henry. "And you're goin' to see him right now."

Chapter Nine

The knock on the front door of her house made Lucinda Hammond flinch as if she'd been struck. She knew she might never be able to hear such a knock again without being reminded of the terrible night Sheriff Dav had murdered her husband.

At least she had forced herself to get dressed today, instead of wearing the same dressing gown she had worn for nearly two weeks straight after Milton's funeral. Her hair wasn't as carefully brushed as it had always been before his death, but it wasn't a wild tangle. She supposed she looked halfway respectable . . . not that it mattered anymore. Nothing mattered.

The front door had a narrow window on each side, covered by curtains. Lucinda moved one of the curtains back to see who was standing on her porch. If it was Dav . . . !

She dropped her other hand to the pocket of her dress and felt the reassuring hardness of the little pistol she carried there. If that bastard had shown up on her doorstep, she would open the door, stick the pistol in his face, and pull the trigger. Dav's gunmen would come for her and probably kill her if she did that, but it would be worth it. She didn't have anything left to live for, anyway.

Her visitor wasn't Samuel Dav. She recognized the slight, long-haired figure of Edgar Wellman.

Lucinda opened the door. She hadn't spoken aloud much these past two weeks, and her voice sounded rusty to her ears as she said, "Edgar. What are you doing here?"

"How are you, Lucinda?" Wellman asked. "No one has seen you in days. You sent your servants away—"

"I didn't feel like eating, and I don't care if the house is clean. I don't care about anything."

"Now, I know that's not true," Wellman said. "You care about this town. You always did. You and Milton both."

Lucinda winced slightly as the newspaperman spoke her late husband's name. She knew what he said was true; as one of the leading citizens of Chico, Milton had always done whatever he could to help the settlement grow and prosper, and she had done her part as well.

But knowing something was true and wanting to hear it were two different things.

Old habits were persistent. She had been raised to be polite, so she said, "What can I do for you, Edgar?"

"Invite me in so we can have a talk?"

Lucinda hesitated. Now that she was standing there with the door open and breathing fresh air for the first time in days, she realized how musty it was inside the house. She ought to air it out before she had company . . .

But what did it matter? She swung the door open farther and said, "All right, come on in."

Wellman stepped in, holding his hat in his hand. He wore a tweed suit, a white shirt, and a string tie. He wasn't a Westerner by birth. He came from back East somewhere, and his voice had an odd, lilting accent to it as if he weren't even a native-born American. But he was a decent man, Lucinda knew, and his newspaper, the *Chico Star*, was the only paper in this part of the territory.

For the past several months, though, Wellman's press had been idle. Sheriff Dav had shut the paper down, saying that it was printing treasonous lies about him and his deputies when all they were trying to do was bring law and order to the town. That was the real lie, of course, but faced with the choice of printing what Dav wanted him to print, having the newspaper office burned down, or not printing anything at all, Wellman had decided to shut his doors for the time being. Until someone came along to help the honest citizens of the settlement, he said.

Lucinda knew that was never going to happen. Wellman insisted there was still a chance. He had taken his buggy and gone to Santa Fe, before Dav had clamped down on travel in and out of Chico, and appealed to Governor Wallace personally for help. Wellman was sure the governor would do something.

Not long after that, three strangers had managed to get into town somehow, one after the other, several weeks apart, and each of them had spent a day or two asking cautious questions about what was going on here.

Then, each of those men had disappeared. Lucinda didn't know if Governor Wallace had sent them, but whether that was the case or not, they were gone, dropped out of sight with no explanation.

Actually, their bodies had been dropped into a ravine somewhere by Dav's deputies, Lucinda believed. That was the most likely explanation for their disappearance.

Those thoughts went through her mind in a flash as she ushered Edgar Wellman into the dim parlor. She pushed a couple of the curtains back to let some much-needed light into the gloomy room.

"That's better," Wellman said. "You can't stay cooped up in here for the rest of your life, Lucinda."

"I don't see why not," she said. "There's nothing out there for me."

"You're wrong about that. You're one of the community's leaders, and the people are depending on you."

Lucinda let out a hollow, humorless laugh.

"Well, they're going to be awfully disappointed,

then," she said. "I can't help anybody. I can't even help myself."

"That's not true. Some of us have been meeting—in secret, of course—and trying to figure out what to do about our illustrious sheriff."

"There's nothing anyone *can* do," Lucinda said. "Dav has twenty deputies, each of them as good with a gun and as ruthless and vicious as he is. No one is going to go up against them."

"There are more than three hundred people in Chico. We outnumber them more than ten to one."

"Three hundred people if you count the women and children. I don't think most of them would be much good in a gunfight."

"Still, there are at least eighty able-bodied men in town," Wellman insisted. "Those are four to one odds."

"*If* you could get everyone to agree to fight. And even then, one of Dav's gun-wolves is probably more than a match for any four men in Chico. You know that, Edgar. If you try to stir up trouble, you'll just get a lot of people killed for no good reason."

Her voice was harsh, and she knew it. She didn't want to see any more innocents die.

Wellman's face flushed, and Lucinda realized to her surprise that he was angry. He was so mild-mannered she didn't recall ever seeing him lose his temper.

"Your husband thought there was a good reason to oppose Dav," the newspaperman said. "It's called the truth."

"And the truth got him killed," Lucinda responded bitterly.

"He knew he had to take a stand—"

"What is it you want from me, Edgar?" Lucinda interrupted. "You want me to come to one of your clandestine meetings and make a speech? You want me to urge the townspeople to take up their guns and fight back against Dav and his men?" She shook her head. "I won't do it. I've seen enough blood to last me, and we both know that if the town stages an uprising against Dav, the streets will be running red."

"Your mind's made up, then?" Wellman asked in a clipped voice.

"Yes, I'm afraid it is."

The newspaperman smiled thinly.

"In that case, I suppose I should just say that I hope you won't lock yourself away in a prison of grief. Milton wouldn't want that, nor would any of your friends."

She felt a surge of anger again, anger that he would presume to try to tell her what her own husband would have wanted, but it lasted only a moment. Even that was too much emotion for her to maintain. It was easier to retreat into dull, unfeeling nothingness.

"Thank you for coming to see me, Edgar," she said.

"I'm being thrown out, is that it?"

"I don't think we have anything else to say to each other, do we?"

"I suppose not," he answered with a sigh. He put on his hat and started toward the door.

"You can show yourself out," Lucinda said.

He looked like he wanted to say something else, but he didn't. Instead he went to the door and opened it.

But instead of stepping out onto the porch, he paused in the doorway and said in what seemed to be genuine surprise, "I wonder what that's about."

Curiosity was just about the last thing Lucinda wanted to give in to, but something impelled her steps into the foyer. She came up beside Wellman and looked along the street, as he was doing. Main Street sloped up slightly to the mansion at the end of it, so from here they had a good view of everything.

Several of Dav's deputies were riding toward the impressive, two-story stone building that housed the sheriff's office and jail. A stranger rode in their midst, surrounded. Even though his hands were free, it was obvious he was a prisoner, at least for the moment.

"Who can that be?" Wellman asked. "We haven't had any strangers in town for a while."

"Not since those three who disappeared."

"I have a strong hunch they were sent here by Governor Wallace," Wellman said. "Maybe this man is another agent working for the governor."

"If he is, God help him," Lucinda said. "Because he's probably as good as dead already."

Chapter Ten

Sheriff Dav was sitting at the desk in his office, nursing a cup of coffee and going through the latest batch of WANTED posters that had arrived in the mail. In what he regarded as a magnanimous gesture, Dav allowed the mail rider in and out of Chico without having to pay a toll to use the road through the pass. The man worked for the government, after all, and so, in a way, did he.

Dav liked to keep track of the reward dodgers. For one thing, he wanted to know if any of them showed up with his men pictured on them. All his deputies claimed not to be wanted in New Mexico Territory, but Dav wasn't sure they were all telling the truth. He wanted to know if there was a chance some bounty hunter would show up looking for any of them.

For another, if some other outlaw with a reward on his head happened to drift into Chico, Dav wanted to know about that, too. When that happened, he could offer to provide a safe haven for a time . . . in return for a price, of course.

Nothing in this life was free, after all.

One of the deputies opened the office door and stepped inside. He said, "Carl and some of the boys are bringin' in a prisoner, Sheriff."

Dav pushed the stack of WANTED posters aside and leaned back in his chair.

"I thought Carl was taking a ride up to the pass with the boys who were supposed to relieve Price and Hoffman."

"He was. But they're all with him now."

Dav shot to his feet angrily and said, "Blast it! If they all came back down here, then who's watching the pass? Anybody could ride through there!"

"I dunno, boss," the deputy said. "I'm just tellin' you who I saw comin' up the street."

Dav stalked out of the office, snagging his hat from a peg in the wall near the door on the way. He stopped on the boardwalk and glared at the men who were reining their mounts to a halt in front of the office and jail.

The six deputies had a lone rider surrounded. The stranger was a fairly young man with ruggedly rough-hewn features and dark hair under a tan hat. His high cheekbones and the reddish tint to his skin made him look a little like an Indian, but clearly he wasn't a savage.

"Carl, what's going on here?" Dav asked. "A

couple of these men are supposed to be up at the pass, guarding the road."

"I know that, Sheriff," Miller replied, "but I thought it might be a good idea to have them come back down here with me, to make sure we got here all right with the prisoner."

"Who the hell is he? Jesse James?"

"No, sir." Miller nodded toward the stranger. "This is John Cobb."

The name was familiar to Dav. After a moment he placed it. He said, "The outlaw and gunfighter John Cobb?"

"That's right, Sheriff."

Dav's eyes narrowed as he studied the stranger. The man didn't really look like a cold-blooded killer, but Dav knew that appearances could sometimes be very deceptive, especially where gunmen were concerned. Some of the deadliest men looked completely mild mannered.

"I reckon there's a story behind this," Dav said. "From the looks of the scrapes and bruises on Hoffman and Price, I'd say they must have tangled with Cobb and come out second best, despite having him outnumbered."

"It wasn't our fault, Sheriff," Hoffman said. "The bastard tricked us—"

Dav held up a hand to stop the deputy.

"I don't care how he did it," Dav said coldly. "I care about results. You two get back up there and guard that pass."

Price said, "But our shifts are over."

"Not anymore, they're not," Dav snapped. "Get going."

The two deputies sighed and turned their horses around. They knew there was no point in arguing with Dav. That could only cause them more trouble in the long run.

"As for the rest of you," Dav went on, "bring the gentleman in."

"Gentleman?" Miller said, sounding surprised.

"That's right." Dav had remembered where he'd seen John Cobb's name just recently. "He and I have business to discuss."

Chapter Eleven

John Henry wasn't sure what sort of "business" Samuel Dav had in mind, but at least it was a somewhat promising beginning. Dav hadn't had him thrown in a cell or killed outright. A business discussion was a definite improvement on either of those two possibilities.

As he swung down from the saddle, he studied Dav. The man was tall and lean, with a narrow dark mustache. John Henry thought the sheriff had a vaguely foreign look about him, although he wasn't sure about that. Dav's voice was flat and hard, with no discernible accent.

Once his boots were on the ground, John Henry glanced up at Miller and said, "I suppose it'd be too much to ask to have my guns back."

Miller snorted.

"I'll bring 'em in. If the sheriff says for you to get 'em back, that's when you'll get 'em back. Not before."

John Henry shrugged. Outnumbered and out-gunned the way he was, there was nothing he could do except play out the hand he'd been dealt.

With Miller and one of the other deputies close behind him, he stepped up onto the boardwalk and followed Dav into the office. It was a large, well-appointed room with a big desk, a polished wooden gun cabinet full of rifles and shotguns, and a heavy, leather-upholstered sofa as well as several armchairs and a swivel chair behind the desk.

A set of stairs on the right side of the room led up to a landing with a thick door that opened off of it. The door had a small, barred window in it, which led John Henry to assume that the second floor was taken up by the cell block. This was the sort of sheriff's office and jail you'd find in a prosperous town . . . the sort of town Chico had been before Samuel Dav took it over and began the process of bleeding it dry.

Dav went behind the desk and said to John Henry, "We haven't been formally introduced. I'm Sheriff Samuel Dav, the law in Chico."

"I reckon that would make me John Cobb, the outlaw in Chico," John Henry said.

A flash of mingled irritation and amusement flickered through Dav's dark eyes. He took off his hat, dropped it on the desk, and jerked a nod toward a red leather chair.

"Have a seat," he said.

John Henry took off his hat and sat down. A glance over his shoulder told him that Miller had taken a seat on the sofa and pulled out the makin's. He was rolling himself a quirly while the other deputy lounged in the doorway with his right hand never straying far from the gun on his hip. John Henry knew that stance; he practiced it most of the time himself.

Of course, his gun belt was lying on the sofa next to Miller right now, along with his Winchester, so he couldn't get his hand anywhere near them.

Dav sat down, looked through some papers on his desk, and selected one of them. He tossed it onto the front part of the desk, close to John Henry, and asked, "Look familiar?"

John Henry leaned forward. He saw that the paper was a WANTED poster, and the printed name "JOHN COBB" jumped out at him. Above the name and a recitation of Cobb's crimes was a drawing of the gunman's face. John Henry was glad it wasn't a photograph; in a drawing like that, one dark-haired man with rugged features looked pretty much like another.

"Not a very good likeness," he commented, just in case Dav was thinking the same thing. He hoped that would disarm any uncertainty Dav might be feeling.

"I disagree," the sheriff said. "I believe I would have known you anywhere, Cobb. What brings you to Chico?"

John Henry shrugged and said, "My horse. The wind. Who the hell knows?"

A smile curved Dav's thin lips.

"I was like that myself once," he said. "Just drifting wherever life took me. I'm more ambitious these days."

John Henry looked around the office and nodded.

"I can see that."

"Oh, I'm not talking about just being a small-town sheriff. I have other plans—" Dav stopped and shook his head. "But that's not important. Tell me about your run-in with Price and Hoffman. They're pretty good men. It's not often someone gets the drop on them."

"Then anybody who wants to just isn't trying hard enough. All I had to do was flip a five-dollar gold piece in the air, and they both watched it instead of my gun hand."

Dav grunted in displeasure. He said, "I'll have to have a talk with them about that. I take it you objected to paying the toll to come through the pass?"

"I thought it was a public road," John Henry said.

"It used to be. Not anymore."

"Since you became the sheriff in these parts?"

"That's right. What happened after you pulled your gun?"

"I didn't cotton to the idea of trouble coming up on my back trail, so I took their guns and horses. And their boots."

Dav smiled again, and this time he appeared to be genuinely amused.

"Their boots," he repeated. "That's pretty good."

"I thought so. Kept 'em from running after me, at least for a while."

From the sofa, Miller put in, "But then me and the other fellas came along, and that sort of ruined Cobb's idea."

"How did Price and Hoffman get those bruises on their faces?" Dav asked.

John Henry used a thumb to point at Miller.

"That was Deputy Miller's idea. He didn't want a shoot-out, so he decided to let Price and Hoffman settle their grudge against me with their fists."

"Only you whipped them both," Dav guessed.

"I'm not claiming it was easy," John Henry said. "They're pretty good scrappers. But I've been in a few brawls in my time, too."

"I'll just bet you have," Dav mused as he leaned back in his chair. His long arm reached out and picked up the WANTED poster. "Says here there's a reward of $500 for your capture."

"You intend to turn me in and collect it?" John Henry asked. He didn't think Dav was likely to, but if the sheriff decided to go that route, it might mean the end of John Henry's plan.

"I mean to collect," Dav said, "but not necessarily a reward."

John Henry frowned and said, "Sorry, but I don't follow you, Sheriff."

"If you want to stay here in Chico . . ." Dav held up the WANTED poster. "You'll have to pay."

"Ah," John Henry said as understanding dawned. "What if I don't have $500?"

"That would be a real shame." Dav let the poster fall back onto the desk.

John Henry wasn't sure Dav would follow through with that implied threat. Since the sheriff ruled Chico with an iron fist, he wouldn't want to draw any more outside attention than necessary. Most owlhoots likely wouldn't know that, however. They would probably be willing to pay just to have a safe place to hole up for a while.

"Maybe we could come to some sort of an arrangement," John Henry suggested.

"Like what?"

"A man in a position of power like yourself . . . I'll bet you could always use another good man to help you out."

"Or another bad man, eh?" Dav asked

"You said it, Sheriff, not me."

"I already have twenty deputies. Just how many do you think I need?"

"The way I see it, you can never have enough guns backing your play," John Henry said. "Besides, I think I proved today that I'm better than at least two of your men."

Miller said, "Hold on a minute. Price and Hoffman are good at their job. You just took 'em by surprise is all."

"A man who works for me shouldn't be surprised," Dav said sharply. "You know that, Carl." His tone eased as he went on, "But I suspect they've learned their lesson, or at least they will have by the time they're finished with that double shift of guard duty. That doesn't change the point Cobb made."

"Wait a minute, boss. You're not thinkin' about takin' this *hombre* on as a deputy, are you?"

"If I am, that's my decision to make," Dav said. His voice had turned flinty again. Clearly, he didn't like being challenged, John Henry thought.

Miller must have realized that, too, because he said quickly, "Well, sure. Of course it is. You're the sheriff, after all."

"And don't you forget it." Dav shrugged. "Anyway, Cobb might not be interested. He might be just passing through Chico and won't want to stay."

"Actually, it looks like a pretty nice town," John Henry drawled. "And I've spent a lot of time on the trail recently. Might be pleasant to stay in one place for a little while, especially if I knew the law wasn't looking for me."

"I'm the only law here," Dav said. "And if you're working for me, it wouldn't make sense for me to give you any trouble, would it?"

"No, I don't reckon it would."

Dav leaned forward and pointed a finger at John Henry.

"But it wouldn't make sense for you to try to double-cross me, either," he said. "Because it wouldn't work, and you'd just wind up dead. *If* you were lucky. You understand what I'm saying, Cobb?"

"I sure do. And you don't have to worry, Sheriff. When a man's outnumbered twenty to one, he'd be a fool to try any funny business."

"I'm not worried," Dav said with an arrogant smirk. "I don't have to worry. I've got this town and everybody in it right in the palm of my hand."

With that, he put his hand out flat, palm up, and then slowly closed it into a fist, as if demonstrating just how easily he could crush any opposition.

"We've got a deal," John Henry said. Dav stood up, and so did he. The two men reached over the desk and shook.

"Give Cobb back his guns," Dav told Miller.

"Sure," the stocky deputy said. He handed over the gun belt, and when John Henry had buckled it on, Miller gave him the Winchester as well.

John Henry saw the wary look in the deputy's eyes, though. Miller didn't trust him, and he didn't think that Dav had made a wise move by hiring him. John Henry figured he would have to keep a close eye on Miller.

He might even need eyes in the back of his head.

Chapter Twelve

A few minutes later, John Henry walked along the street with Miller beside him. He had a deputy's badge pinned to his shirt now. It was a cheap tin star, not nearly as impressive as the deputy United States marshal's badge that was hidden away safely in his gear, but the sight of it made the townspeople move aside and glance warily at him anyway.

He could still feel the deputy's hostility, but Sheriff Dav had told Miller to take John Henry down to the Collinses' place.

"You'll need a place to stay, Cobb," Dav had said. "Old Jimpson Collins runs a decent boardinghouse. Carl can show you the way."

"I'm obliged," John Henry had said with a nod.

"Yes, you are," Dav had agreed with a smile, "but you'll work off that obligation. I'll see to that."

Now as they walked toward the boardinghouse with John Henry leading Iron Heart, he said to Miller, "I'll need a place to keep my horse, too."

"Collins has a barn and a corral behind his house," Miller said. "You can keep the horse there instead of having to put it in a stable."

"Cheaper that way, I imagine."

That brought a harsh laugh from Miller.

"It would be if we paid for anything around here. The townspeople are so grateful to us for bringing law and order to Chico, our money's no good."

Miller's smug arrogance rubbed John Henry the wrong way, but he didn't let that reaction show. He was just glad he had been able to ride into Chico and get in Sheriff Dav's good graces right from the start, at least provisionally. That gave him the opportunity to scope out the lay of the land without asking a bunch of questions that might make Dav suspicious of him.

John Henry thought it was pretty unlikely that he would be able to take on all of Dav's deputies in a fight and emerge victorious. Twenty-to-one odds were impossible. His best bet along those lines might be to catch some of the deputies alone, overpower them, and take them prisoner. If he could manage that, he would need some place to stash them, which would mean trusting someone here in town to help him. All of that would take time to figure out.

It was also possible that he could take Dav by surprise some time, capture him, and sneak out of the settlement with him. If he took Dav back to Santa Fe as a prisoner, would the gang collapse without him?

Or would someone like Carl Miller just take over, so that things went on as before, possibly even worse?

Only time would tell which of those options would work out the best. Luckily for John Henry, his run-in with Cobb at that river settlement had given him that time by allowing him to pose as the gunman.

He and Miller came to a two-story frame house that appeared to be well cared for. A fresh coat of whitewash gleamed on its outer walls, and flowers bloomed in a bed along the front of its porch.

"This is the boardinghouse," Miller said. "Collins ought to have a room. If he doesn't, we'll kick somebody out."

John Henry didn't want to do that, but he might be forced to, he told himself. The gunfighter John Cobb wouldn't care about displacing some tenant, so John Henry Sixkiller couldn't allow himself to, either.

He tied Iron Heart's reins to the picket fence around the yard, then he and Miller went up a stone walk and climbed three steps to the porch. Miller hammered on the door with a fist.

The man who opened it was hunched a little with age, but he was still pretty big. His hair was white, and so was his drooping mustache. He looked at Miller and made a face like he had just bitten into a rotten apple.

"It's you," he said.

"Damn right it's me, Jimpson," Miller said.

"That's Mr. Collins to you," the old man said.

Miller ignored that and went on, "Got a new tenant for you, Jimpson. This is John Cobb, the newest deputy in Chico."

"The newest no-good owlhoot, you mean?"

Miller's heavy jaw thrust out belligerently as he stepped closer to Jimpson Collins.

"You'd better watch your mouth, old man," he snapped. "Bad things happen to people who are too loose with their talk."

"Like Milton Hammond and poor Willie Heinsdorf?" Collins snorted in disgust. "You can threaten me all you want, Miller, but you can't shut me up, and I'll be damned if I'll harbor another one of you polecats under my roof!"

Miller said, "Why, you—" and clenched a fist. John Henry wondered if he was going to have to step in and prevent Miller from giving the old man a beating. That wouldn't help his plans, but he couldn't stand by and watch such brutality, either.

He was saved from having to make that decision by a woman's voice, clear and sweet as the music of a mountain stream, saying, "That's enough, Grandfather. Let them come in."

Old Jimpson Collins looked like he wanted to ignore what the woman told him, but after a moment he reluctantly stepped back out of the doorway.

The woman who came forward was probably around twenty years old, John Henry guessed, but her green eyes looked older than that, testifying that she had seen some hardship in her life.

Everything else about her was young and vibrant, from the smooth curves of her body in a cotton dress to the long red hair that framed her features to the creamy skin of her face.

"What can we do for you deputies?" she asked.

Miller gave her a leering smile. John Henry's first impulse was to smash the expression off the man's face, but he suppressed the urge as Miller jerked a thumb at him and said, "Cobb here needs a place to stay. Sheriff Dav had the idea that you folks could put him up."

"Three of your men are already staying here," the young woman said. "Without paying, I might add."

"You know what the town council said. It's everybody's duty to pitch in and help out our dedicated peace officers."

The redhead looked like she wanted to say something, but her lips thinned as she held in the words. After a moment she nodded.

"We have one more empty room." She looked at John Henry. "You're welcome to stay, Deputy . . . Cobb, was it?"

"That's right, miss," he told her. Her welcome sounded like it tasted bitter in her mouth. He would have eased her mind if he could, but that was out of the question right now. "Deputy Miller tells me you've got a corral out back?"

She nodded and said, "That's right." Her attitude eased slightly as she glanced at Iron Heart. "Your horse looks like a fine animal."

"He is," John Henry agreed.

"You can put your saddle in the barn."

"Much obliged."

Miller said, "All right, you don't need me to hold your hand while you get settled in. When you get your gear put up, come on back down to the office."

"I'll do that," John Henry replied with a nod.

Miller grinned at the redhead again and said, "So long, Katie."

"My name's Kate," she said to his back as he turned away. He didn't respond, just went down the steps and back along the walk.

She glared after him for a second, then turned to John Henry.

"Don't just stand there," she told him. "Take your horse around back. I'll meet you at the back door."

John Henry touched a finger to his hat brim and said, "Yes, ma'am, Miss Collins."

She looked angry for a second, as if she thought he was mocking her, and then she just looked confused. Obviously, such courtesy from one of Sheriff Dav's men was unexpected.

John Henry heard Kate say, "Come on, Grandfather," as she went back into the house. Old Jimpson Collins snorted disgustedly as his granddaughter closed the front door.

John Henry untied Iron Heart and led the horse

along the side fence, which ended when it was even with the rear corner of the house. The fence was just for show; open at the back like that, it woudn't keep anything out.

The barn was made of rough-hewn lumber, and the corral attached to one side of it was built with planed poles. There was no gate in the corral fence, which meant it had to be entered through the barn. Three horses stood inside the corral, which reminded John Henry of how Kate Collins had said three deputies were already staying here. John Henry was confident the horses in the corral belonged to Dav's men.

He took Iron Heart into the barn, which had half a dozen stalls in it, three on each side of the center aisle, all of which were empty at the moment. He opened a door and found a tack room. After unsaddling Iron Heart he left saddle, harness, and blanket there. Iron Heart cast a wary gaze on the other three horses as John Henry opened the gate into the corral, but he walked out there with his head held high. If those other horses had any ideas about trying to intimidate the newcomer, they would give them up pretty quick-like, John Henry knew.

Taking his rifle and saddlebags, he went to the house. Kate Collins was waiting at the back door, as she had said she would be.

"This is the kitchen," she said to John Henry as he came in. "You don't really need to know that, since you've no business in this part of the house. I handle all the cooking."

"Yes, ma'am," John Henry said. "I guess I should call you miss, though, since I don't see a wedding ring on your finger."

"Never you mind about whether I'm married or not," she told him in a brisk tone. "Come along through here . . . This is the dining room. Meals are at six, noon, and six o'clock. I'm a stickler for being on time, so if you're not here, you don't eat." She paused. "I don't know why I'm telling you about breakfast. You deputies are hardly ever up in time to eat it."

"Well, lawmen sometimes don't keep regular hours," John Henry said.

She looked at him for a second, then scoffed, "Lawmen." He didn't respond to that, so she turned away and motioned for him to follow. "If you miss breakfast here, you can always get something to eat at Abernathy's Café, across the street from the bank. The food's not as good as what I prepare, but it'll keep you from starving."

"I expect it will," John Henry said. "You've got me curious enough, though, that I'm going to make an effort to sample your breakfasts."

She ignored that and waved a slender hand toward a staircase.

"I'll show you your room."

As they went up the stairs, John Henry asked, "Are any of Sheriff Dav's deputies here right now?"

"As a matter of fact, yes. A couple of them are in their rooms, sleeping. I suppose they'll be on duty tonight."

"What are their names?"

She hesitated as if she wasn't sure she wanted to answer, but she must have decided it wouldn't do any harm. She said, "Steve Buckner and Aaron Kemp."

The names didn't mean anything to John Henry. He had a hunch that most of Dav's men had been outlaws at one time or another, but if they'd operated mostly in the Southwest he wouldn't have any reason to know them. Until recently his entire life had been spent in Indian Territory, Kansas, Missouri, and Arkansas.

That was changing, he realized. As a federal lawman, his authority was good all over the country, and although most of his assignments might still find him in Indian Territory, Judge Parker had the ability to send him just about anywhere.

Kate showed him to a clean, comfortable-looking room on the second floor. It had a nice bed, a rug on the floor, and yellow curtains over the window. John Henry looked around and nodded in satisfaction.

"Thank you, Miss Collins. I'm sure I'll be very comfortable here."

She stood in the door with her arms crossed, regarding him curiously.

"You're a little different from the rest of the sheriff's deputies," she said. "You know that, don't you?"

He tossed his saddlebags on the bed and asked, "Different how?"

"Well, for one thing, you're not a crude, arrogant boor."

Uh-oh, John Henry thought. He had almost let his natural politeness and chivalry lead him into making a mistake. He wanted Dav to trust him, so he had to fit in with the other deputies, no matter how abhorrent he found their behavior.

He leaned his Winchester in a corner and smiled.

"I'm glad to hear you say that," he told Kate as he tossed his hat on the bed next to his saddlebags. "Maybe you won't mind me doing this."

He stepped close to her, moving fast enough that she had no chance to duck away from him, and put his arms around her waist. She let out a startled gasp as he pulled her toward him and planted his mouth on hers in a passionate kiss.

She was stiff as a board in his embrace. Her hands pushed against his chest. That reaction changed abruptly as she softened her resistance. Her lips went slack under his for a second, then clung with renewed urgency. John Henry managed not to raise his eyebrows in surprise, just in case she had her eyes open. Which seemed unlikely.

Then she changed again in the blink of an eye. She tore her mouth away from his, let out a furious "Oh!" and tried to slap him. His hand came up with the same speed he used in drawing a gun and caught her wrist before the blow could land on his face. Her hand trembled inches from his cheek.

"You mean this isn't part of the service in this boardinghouse?" he asked with a sly, lazy smile.

"You . . . you . . ." Apparently she couldn't find a

word strong enough to express her contempt for him. "Let go of me!"

"Sure," John Henry said. He released her and stepped back out of reach so she couldn't slap him. He wouldn't have been surprised if she came after him anyway, but she didn't.

Instead she stood there shaking with anger and said through clenched teeth, "Meals are at six, noon, and six, like I told you. Fresh linens once a week. Other than that I don't see any reason for us to have anything to do with each other."

"I'm sorry you feel that way," John Henry told her. "Maybe you'll change your mind when you get to know me better."

"I don't think so." She turned away sharply but paused in the doorway to glance back at him. "For a minute there, I thought you were different. But I was wrong. You're just another no-good outlaw masquerading as a deputy, just like the rest of them!"

She had that backward, John Henry thought as she stalked off down the hall, but for the sake of his mission he hoped everybody in Chico felt the same way about him for the time being.

Chapter Thirteen

Dav had told John Henry to come back to the sheriff's office once he was settled in at the boardinghouse, but John Henry didn't see any harm in carrying out that order in a leisurely fashion. The Collins house was set on a side street, around the corner from Main. He strolled back to that corner and paused there for a moment to study the town.

It resembled many others he had seen, with a variety of businesses dominated by a two-story brick building that housed the Territorial Bank of Chico and the big Chico General Mercantile that took up an entire block. John Henry spotted a newspaper office on the other side of the street, but it appeared to be closed. He saw Abernathy's Café, which Kate Collins had mentioned, as well as a hash house called Rudy's. Down the street was Li Po's Laundry, with a sign in front of it that also sported a lot of Chinese characters; they reminded John Henry of chicken scratchings and made just about as much sense to him. A blacksmith shop, a saddle maker, a cobbler, a gunsmith . . . all of those establishments and others had set up shop in Chico, but they didn't appear to be doing much business at the moment. In fact, the boardwalks were almost deserted.

John Henry had a hunch that was because everybody was afraid of Sheriff Dav and his deputies. Faced with the sheriff's tyrannical reign, the smart thing to do was to hunker down and hope not to be noticed.

That might work in the short term, but in the long run such an attitude would doom the town. Eventually all the businesses would fail. Chico would dry up and blow away. But not before Samuel Dav had leeched every penny he could out of it.

There were exceptions to the lassitude that gripped the rest of the settlement. Half a dozen horses were tied up in front of the Buzzard's Nest Saloon, and John Henry could hear the music of a player piano coming from it. Even in bad situations, people still liked to drink. *Especially* in bad situations, he thought wryly.

The Buzzard's Nest wasn't the only saloon in town. He saw at least two others, although they didn't look as prosperous. He was sure he would become familiar with all of them if he was here long enough, since a lawman's job often took him into a settlement's most unsavory places.

Sheriff Dav was probably starting to wonder

where he was by now. Telling himself that he would look around town more later, John Henry started toward the sheriff's office.

When he got there, Miller was sitting on the sofa smoking again. John Henry didn't see Dav.

"Took you long enough," Miller commented.

John Henry grinned and said, "Well, as long as that pretty little redhead was showing me around the boardinghouse, I wasn't going to get in any hurry."

Miller chuckled.

"Yeah, she's a peach, ain't she? She doesn't seem to want to warm up to any of us, though."

"We'll see about that," John Henry said confidently.

"I guess we will." Miller tossed the butt of his quirly into a spittoon and stood up. "Come on. We got work to do."

"Where's the sheriff?"

"Tendin' to some business of his own. Don't ask me what, because he only fills us in on what he figures we ought to know, so you'd better get used to that. But before he left, he told me what he wanted you and me to do. We're gonna pay a visit to the blacksmith shop."

"I don't need any horseshoeing done."

"You just follow my lead when we get there," Miller said.

"I was curious what it's about, that's all."

Miller gave John Henry a narrow-eyed look and said, "You'll learn pretty quick that curiosity ain't all that welcome around here. Do what you're told and don't ask questions."

John Henry shrugged.

"Fine," he said. "That's what I'll do from here on out."

"Questions make people nervous," Miller continued as they went out onto the boardwalk. "Especially when they're from somebody we don't really know yet."

John Henry held up his hands in a gesture of surrender.

"No more questions," he promised.

Being too inquisitive was probably the mistake Governor Wallace's previous agents had made, John Henry thought. He'd been given a chance to avoid the same fate, and he intended to take advantage of that.

The two men walked toward the blacksmith shop that John Henry had taken notice of a few minutes earlier. Smoke came from the chimney, so the smith had a fire going in the forge. As they came closer, John Henry heard the ringing reports of a hammer striking metal.

The big double doors on the front of the shop stood open. Miller walked in with John Henry beside him. The interior of the shop was dim and smoky. A red glow came from the forge.

Two men stood next to an anvil. One of them held a horseshoe with a pair of tongs while the other man hammered it into shape. Both of them wore thick leather aprons to protect their clothes from sparks. Long gloves came almost to their elbows and served the same purpose.

The man wielding the hammer was the older of the two. He was only medium height but powerfully built, with broad, heavily muscled shoulders. His graying dark hair was a wild tangle, and the beard that jutted out from his jaw was bushy, as well.

The man with the tongs was younger and even bigger. John Henry saw the resemblance between them right away, even though the younger man didn't have a beard. He knew they were father and son.

The older man glanced over at Miller and John Henry, and the blows he struck with the hammer seemed to fall a little harder, as if he were taking out some anger on the horseshoe. His son looked toward them, too, and glared.

The smith didn't stop what he was doing until he was satisfied with the shoe. Then he stepped back and nodded to his son, who plunged the still faintly glowing horseshoe into a bucket of water. The water sizzled, and a few wisps of steam rose from the bucket.

Still holding the hammer, the smith turned to the two visitors and asked in a gravelly voice, "What do you want, Miller?"

"That's Deputy Miller to you, Farnham. Anyway, I'm not lookin' for you." Miller nodded toward the younger man. "It's your boy I need to talk to."

The blacksmith frowned.

"Nate's got nothing to do with you," he said.

"That's where you're wrong," Miller said. "Deputy Ralston brought a horse with a loose shoe by here yesterday, and the boy refused to fix it."

Nate Farnham shook his head and said, "No, I didn't, Deputy. I was busy with another job, and I just told Ralston he'd have to wait until I was finished with it. Then I would have fixed that loose shoe. But he just got a mean look on his face and left."

In listening to the young man speak, John Henry realized that Nate Farnham maybe wasn't quite right in the head. He sounded more like a ten-year-old than a grown man in his midtwenties.

"You call him Deputy Ralston or Mr. Ralston, you hear?" Miller snapped. "And you should've dropped that other job and tended to what he wanted right away. Don't you know that the needs of the law come first?"

"I'm sorry, Mr. Miller," Nate said.

"You don't have anything to apologize for, son," his father said. Farnham's rough voice was almost a growl as he looked at Miller and went, "The boy was just doing what I taught him to do. When I'm not here he takes each customer in turn. That's the only fair way to do it."

"No, what's fair is respectin' the law," Miller said. "You're gonna have to come with me, Nate."

Farnham stepped forward.

"Wait just a damned minute," he said. "What are you plannin' on doing with him, Miller?"

"He's got to spend a night in jail. That's what

Sheriff Dav decided. That'll teach him not to say no the next time one of us asks him to do somethin'."

Nate's eyes got big, and he started to shake his head back and forth. John Henry thought the young man looked terrified.

"You can't do that," Farnham said. He looked a little scared, too. "You know Nate couldn't stand that—"

"The decision's been made," Miller said flatly as he took a step toward Nate. He put his hand on the butt of his gun. "You come along with me, kid—"

That was as far as he got. Nate howled, "Noooo," put his head down, and charged at Miller, swinging the tongs.

Chapter Fourteen

Edgar Wellman had stayed at the Hammond mansion with Lucinda until the man who had been brought into town by Carl Miller and the other deputies emerged from the sheriff's office with Miller and walked off leading his horse.

"Well, I guess they're not going to kill him after all," Lucinda said as she stood in the foyer with her arms folded. She sounded relieved.

"No, it appears not," Wellman agreed. He didn't know who the stranger was, and in anything other than the most basic human terms, he didn't care. He was just glad to see Lucinda taking an interest in something again.

True, it really hadn't been that long since her husband was killed, and you couldn't expect someone to bounce back from that right away. But Wellman had worried that Lucinda would never truly recover, and he didn't want that.

She would have to get over losing Milton before

he could begin trying to convince her that she ought to turn to *him* for comfort and affection.

Once Miller and the stranger left the sheriff's office, Lucinda lost interest in things again. Her eyes turned dull, and Wellman knew he had overstayed his welcome. He tipped his hat to her and said, "I'll say farewell again, I suppose."

"Good-bye, Edgar," she said. She closed the door in his face before he could even try to add anything else.

Wellman knew when he was beaten . . . for the moment. He turned and left the mansion, walking along Main Street toward the newspaper office. His living quarters were behind the office, in the same building.

As he walked, he thought about Lucinda Hammond, as he often did. At her best she was a gorgeous woman, absolutely breathtaking. He had wanted her from the very first time he saw her, four years earlier when he first came to Chico to take over the *Star*.

But she was married, of course, and seemed to be genuinely in love with her husband, something that Wellman had found to be relatively rare among married couples, most of whom, it seemed to him, barely tolerated each other after they'd been together for a few years.

Not only that, but as Wellman got to know Milton Hammond, he found that he actually liked the man. Wellman wasn't above setting his sights on a married woman, but circumstances like that made it more difficult.

A married woman, in fact, had been a partial influence on his decision to leave Dallas rather hurriedly, along with the pending discovery of how he had embezzled a bit of money from the newspaper where he'd been working as a reporter. He had gotten out of Texas quickly and used his ill-gotten gains to buy a defunct newspaper, press and all, in Chico. He thought that might be far enough away from both the Texas authorities and a jealous, irate husband.

All in all, it had been a splendid move, his best so far. He had gotten out of New Orleans one step ahead of the law, too, just as he'd made a hurried departure from Boston and from Liverpool before that. His appetites had always had a habit of leading him into trouble.

But he was clever and had a knack for turning a phrase, so he could always get work anywhere there was a newspaper. Having a paper of his own had been the best, though, and he had given some thought to staying here in Chico and turning his façade of respectability into the real thing.

Then Samuel Dav had come to town.

The previous sheriff, Buck Tannehill, had been well liked, but he was an amiable incompetent and everybody knew it. When a gang of outlaws robbed the bank a month or so before the last election, Tannehill had dithered around about forming a posse until it was almost too late to go after the robbers.

That was when Dav stepped in, volunteering to take over, and after being deputized he had led a group of men in pursuit of the outlaws, catching up to them before they were able to slip away in the mountains. A fierce exchange of gunfire had broken out, and although none of the robbers had been captured, the one carrying the loot had dropped it in all the confusion, and Dav had recovered the money. Upon his return to Chico with the posse, he had been hailed as a hero.

When he announced that he was going to run for sheriff, the outcome was a foregone conclusion. The voters wanted a real lawman to be in charge of things, not the pleasant but ineffective Buck Tannehill. Wellman himself had editorialized frequently about the need to elect Dav.

It was a landslide.

And then, as soon as Dav was in office, he'd begun to surround himself with new deputies, men who were clearly not much better than outlaws themselves . . . if indeed they were any better. Wellman suspected that many of them were wanted elsewhere and regarded Chico as a sort of safe haven. In short order, intimidation, extortion, and mysterious disappearances became common. Dav paraded around town with an arrogant smirk on his face, confidently secure in his new power.

After a while, Wellman began to suspect that there was something fishy about the bank robbery that had started Dav on his path to the sheriff's office. Wellman wondered if the men who had held up the bank now strutted around Chico wearing tin stars. After all, none of the robbers had been captured in the battle. They could have put on a good show for the honest citizens who had gone along with the posse, the citizens who had come back to Chico and enthusiastically supported Dav in his campaign because he had recovered the money.

They had all been used and manipulated, himself included, Wellman finally concluded. He felt a little guilty for his part in it, for letting himself fall for Dav's spiel, but it was too late to do anything about it now, other than slipping a few veiled suspicions into the newspaper.

He had folded quickly when the sheriff took offense to the things he'd printed. He had never been a courageous man, nor had he ever felt the noble calling some journalists claimed they did. It was easier just to go along with those in power, even though he sometimes woke up with a sour, bitter taste in his mouth.

When he reached the newspaper office, he went around to the back to let himself into his living quarters, rather than unlocking the front door and going through the office. He didn't want to look at the empty desk up there where he used to write the news stories and his fiery editorials, or at the press sitting unused and growing dusty.

In the back room with its stove, table, and bunk, he hung his hat on a nail and took a bottle and a glass from one of the shelves. He poured himself a shot of whiskey, looked at the amber liquid for a second, and then tossed it back. The stuff warmed his insides and dulled some of the pain in his soul.

A knock sounded on the door.

Wellman's fingers tightened on the empty glass. Only one person came to visit him in these quarters. None of the townspeople wanted much to do with him these days, anyway. They saw him as a coward who had buckled under to the corrupt sheriff. That was right, of course, but it ignored their own kowtowing to Dav.

Nothing unusual about that, Wellman thought. People were always much quicker to see the flaws in others than they were to recognize their own.

He went to the door and asked, "Who is it?" even though he already knew.

"Let me in, Edgar."

Wellman sighed and opened the door.

Sheriff Samuel Dav stepped into the room and heeled the door closed behind him.

Chapter Fifteen

As Nate Farnham charged him, Miller clawed at the gun on his hip, and John Henry knew exactly what was going to happen here in the blacksmith shop in the next couple of seconds.

Miller was going to pull his gun and blow a hole in Nate before the young man could bash his brains out with those tongs.

John Henry wasn't going to let that happen. He threw himself forward, bulling into Miller and taking him by surprise. The impact knocked the deputy to the side and sent him sprawling off his feet.

That put John Henry right in the path of Nate's charge. The heavy metal tongs swept at his head. With the power of the young man's massive form behind them, they would crush his skull if they landed.

John Henry made sure they didn't by ducking swiftly. The tongs hit his hat and knocked it flying off his head, but that was all they hit.

Nate was still plenty dangerous, though. He barreled into John Henry like a runaway freight. John Henry flew backward and crashed to the ground.

"Nate, no!" Farnham yelled. "Stop!"

Nate didn't listen. He roared in defiance—defiance motivated more by fear than by anger, John Henry knew—and brought the tongs down, still intending to crush the skull of the man on the ground. John Henry managed to roll aside just at the last second. He felt the tongs as they swept down past his ear.

He lashed out with a foot, hooked it behind one of Nate's ankles, and heaved. Nate stumbled, thrown off balance by the move. John Henry launched a kick with his other foot. The heel of his boot drove against Nate's thigh.

It was like kicking a tree and did about as much good. Nate yelled in pain but didn't budge.

He dropped the tongs, reached down, and dug sausage-like fingers into the front of John Henry's shirt. Suddenly John Henry felt himself lifted. Nate Farnham handled him like he didn't weigh anything. John Henry found himself flying through the air.

An instant later he slammed into a wall of the blacksmith shop with stunning force.

The world spun crazily around John Henry as he bounced off the wall and dropped to the ground again. He couldn't marshal his thoughts, and he couldn't force his muscles to work as Nate stampeded toward him. In a matter of seconds, John Henry would be trampled under that charge.

And there wasn't a blasted thing he could do about it.

At the last moment, Carl Miller loomed behind Nate. The gun in his fist rose and fell, thudding against Nate's skull when it landed. Nate stumbled. His feet got tangled up, and he fell to his knees. Miller hit him again with the gun. Nate pitched forward.

John Henry saw that through blurry eyes. His vision cleared just in time for him to see the black-smith come up behind Miller with the hammer lifted. That big hammer would shatter the deputy's skull like an eggshell. John Henry pulled his Colt and fired, hoping that his shaky condition wouldn't make him miss.

Instinct guided his shot, which was as unerring as ever. The slug burned through the air past Miller's head and struck the hammer's head with a ringing report. The bullet's impact tore the handle from Farnham's grip. It must have stung, because Farnham yelled in pain.

Miller's eyes were wide. For a second he must have thought that John Henry was shooting at him, because the bullet had passed so close to him. The clang of bullet on hammer and Farnham's subsequent outcry told a different story, though. Miller whirled around and thrust his gun at the blacksmith.

"Don't kill him!" John Henry said as he used his free hand to push himself up to a sitting position. "I've got him covered!"

Miller hesitated with his finger on the trigger. Then his face contorted in a snarl and he stepped forward to slash the gun across Farnham's face. Farnham staggered back a step as blood flowed from the gash on his cheek the gunsight had opened up.

John Henry climbed wearily to his feet. Nate Farnham lay senseless on the ground, still stunned from the pistol-whipping Miller had dealt out to him. John Henry circled the big form and kept his gun pointed at Nate's father.

Farnham rubbed the tingling fingers of his right hand with the other hand and snarled at Miller, "You didn't have to do that. You didn't have to hurt my boy!"

"He was about to stomp Deputy Cobb to death," Miller said coldly. "You saw it with your own eyes, Farnham."

"I could've stopped him if you'd just given me the chance!"

"I don't take chances with addlepated animals like that boy of yours."

"Don't talk about him like that," Farnham said. His voice shook with emotion. "Nate's a good boy. He's sweet and obedient and he'd never hurt anybody unless he was pushed into it."

Miller sneered and let out a contemptuous snort.

"Yeah, he looked harmless when he was tryin' to stove our heads in with those tongs," he said. "Drag him over to the jail, Farnham. He could've just spent one night behind bars for disrespectin' the law. The attempted murder of two peace officers is a lot worse. He may not see the outside of a cell for a long time."

"You can't do that," Farnham said. Desperation crept into his voice. "You just can't."

"Oh, don't worry. You'll be keepin' him company. You tried to kill me, so you'll be locked up, too. You came at me with that hammer." Miller glanced at John Henry. "You'll testify to that, since you're the one who shot it out of his hand." He added, "That was mighty good shootin', by the way."

"Thanks," John Henry said. His insides were in a turmoil, but he made an effort not to show it. The idea of locking up the two Farnhams and charging them with attempted murder went against the grain. Technically, he supposed the charges were true enough, but Miller had goaded the father and son into reacting violently.

John Henry couldn't do anything to try to stop it, though, without casting suspicion on his pose as John Cobb. He didn't want to do that when his mission here in Chico was just getting underway.

At gunpoint, Farnham reached down, grasped Nate's ankles, and dragged him out of the blacksmith shop. The few citizens on the street scattered at the sight of them, not wanting to get involved in whatever was going on, John Henry supposed.

As he and Miller followed with their guns still drawn, Miller frowned and asked, "Hey, what was the idea of runnin' into me like that, Cobb?"

"I didn't really mean to," John Henry replied. "I

was just going for the kid, trying to stop him from jumping you. Sorry about knocking you down."

Miller appeared to accept that explanation. He said, "All right, but we'll just keep that part of the story to ourselves, you hear?"

"That's fine by me," John Henry agreed.

Farnham stopped halfway to the sheriff's office and jail. His chest heaved. He was winded from the effort of dragging his unconscious son that far.

"Blast it, Nate's too big to do him this way," Farnham complained. "Not only that, but shouldn't he be waking up by now? I swear, if you've done him any real harm, Miller—"

"You think threatenin' a law officer's gonna make things better for you, Farnham?" Miller interrupted. With a flourish of the gun in his hand, he went on, "Take him over there and dump him in that horse trough. That ought to wake him up."

"I may be strong, but I don't know if I can lift him by myself like that."

Miller scowled impatiently and said, "All right. Cobb, give him a hand. Don't worry, I'll keep the varmint covered."

John Henry wasn't really worried about Farnham. The blacksmith was too worried about his son to try anything. John Henry holstered his gun and went over to Farnham. He got hold of Nate's right leg, Farnham took the left, and together they hauled Nate over to the horse trough Miller had mentioned.

Once they got him there, they lifted him with

much grunting and straining and draped his upper half on the edge of the trough. Then John Henry held Nate in position while Farnham lifted his son's legs and let gravity do the rest. Nate rolled into the trough and hit the water with a great splash.

The splashing got even worse as Nate floundered back up, kicking his legs and waving his arms. The water had revived him. John Henry was glad to see that. Like Farnham, he had worried that the pistol-whipping might have done some real damage to Nate.

He appeared to be all right, though, now that he had been shocked back to consciousness. Farnham leaned over and grabbed Nate by the shoulders to stop him from flailing around.

"Take it easy, boy, take it easy," Farnham said. "It's all right, Nate. Just stop fighting, lad, and settle down."

After a moment Nate ceased struggling and just sat there in the horse trough, water streaming off his head and shoulders as he breathed heavily. He gulped down some air and said, "I . . . I thought I was drowning, Pa."

"I know you did," Farnham said gently. "But it's all right now."

Miller said, "If you consider bein' locked up in jail all right. Get him up now, Farnham. He can walk the rest of the way."

John Henry stepped back and drew his gun again. He didn't know how Nate was going to react to being ordered to jail again. If there was another violent outbreak from the young man, John Henry intended to do what he could to keep Miller from killing him.

All the fight seemed to have gone out of Nate, though. When Farnham grasped his arm and said, "Come on, now," Nate stood up, stepped out of the trough, and walked docilely enough toward the two-story stone building that housed the sheriff's office and jail. His head hung low and he shuffled along, reminding John Henry of a bear.

Sheriff Dav still wasn't there when the little group reached the office. Miller gestured with the gun and ordered the prisoners, "Get up those stairs now."

Nate whimpered a little and asked, "Do I have to, Pa?"

"Just for a little while," Farnham said. "It won't be too bad." He gave Miller and John Henry a glance filled with rage and went on, "Don't worry, son, I'll be with you."

"All right, Pa," Nate said, but he still didn't sound happy about it.

Miller took a ring of keys from a peg and tossed them to John Henry.

"Get up there and unlock the cell block door."

John Henry went up the stairs in front of the Farnhams. He had to try a couple of the keys before he found the one that worked on the cell block door, but he had it open by the time they got there. He backed into the cell block in front of them.

There were ten cells, he saw at a glance, five on either side. All of them were empty at the moment.

He nodded toward the first one on the right. Farnham led Nate into the cell.

"You reckon we ought to split them up?" Miller said.

"I don't see why," John Henry replied. "They'll probably be easier to handle if they're together."

"Yeah, you're right." Miller slammed the door on the cell that now held the blacksmith and his son. The sound had a grim finality to it.

Nate whimpered again. John Henry's jaw tightened. He still had the keys. Doubtless one of them would unlock that cell. He could get the drop on Miller and turn the Farnhams loose.

That would put him in open opposition to the sheriff's gang, though, and right now that would be the same thing as signing his own death warrant. Farnham and Nate would just have to put up with their captivity for a while, until John Henry figured out a way to break Samuel Dav's iron grip on this town.

Maybe it wouldn't be too long.

"What's going to happen to them?" John Henry asked Miller when they were downstairs in the sheriff's office again.

"What's it matter to you?"

"It doesn't," John Henry said with a shrug. "It's just that locking up that boy seems a little like putting a wild animal in a cage. It's liable to break him, make him go *loco*."

"He's already *loco*, in case you didn't notice. And why do you care about the big dummy? He tried to kill you, too."

"Yeah, you're right," John Henry forced himself to say. "Let 'em rot up there."

"Anyway, it's not up to us," Miller went on. "The sheriff will decide what to do with them as soon as he gets back."

Chapter Sixteen

"What do you want, Sheriff?" Wellman asked. He tried not to sound too unfriendly, but at the same time, having Samuel Dav in his room was sort of like looking down to see a rattlesnake coiled at your feet.

Dav smiled that thin, cold, reptilian smile of his and said, "Don't you mean to say, what can I do for you, Sheriff? That's the way a good citizen would greet a visit by an officer of the law, don't you think?"

Wellman tried not to sigh. He said, "What can I do for you, Sheriff?"

"That's better," Dav replied with a laugh. "For a second there, you almost sounded like you meant it."

A flash of anger went through Wellman. The sheriff was mocking him. He hadn't done anything to deserve that. He had been helpful to Dav's campaign, after all, and he had folded easily enough after his feeble attempt to make up for that later.

Dav waved a hand and went on, "Never mind. I

don't care whether you cooperate with me because you believe in what I'm doing, or because your bowels get loose when I walk by, as long as you do what you're supposed to do. What I want from you today, Edgar, is for you to tell me something."

"What's that, Sheriff?"

"How's the Widow Hammond doing?"

Surprise went through Wellman at the question. He couldn't even speak for a moment. When he could, he said, "What . . . what do you mean?"

"I want to know how Lucinda Hammond is doing these days." A trace of impatience came into Dav's voice as he went on, "I saw you up there at her house a while ago. You were standing in the doorway with her, watching while Miller and those other deputies brought in that prisoner. I figured that since you've been visiting her, you'd know how she's getting along these days."

"How do you think she's getting along?" Wellman asked. The question came out sharper than he'd intended, but he couldn't help it. "She's in mourning. She's deeply grieving the loss of her husband."

The husband that you *murdered,* he thought, but at least he had enough sense not to say it.

"I suppose you're disappointed by that."

Dav's comment made Wellman frown.

"What do you mean?" he asked again.

"Well, you've got your eye on her, don't you? You think that as soon as she gets over that well-meaning boob she was married to, you'll move in and scoop her up for yourself."

Wellman's mouth opened and closed a couple of times before he was able to say, "I . . . I won't dignify that with a response."

Dav threw his head back and laughed.

"The way you go around with your tail tucked between your legs, like everybody else in this town, I don't reckon you'll dignify much of anything ever again, Edgar. But to get back to Lucinda . . . She's eating enough? She's taking care of herself?"

"Why would you care?"

"She's a citizen of this town. As sheriff, I'm charged with seeing to her welfare, just like I am that of everybody else."

Wellman wanted to laugh this time. Dav didn't give a damn about anybody's welfare but his own, and that was obvious to anyone with a pair of eyes.

But instead he told the truth, saying, "I'm a bit worried about her. She's taken Milton's death very hard. The way she's withdrawing into herself, I wouldn't be too surprised if she never sets foot outside that house again."

"We can't have that," Dav said with a shake of his head. "I have plans for Mrs. Hammond."

Good Lord, thought Wellman. *He wants her for himself.*

"But that's my business, not yours," the sheriff went on. "There's something else you can do for me, Edgar."

"What's that?" Wellman asked, although he didn't really want to know.

"I want you to start printing the *Star* again."

Wellman's eyes widened in surprise. He had lost track of how many times that had happened during this unexpected conversation.

"I closed it down because you were upset with what I was printing," he reminded Dav.

"No, I gave you the choice of either closing down or printing the things I wanted you to print. The right things." Dav shook his head. "I'm not giving you that choice anymore."

Wellman struggled to grasp what the sheriff was saying.

"You want me to . . ."

"I'll tell you what to print, and you'll print it," Dav said. "Simple as that."

"A newspaper doesn't work that way."

"Of course it does. Every newspaper in this country is in the pocket of one politician or another. How do you think so many crooked, incompetent men keep getting elected? Because the newspapers tell people to vote for them, and people are too stupid to know any better. From now on the *Star* is going to be my newspaper."

Wellman shook his head and muttered, "I won't . . . I won't—"

Striking swiftly like the snake he reminded Wellman of, Dav stepped closer to the publisher and grabbed the front of his coat. Wellman let out a frightened croak as Dav jerked him up onto his toes.

"Listen to me, you little weasel," Dav said in a low, dangerous voice. "I need a newspaper on my side. I've got plans that go far beyond this town, and in order to make them work, I have to have a voice on my side, trumpeting my accomplishments and letting the world know that I'm on my way to bigger things. Do you understand that?"

"But why . . . why me?" Wellman gasped.

"Because you're here." Dav gave Wellman a shove that sent him staggering back a couple of steps. "You know how to put out a paper already, and people seem to trust you for some reason. I'm not sure why. I can see right through you, Wellman. You're yellow, and you're as corrupt as you like to accuse other people of being. But as long as you do what you're told, I'm willing to work with you. I can bring in my own man to publish the paper if I have to, but it'd be easier if you'd just cooperate."

Wellman realized that he was trapped. If he refused, Dav would just have him killed. He would go down as another of the mysterious disappearances that had plagued Chico ever since Dav took over.

But if he cooperated—or at least pretended to cooperate—maybe he could find out what those mysterious plans that Dav had alluded to really were.

That might turn out to be the sort of story that an actual journalist would want to go after.

He swallowed, straightened his coat where Dav

had crumpled it, and said, "What do you want me to print?"

A grin of triumph spread across Dav's lean face.

"That's more like it, Edgar," he said. He reached into his shirt pocket and pulled out a folded piece of paper. "I've taken the liberty of writing a little editorial that ought to go on the front page of the first edition the *Star* publishes after its temporary hiatus. You can put it into your own words, of course. In fact, I wish you would. You're a good writer, you know."

Dav held out the paper.

Wellman hesitated. If he took it . . . if he published Dav's lies, whatever they were . . . he might be taking a step from which he could never retreat. Ultimately, he might wind up being partially responsible for whatever damage the man did. The blood of innocents might be on his hands.

But if he refused, his own blood might be on the floor of this room, right here and now. Dav's agate-like eyes revealed that in the end, he didn't really care what Wellman's decision was. He would get what he wanted, one way or the other.

Wellman reached out and took the folded sheet of paper.

"That's being smart, Edgar," Dav said. "When can you have the next edition of the paper ready?"

"When do you want it to be ready?" Wellman asked hollowly.

"The sooner the better. We have a lot of work to

do, to make this territory over into what it needs to be."

Wellman nodded and said, "All right. Give me a few days."

"Sure. I'm looking forward to seeing what you'll do with that editorial." Dav started to turn toward the door, but he paused. "There's one more thing."

"What's that?" Wellman's voice was dull and dispirited in defeat as he asked the question.

"The next time you talk to the Widow Hammond, I'd take it kindly if you'd mention my name."

Wellman's head came up as he was surprised yet again.

"Tell her I'm sorry about what happened to her husband. Tell her that you've gotten to know me, and you've realized what a fine man I am after all. Tell her that there are going to be some big changes around here, changes for the better, and that they're not going to be confined just to Chico, either. Tell her that pretty soon I'm going to be the most powerful man in this territory."

"You're insane," Wellman whispered.

"Maybe you'd better not print *that* opinion," Dav said with a smile. "Not unless you want the new editor of the *Star* to put your obituary on the front page."

Chapter Seventeen

Sheriff Dav seemed pleased with himself when he came into the office a short time after John Henry and Miller had locked up the Farnhams. He was even whistling a little tune. John Henry had been around Dav only a very short period of time, but that seemed incongruous even to him. Whatever Dav's business had been, it must have gone well.

Miller pointed to the ceiling with a thumb and said, "Got a couple of prisoners up in the cell block, Sheriff."

"Prisoners?" Dav repeated. "Who'd you lock up?"

"Peabody Farnham and that simpleminded son of his."

"The blacksmith and his boy?"

"You told me to have a word with 'em about how the boy refused to fix that shoe on Ralston's horse yesterday," Miller reminded the sheriff.

Dav looked annoyed, as if such matters were beneath his concern.

"I figured you'd just put the fear of God into them, Carl," he said. "Maybe lock up the boy for a night. Not both of them, though. What's the town going to do for a blacksmith if they're both behind bars?"

Miller frowned and said, "Reckon I didn't think about that. But the kid went *loco* and tried to kill me and Cobb, and Peabody was set to bash my head in with his hammer when Cobb shot it out of his hand. That's attempted murder of a peace officer for both of 'em."

Dav didn't seem all that concerned about the attempted murder of two of his deputies. Instead he looked at John Henry and said, "You shot the hammer out of Farnham's hand?"

"I got lucky," John Henry said with a shrug. "Or unlucky, depending on how you want to look at it. I was trying to put the bullet through his head."

That was a lie, of course, but just the sort of thing that a callous, cold-blooded killer like John Cobb might have said and done.

John Henry went on, "Now that I think about it, I suppose it's a good thing I didn't blow his brains out. Like you said, Sheriff, what would folks around here do for a blacksmith? I don't think the boy's smart enough to handle the job full-time on his own."

"You're right about that," Dav agreed. He stroked his chin as he frowned in thought. After a moment he said, "All right, leave them up there for now. Judge Curwood can sentence them to a week in jail for disturbing the peace. I'll talk to the judge tomorrow."

"What about the way they tried to kill us?" Miller asked, clearly not satisfied with Dav's decision.

"I think we can dispense with that because of extenuating circumstances."

"Exit . . . extent . . . what?"

"Chico still needs a good blacksmith," Dav explained. "But I already have plenty of deputies. One thing trumps the other."

"Fine," Miller grumbled. "Whatever you say, boss."

"That's right, and you'd do well to remember it." Dav hung up his hat and sat down at the desk. He leaned back and clasped his hands over his belly as he looked at John Henry. "You've had a full day today, Cobb. First you tangle with Harry Price and Ben Hoffman, and then you mix it up with that monster of a blacksmith's son."

Miller said, "Nate picked up Cobb and threw him clear across the shop like a kid with a rag doll."

"It wasn't quite that bad," John Henry said, but the aches and pains he already felt from the pair of ruckuses testified to a different story. He knew his muscles would be plenty stiff and sore in the morning.

"Well, you can take it easy for the rest of the day," Dav said. "It's almost suppertime. Consider yourself off duty, Cobb. Go on back down to the boardinghouse. You don't want to miss supper on your first day there." The sheriff chuckled. "That pretty little redhead who runs the place wouldn't be happy, and it's never smart to make a good-looking woman mad at you. They hold grudges longer than the homely ones do."

"I wouldn't know about that," John Henry said. "A gentleman considers all women good-looking, doesn't he?"

Dav looked at him for a second, then laughed.

"Go on, get out of here," he said. Then his tone sharpened as he added, "Not you, Carl. You and I still have business to talk about."

John Henry would have preferred to stay and find out what sort of "business" Dav wanted to discuss with Miller, but to do so would be pushing his luck. He said, "I'll be back in the morning, Sheriff. If you need me between now and then, you know where to find me."

"Indeed I do," Dav agreed.

John Henry left the sheriff's office and walked toward the cross street where the Collinses' boardinghouse was located. A few people were on the boardwalks again, and he took note of the sullen, furtive looks they gave him as he passed.

He figured that had something to do with the blacksmith and his son being arrested. Enough people had seen the Farnhams being arrested that the news would have gotten around town by now. The citizens would regard the situation as just another example of the brutal, tyrannical rule by Dav and his deputies, John Henry mused.

He checked his watch as he came into the boardinghouse. The time was a few minutes shy of six o'clock. He went into the dining room and found that several people were already sitting at the long table with its white linen cloth. A platter with fried chicken on it, along with another full of biscuits, rested in the center of the table.

Kate Collins came through a door on the other side of the room that led to the kitchen, John Henry recalled. She carried a bowl of mashed potatoes in one hand and a gravy boat in the other. When she caught sight of John Henry she paused for a split second, then her face began to turn pink as she set the potatoes and gravy on the table.

He wondered if she was remembering the kiss from that afternoon.

"Deputy Cobb," she greeted him curtly.

"Miss Collins," John Henry replied with a smile. "Six o'clock, just like you said."

"If you'll be so kind as to remove your hat."

"Oh." John Henry reached up and took off his hat. He looked around for a place to hang it, and not seeing one, he settled for bending over and placing it on the floor beside one of the empty chairs. Might as well sit there, he thought.

"And if you wanted to remove your gun," Kate went on, "that gesture would be appreciated as well."

John Henry had already noted that two of the men at the table were packing iron. He had them pegged as two of the other deputies who lived here.

"Sorry, Miss Collins, but I feel downright undressed without my gun, and that wouldn't be proper at all."

She gave a soft little snort and turned to go back out to the kitchen.

One of the other armed men stood up, grinned, and extended his hand to John Henry.

"Don't let Kate put a burr under your saddle, *amigo*," he said. "She can be a mite prickly, but once you're tasted her cookin', you'll agree she's worth puttin' up with it. She's pretty easy on the eyes, too."

"She is, at that," John Henry agreed as he gripped the man's hand. "Name's John Cobb."

"I'm Steve Buckner." He inclined his head toward the other armed man. "That sour-faced cuss is Aaron Kemp. We work for Sam Dav, same as you."

"I figured as much." John Henry shook hands with the stocky, dour Kemp, who had graying dark hair and a thick mustache. Buckner was younger, not yet thirty, with a lean body and a shock of sandy hair.

The two other people at the table, a man and a woman, weren't joining in the conversation. In fact, they kept their eyes downcast as they sat together, as if they didn't want to attract the attention of the three lawmen.

Buckner didn't let that go past. He waved a hand toward the couple and said, "Over yonder on the other side of the table is Mr. and Mrs. Peterson. They've got a store that sells clothes for gentlemen and ladies. Which same is sometimes in short supply in Chico, but we're tryin' to civilize the place as best we can, ain't we, Aaron?"

Kemp just grunted and didn't say anything.

John Henry nodded politely to the Petersons and said, "Howdy, folks."

Mrs. Peterson didn't look up or acknowledge the greeting, but Mr. Peterson replied in a high-pitched, tentative voice, "Deputy."

"I'm pleased to meet you," John Henry went on. "If I need any duds while I'm here, I'll know right where to go."

Buckner chuckled and said, "You'll get a good price at their store, that's for sure. Of course, we get a good price just about everywhere in Chico, don't we, Aaron?"

"Huh," Kemp said.

Kate came back into the dining room, bringing a bowl of greens with her. Her grandfather walked in behind her, carrying a pie. Buckner started licking his lips at that.

"Kate's apple pie is just about the closest thing you'll find to heaven on this earth," he told John Henry. "That's one reason I think she's really an angel."

"I've told you I prefer to be called Miss Collins, Deputy," she said to him.

"Oh, I beg your pardon, Miss Collins," Buckner said, but despite his words it was clear that he was mocking her. "I'll try to remember that."

"Everyone sit down and eat."

"Not everybody's here yet," Buckner objected. "Where's ol' Turnage?"

"Mr. Turnage came in earlier and told me he

didn't feel well," Kate said. "I gave him a bit of food and told him to go on upstairs and lie down."

"I reckon I know how he feels. It'd make me plumb sick to work in a bank, too, handlin' other folks' money all day and knowin' the whole time that I was poor as a church mouse."

John Henry and Buckner took their seats, as did Kate and her grandfather. The deputies dug in. So did John Henry, following their lead. Under the circumstances, it wouldn't pay to be too polite.

After a few minutes, Buckner said around a mouthful of fried chicken, "Heard about you tanglin' with Nate Farnham, Cobb. I'm a mite surprised you're still walkin' around. That boy's as big as a mountain . . . and just about as dumb as one, too."

"I suppose I was lucky," John Henry said.

Kate spoke up, saying, "I think it's awful that you arrested Peabody and Nate." She ignored a warning look from old Jimpson and went on, "Poor Nate is harmless."

"Well, he didn't really seem all that harmless when he was throwing me halfway across the blacksmith shop into a wall," John Henry said. "And I suspect that Peabody Farnham with a hammer in his hand is a far cry from harmless, too."

"What are you going to do with them?"

John Henry shrugged and said, "That's up to the sheriff." He knew what Dav planned to do about the Farnhams, but he didn't think the sheriff would appreciate him spreading that knowledge around.

Mr. Peterson surprised John Henry by speaking up again.

"If there's a fine or something they need to pay, I'm sure the townspeople could take up a collection to cover it," Peterson suggested.

"That's a good idea," Buckner said. "I'll be sure and tell the sheriff you thought of it."

Peterson muttered something unintelligible and looked down at his plate again.

After the meal was over, Buckner asked John Henry, "Are you goin' back out on rounds?"

"The sheriff told me I was off duty," John Henry replied with a shake of his head.

"Well, Aaron and me are just fixin' to go *on* duty, and we always start our shift by stoppin' by the Buzzard's Nest and havin' a little eye-opener. Why don't you come along with us, and we'll introduce you around?"

John Henry considered the invitation for a second. Buckner was the friendly, garrulous sort, and once he got to talking, there was no telling what he might say, especially if he had a drink or two in him. It was unlikely that Buckner or Kemp knew anything about what Dav's ultimate plans were, but John Henry couldn't rule out the possibility.

"Sounds good to me," he said. "I think I'll join you."

Buckner grinned and slapped him on the shoulder.

"You can tell us all about rasslin' with that bear,

by which I mean Nate Farnham. So long, Kate. I mean, Miss Collins. See you in the mornin'."

Kate just sniffed and didn't say anything.

The other two deputies got their hats. Kemp worked at his teeth with a toothpick as they left the house.

"See what I meant about Kate's cookin'?" Buckner asked John Henry.

"It was good, all right."

"She's gonna warm up to me one of these days," Buckner went on. "I been workin' on her with my charm."

"How long have you been here in Chico, Steve?" John Henry asked.

"Couple of months. Why do you . . . Oh, I get you. You think that if charm was gonna work, it would have by now."

"Miss Collins's dislike for us seems to be a formidable obstacle. She's a determined woman."

"You could call her that." Buckner laughed. He dug an elbow into John Henry's ribs. "Or you can just call her the future Mrs. Buckner, know what I mean?"

John Henry stifled the irritation and thought that Kate Collins turning out to be the future Mrs. Buckner was about as likely as hell freezing over.

Chapter Eighteen

The Buzzard's Nest, despite its inelegant name, was a pretty nice place, John Henry thought as he and Buckner and Kemp pushed through the batwings and made their way to the bar. That gleaming hardwood fixture extended down the length of the room's left side for a good forty feet, and two aproned bartenders were working behind it, keeping up with the orders of more than a dozen men who stood there drinking.

Tables extended across the room, filling the floor. Men sat at most of the tables, and a couple of girls in low-cut dresses brought them their drinks. There were booths with bench seats along the right-hand wall. A player piano stood in the front corner, silent now. Toward the back of the room were a couple of poker tables and a faro layout. Oil lamps in wagon wheel fixtures hung from the ceiling and cast their yellow light through air that was thick with smoke from numerous quirlies, cigars, and pipes.

Despite the crowd, the atmosphere in the Buzzard's Nest was rather subdued, almost hushed. It had gotten that way as soon as the three deputies stepped inside, John Henry realized. Somehow everybody in the place knew they were there, even the men who had their backs turned.

Most of the men at the bar wore range clothes. John Henry figured they were cowhands from the ranches scattered along the lower slopes of the San Juan Mountains. The men at the tables were a mixture of miners and townies.

John Henry had known a lot of cowboys and mining men in his life. Without exception, they were all tough *hombres* who didn't like to back down from trouble, ever. The fact that Sheriff Dav and his deputies had this area so thoroughly buffaloed was evidence of just how deadly they really were.

In fact, as John Henry and his companions approached the bar, the men standing there began to drift down toward the other end, leaving a large spot bare. Buckner took notice of that and grinned.

"Hope you ain't thin-skinned, Cobb," he said. "If you are, you're liable to get your feelin's hurt around here."

"Not me," John Henry said. "My hide's nice and thick, like a buffalo's."

"Not thick enough to stop a bullet, I expect. Which means you'd be smart to keep your eyes open all the time."

"You don't think any of these people would try to bushwhack us, do you?" John Henry asked.

"They ain't showed that much fight so far . . . but you never know."

Buckner was right about that, John Henry thought. Push anybody, no matter how peaceful, far enough, and sooner or later they would strike back.

"Three whiskies, Jack," Buckner told the bartender who came along the bar to take their order.

"Sure thing, Deputy," the man replied with a friendly nod that John Henry sensed wasn't completely sincere. He took three glasses from a shelf on the wall behind him, set them on the bar, and then reached for a bottle on the same shelf.

"Not that stuff," Buckner said. "The bottle I want is under the bar, Jack."

The bartender hesitated.

"That's Mr. Rembard's private stock," he said.

Buckner's eyes narrowed as he looked across the bar.

"Are you sayin' we ain't good enough for private stock?" he asked.

The bartender didn't hesitate this time. He shook his head immediately and said, "No, sir, that's not what I'm saying at all. I'd be mighty glad to pour some for you and your friends, Deputy Buckner."

"That's more like it," Buckner said with a satisfied nod.

The bartender took a bottle from underneath

the bar, uncorked it, and poured three fingers of amber liquid into each glass.

Buckner looked critically at the drinks and said, "Top those off just a *leeeetle* more."

The bartender didn't say anything, but he didn't look happy as he splashed more whiskey into each glass.

"That's better," Buckner said. He picked up his drink and motioned for John Henry and Kemp to do likewise. As he raised the glass, he went on, "To the future, gents. To the day we'll all be rich men."

"I'll drink to that," Kemp said, which was the most words John Henry had heard come out of the man's mouth so far.

All three of them tossed the drinks back. The liquor was smooth going down and immediately lit a fire in John Henry's belly. He could see why the owner of the Buzzard's Nest kept it as his private stock.

Since he was half-Cherokee—which nobody in Chico knew about, of course—people sometimes assumed that John Henry couldn't handle his liquor. But he was half-white, too, and when anyone questioned his consumption of alcohol, he always replied that it was his white half doing the drinking. Although he didn't really have a taste for the stuff and he disliked what he had seen it do not only to some of his people but to many others as well, he didn't actually have a problem handling it when he needed to drink to blend in.

He licked his lips now as he set the empty glass on the bar in front of him.

"That's mighty fine drinking whiskey," he said.

Buckner grinned at him.

"You can see why Aaron and me stop here for an eye-opener every evenin'. Want another?"

John Henry shook his head.

"I'd better not," he said. "Miss Collins probably wouldn't like it if I came stumbling in drunk the first night I was staying at her house."

"I understand." Buckner's voice took on a slight edge. "Just don't get too many ideas in your head about her, Johnny. Like I told you, that's my future bride you're talkin' about."

"Don't worry," John Henry assured him. "I plan on letting you keep on trying to thaw her out."

He didn't say anything about the kiss he had shared with Kate that afternoon. He would have been willing to bet his hat, though, that that intimacy was more than Buckner had ever been able to achieve with her.

"I guess we'd better be gettin' down to the office and check in with the sheriff before we start our rounds," Buckner said after looking longingly at his empty glass for a moment. "If he ain't there, Miller probably will be."

"Miller is Sheriff Dav's *segundo*?" John Henry asked as the three men turned away from the bar.

"Yeah, I reckon. There ain't nothin' official about it, you understand. All the deputies are equal. But everybody sorta knows that Miller's *more* equal, if you get my drift. He's the one who passes on Dav's orders to the rest of us a lot of the time, and he's got the sheriff's ear more than anybody else, I reckon. But he's a good *hombre*, so it's all right."

They approached the batwings while Buckner was talking, but they hadn't gotten there yet when a man suddenly stood up from one of the tables. He moved to his left, and that put him directly in the path of the three deputies.

The man's lace-up work boots, canvas trousers, and flannel shirt marked him as a miner. So did the thick slabs of muscle on his shoulders and arms put there by long hours of swinging a pick every day to dig out the ore. His features were as rugged as if they had been hewn from the mountain, as well.

Buckner, Kemp, and John Henry came to a stop. Buckner glared at the miner who stood in their way. The deputy demanded, "What do you want, Spivey?"

"You shouldn't be in here," the miner called Spivey rumbled. "By God, there ought'a be one place in this town where we're safe from you vultures who call yourselves lawmen."

"That's no way to talk," Buckner snapped. "We just had ourselves a peaceful drink, and now we're on our way out. Move aside, and I'll forget that you're treadin' on mighty shaky ground there, Spivey."

"Ain't goin' nowhere," Spivey said. "I aim to teach you a lesson, you high-handed sons o' bitches."

Buckner tensed. John Henry was keeping a close

eye on him, in case Buckner whipped out his gun with the intention of shooting the troublesome miner. If that happened, he would have to try to prevent the killing somehow without being too obvious about what he was doing, the same way he had kept Miller from gunning down Nate Farnham.

Another man dressed like a miner hurriedly got up from the table where Spivey had been sitting and came over to them. He put a hand on Spivey's brawny arm and urged, "Come on, Lou. You don't want to do this."

Spivey shrugged off his friend's grip.

"The hell I don't!" he said. "These varmints have been asking for trouble ever since they came to Chico!"

"But they've got the badges . . . and the guns," the smaller man argued. "And there are three of them."

"You'd better listen to your friend, Spivey," Buckner warned. "You open that piehole of yours one more time, I'm gonna arrest you for disturbin' the peace. They won't like it up at the Lucky Seven when you don't show up for work. The foreman's liable to fire you."

"I don't give a damn about that," Spivey insisted. His hands clenched into knobby-knuckled fists.

John Henry's keen hearing suddenly picked up the faint creak of a floorboard somewhere behind them. He glanced over his shoulder and saw several more burly miners creeping toward them. In that instant, he realized that Spivey and probably the second man as well were nothing more than distractions. The confrontation had given the other men time to get into position to jump them from behind.

"Buckner! Kemp!" he snapped. "It's an ambush!"

"Get 'em, boys!" Spivey roared.

The miners charged at the deputies from both sides, fists cocked to deliver sledgehammer blows.

Chapter Nineteen

Four men had come up behind the deputies, so when Spivey and his friend joined the attack from the front, that meant John Henry, Buckner, and Kemp were outnumbered two-to-one. The guns the lawmen carried would have gone a long way toward evening the odds, but they didn't have time to pull the irons before the miners crashed into them.

In the blink of an eye, the angry confrontation turned into a wild melee. One of the miners tackled John Henry and drove him into one of the tables. The men who had been sitting there drinking scattered frantically as John Henry and his attacker landed on top of the table. With sharp cracks, a couple of the legs broke and the table collapsed, dumping the two men down among the debris.

The miner slugged at John Henry as he lay on top of the broken table. How many of these ruckuses could he be forced to endure in one day? he asked himself as the man's fists thudded into him.

John Henry flung his arm out and closed his hand around one of the broken table legs. He could have killed his opponent by ramming the jagged end of the leg into his body. He didn't want to do that, though, so he swung it as a club instead and pulled back at the last second so that the makeshift bludgeon rapped the man's head with stunning force but not enough to fracture his skull.

John Henry grabbed the man's shirtfront and threw him to the side. Freed of the miner's weight, he was able to scramble to his feet, but just as he came up he caught a flicker of movement from the corner of his eye.

One of the other miners had picked up a chair and was swinging it at his head.

John Henry twisted and ducked forward, taking the blow on his hunched shoulders. It hurt enough to make him gasp in pain anyway. He ignored that and swung the piece of table leg. It caught the miner on the upper arm. The man howled and dropped the chair.

John Henry pivoted and threw a left cross that landed solidly on the man's jaw and flung him backward. The man hit the bar with enough force that he flipped up and back, going all the way over. As he came down his legs smashed into a row of bottles on the back bar, shattering them with a great crash of glass.

John Henry turned and saw that Buckner and Kemp were getting the worst of it. Each deputy had been grabbed from behind by one of the miners.

With their arms pinned, they couldn't put up much of a fight as the remaining two miners pounded them with hard, bony fists.

He had run into the same thing with Price and Hoffman, John Henry recalled from earlier in the day, but here in this crowded saloon, Buckner and Kemp didn't have room to draw their legs up and kick out at their assailants.

Despite the fact that they worked for the man whose schemes he had come here to destroy, John Henry waded in to help the other two deputies. He smashed the table leg across the back of one of the miners, staggering him. Whipping it around, he forced the other man to duck, which put the man in position for the kick that John Henry lifted into his belly. As that man doubled over in pain, John Henry smacked his head with the table leg and sent him to the floor.

Buckner and Kemp were stunned from the beatings they'd been getting, so the men holding them turned them loose and charged John Henry instead. John Henry twisted away from one man but caught a punch on the jaw from the other. The miner followed with a blow hooked into John Henry's midsection.

Three of the miners were still on their feet, and three-against-one odds were pretty bad. John Henry wasn't the sort to give up, though, so he ducked the next punch and stepped in to plant a short jab on a man's nose. Blood spurted under the impact of John Henry's knuckles. The man yelled in pain and stumbled backward, clutching at his bleeding, flattened nose.

Another man tried to grab John Henry from behind. He lifted his elbow under the miner's chin and sent him spinning away. He had dropped the broken table leg in the struggle, but it was still lying on the floor near his feet. As the remaining miner charged him, John Henry kicked the table leg under the man's feet. The miner tripped on it and let out a startled shout as he fell forward, out of control.

John Henry was ready. He clubbed both hands together and swung them in a powerful round-house blow that smashed into the miner's jaw and used the man's own momentum against him. The miner hit the floor so hard John Henry felt the planks tremble through the soles of his boots.

All the miners were down now, some of them unconscious, the others groaning. None of them seemed to be interested in fighting anymore.

That was good, John Henry thought as he stood there with his chest heaving, because he was just about out of stamina.

A few feet away, Kemp leaned on one of the tables with both hands. His head drooped so that his graying hair fell in his eyes. He shook his head slowly, evidently trying to clear the cobwebs from his brain.

Over by the bar, Buckner had propped himself up against the hardwood while he tried to catch his breath and get his wits back about him. He stared at John Henry and then at the bodies scattered around on the sawdust-littered floor.

"Son of a *bitch*!" Buckner said. "You're a one-man wreckin' crew, Cobb."

"These *hombres* . . . didn't give me much choice in the matter," John Henry managed to say.

Buckner straightened and pulled his gun. John Henry hoped he didn't intend to start shooting the fallen miners.

Luckily, that wasn't what Buckner had in mind. He gestured with the Colt in his hand at some of the other patrons of the Buzzard's Nest and ordered them to drag the miners over to the jail.

"Don't make me tell you again!" he added harshly.

With obvious reluctance, the men got to work. It took a dozen of them to haul the miners out of the saloon. After retrieving their hats, John Henry, Buckner, and Kemp followed. John Henry had his gun out now, too.

"At this rate, the jail's gonna be full before the night's over," Buckner commented. "Oh well, it wouldn't be the first time."

"I thought you said the townspeople weren't going to fight back," John Henry said.

"I said they hadn't done much of it so far. Looks like that might be about to change, unless we can keep the fight knocked out of 'em." Buckner laughed. "The way you whaled the tar outta this bunch might be enough to make the rest of these yokels think twice before they try anything like this again."

John Henry hoped so.

Three big brawls in one day was enough.

More than enough, his aching muscles told him.

Chapter Twenty

Sheriff Dav was gone when John Henry and the other two deputies reached the office with the prisoners, but Deputy Carl Miller was still there. Miller stared at them as they trooped in. Some of the miners who had jumped the deputies in the Buzzard's Nest had regained consciousness enough to walk with help from the men Buckner had pressed into service. Some of the others were still out cold.

"What the hell!" Miller exclaimed. "Steve, what have you and Aaron gotten into?"

"These varmints ganged up on us in the saloon," Buckner explained.

"I didn't hear any shots."

Buckner grinned and said, "That's because there wasn't any shootin'. Cobb there laid into 'em with a broken table leg like ol' Samson with the jawbone of an ass in the Bible."

John Henry was a little surprised to hear Buckner make a reference to the Good Book, but he supposed that even crooked deputies might have once been little boys dragged to church by their mamas.

Miller looked at John Henry and said, "I thought the sheriff told you to take the rest of the day off."

"He did," John Henry agreed, "but after supper at the boardinghouse, I decided to walk back downtown with Deputy Buckner and Deputy Kemp."

"And naturally the three of you wound up in the Buzzard's Nest."

Buckner said, "You know how we like to start our shift off with a little eye-opener, Carl."

Miller grunted. He waved a hand toward the stairs and said, "All right, take 'em up to the cell block. It's a good thing we've got enough empty cells. Things better stay quiet the rest of the night, though, or else I don't know where we'll put any more prisoners."

"We'll put 'em three to a cell," Buckner said. "That way there'll be plenty of room left for other miscreants."

It didn't take long to get the prisoners locked up. The townspeople who had lent an unwilling hand to get them over there left in a hurry, obviously not wanting to spend any more time in the jail than necessary.

When the deputies came downstairs, Miller asked them, "What do you want to charge 'em with, attempted murder?"

Buckner frowned and said, "I ain't sure they

meant to kill us, Carl. More than likely they just figured to give us a good stompin'. I'd lean toward callin' it assault on a peace officer. How about you, Aaron?"

Kemp grunted his assent.

Miller turned to John Henry.

"What do you say, Cobb?"

"Well, the town's not depending on them for their blacksmithing skills, like the case with the Farnhams," John Henry replied. "Do they all work at the same mine?"

"Yeah, the Lucky Seven," Buckner said.

"Having all six of them locked up for very long might put a big dent in the crew up there," John Henry said. "And the town gets a lot of business from the mines, I expect. So it would be a good gesture to maybe give them a stiff fine and then turn them loose. The mine owner might even pay the fine."

Miller scratched his heavy jaw with a thumbnail and frowned in thought. After a moment he said, "I'll have to clear it with the sheriff, but that's not a bad idea, I guess. They can cool their heels overnight." He looked at John Henry and added, "Anyway, it looked like you'd already doled out some punishment to 'em, Cobb. Tell me, do people just naturally try to kill you wherever you go?"

"Sometimes it seems like it," John Henry said.

* * *

The boardinghouse was dark when he got back to it. John Henry supposed the people who lived there turned in early.

Most *honest* people went to bed when it got dark, or shortly after that, he reminded himself with a wry smile. It was the lawbreakers, and those who had to deal with them, who made up the majority of the night's population.

The front door wasn't locked. Businesses might lock their doors at night, but private residences were always left open. John Henry remembered enough from his tour of the house that afternoon to make his way to the stairs and climb them to the second floor.

His naturally observant nature helped him recall which room was his. He didn't want to make a mistake and walk in on someone else, so when he came to the door he thought belonged to his room, he knocked softly on it before he grasped the knob with his left hand and turned it.

Habitual caution kept his right hand on the butt of his revolver as he opened the door and stepped into the room.

Nobody shot at him, so after a moment he closed the door. He took a match from his pocket and snapped it to life with his thumbnail. The flame's glow showed him that the room was empty. He lit the lamp on the small table.

A knock as soft as the one he had laid on the panel a few seconds earlier sounded behind him.

Not knowing who it might be, John Henry drew

his gun. He went to the door, and instead of calling out and giving somebody on the other side of the door with a rifle or a shotgun something to shoot at, he grasped the knob instead, twisted it, and jerked the door open.

Kate Collins took an involuntary step backward at the sight of him standing there with a gun in his hand, but she kept her lips pressed tightly together and didn't let out a startled gasp. Instead she said curtly, "Put that away."

Since she didn't seem to be any real threat, standing there in a dressing gown that was tightly belted around her, with her red hair loose around her shoulders, he did as she requested and slid the Colt back into leather.

"What can I do for you, Miss Collins?" he asked.

"I heard you come in a minute ago. My grandfather and I don't like to have our boarders disturbed, so it's probably best if everyone is in their rooms before this time of night."

"I was pretty quiet," John Henry pointed out. "I don't think I disturbed anybody."

"If I heard you, some of the other boarders could have, too," Kate said.

John Henry supposed that was true, but he thought it was unlikely, too. Kate must have been listening for his return, he thought. She knew he had left with Buckner and Kemp, but unlike the two of them, he was off duty tonight and Kate knew that. She knew he would be coming back to the boardinghouse sooner or later.

So why had she been waiting for him? John Henry couldn't help but ask himself that question, and as he did, he was reminded of the kiss he'd shared with Kate that afternoon. All he'd been doing was trying to maintain his pose as one of Sheriff Dav's crooked deputies, but for a second there, Kate had responded to him. At least, he believed she had.

"I'm sorry," he said. "I'll try to be more discreet in the future."

"Thank you," Kate said with a nod. "I appreciate that." She started to turn away but paused. "You know, I don't believe I've ever heard the sheriff or any of his men apologize for anything since they've been in Chico. You're . . . unusual, Mr. Cobb."

"No, I'm just like the others," John Henry said. He could prove it by making advances toward her again, he thought, but somehow he couldn't bring himself to do that.

"Maybe," Katie said speculatively. "Maybe not."

With that she turned away and started along the hall toward her room. John Henry quietly closed the door. He wasn't sure what to make of Kate's reaction to him.

He just hoped that he could get to the bottom of Dav's plans quickly and take action to bring the so-called sheriff to justice.

He didn't like who he was pretending to be.

The rest of the night passed quietly. John Henry rose early, as he was in the habit of doing, so he was downstairs in the dining room when Kate Collins began putting breakfast on the table a few minutes before six. She raised her eyebrows in surprise when she saw him.

"I didn't think you men ever got out of bed until the day was half over," she commented.

"After that supper last night, I didn't want to take a chance on missing breakfast," he said with a grin. He was stiff and sore from all the pounding on him that had been done the day before, but he tried not to show it.

Kate just said, "Hmmph," and returned to the kitchen.

None of John Henry's fellow deputies showed up for breakfast, but he got a chance to meet the other boarders in the house. In addition to the Petersons, who had been there for supper the night before, he met Alvin Turnage, who was a teller at the bank, Clara Mims, a middle-aged spinster who clerked at the Petersons' store, and George Hooper, the manager of the local freight line office. All of them greeted him warily because of the badge pinned to his shirt, but John Henry was polite, if not overly friendly. Masquerading as a cold-blooded gunman went against the grain for him, so all he could do was manage it as best he could.

Not surprisingly, the bacon, hotcakes, and fried eggs were delicious, even more so when washed down with several cups of hot, strong coffee. John Henry enjoyed the meal a great deal. It would have been even better with some good conversation, but the other people at the table were quiet and subdued, probably because they were all afraid of him. He would have liked to tell them who he really was and set their minds at ease, but that was going to have to wait.

After breakfast was over, John Henry drank the last of the coffee in his cup and stood up.

"That was mighty fine, Miss Collins," he said. "I'm much obliged to you for the meal."

"You continue to surprise me, Deputy," she replied coolly. "Not only do you apologize, but you say thank you as well."

"I was raised to—" He stopped short. He'd been about to say that he was raised to treat people decently, but that wasn't something John Cobb would say.

"You were raised to do what, Mr. Cobb?" Kate asked.

"Mind my own business," John Henry said brusquely. He turned away from the table and strode out, feeling the hostile glances that followed him.

That didn't go very well, he told himself as he walked toward the sheriff's office.

Samuel Dav wasn't there when John Henry reached the office, and neither was Carl Miller. Instead, a man he hadn't seen before was sitting behind the desk. A deputy's badge was pinned to his vest.

"Howdy," the man greeted him in a voice like a

washtub full of railroad spikes being dragged across a gravel road. "You must be the new fella."

"That's right," John Henry said. "Name's Cobb."

"Oh, I know who you are. Heard all about you," the man rasped. "I'm Gil Hobart."

He stood up and shook hands with John Henry. Hobart was a broad-shouldered man with a craggy face to match his voice, dark hair, and a mustache.

"I take care of the jail durin' the day," he went on.

"When does the sheriff come in?"

"Shouldn't be too much longer. Between you and me, I don't reckon Sheriff Dav sleeps more'n a few hours ever' night. He's almost always around." Hobart chuckled. "A while back, the Dutchie who runs the bakery was spreadin' rumors that the sheriff was some sort of monster they got legends about over yonder in the Old Country. Don't know what you call it, but it ain't really alive, nor dead, neither. Bunch o' hooey, of course. The sheriff got a good laugh out of it 'fore he set ol' Heinsdorf straight."

Like Steve Buckner, Gil Hobart appeared to be the talkative sort. John Henry went to the stove and poured himself a cup of coffee from the pot sitting there staying warm. He took a sip of it— nowhere near as good as Kate's coffee, he judged, but drinkable—and said, "That's a mighty odd story. The sheriff seemed human enough to me."

"Oh, he's human, all right. Human enough to be ambitious."

That was just the sort of thing John Henry wanted to hear about, but before he could prod

Hobart into revealing anything else, the door opened and Sheriff Dav himself walked in.

From the look on the sheriff's face, somebody was already in bad trouble . . . and it was about to get worse.

Chapter Twenty-one

Dav barely spared a glance for John Henry as he said, "I just heard about what happened last night. Where are those damned miners?"

"Don't worry, Sheriff, they're safe and sound upstairs," Hobart said. "I was fixin' to take 'em breakfast in a little while—"

"Don't bother," Dav interrupted. "I don't feel like feeding them."

Hobart frowned in confusion and asked, "You want me to go ahead and turn 'em loose, then?"

"Loose, hell! Those bastards set a trap for some of my men. They have to pay for what they've done." Dav turned to John Henry. "You were there in the Buzzard's Nest, I understand?"

"That's right." John Henry rolled his shoulders. "My aching muscles sure know it this morning, too."

"Then you understand why we can't let them get

away with this," Dav snapped. "We have to make an example of those men."

"I thought the judge would just fine them—"

"Oh, they'll pay a fine, all right." Dav's face was dark with fury. "They'll pay a price in blood and hide!"

John Henry didn't like the sound of that. He didn't know if he could go along with whatever Dav had in mind.

The sheriff didn't argue the matter. He ordered curtly, "Get out there on patrol, Cobb."

"You mean just walk up and down the streets?"

"That's exactly what I mean," Dav said, his voice cold. "Get moving."

If he wanted to keep up his pose, there was nothing John Henry could do except follow the sheriff's order. He nodded and left the office, but the wheels of his brain were turning over rapidly. He didn't know what Dav planned to do, but he was sure it wouldn't be anything good.

For the next couple of hours, as Chico came to life, John Henry walked the settlement's streets. He stopped in various businesses and tried to engage the owners in conversation, hoping to get to know them better, but what he got in return were mostly nervous monosyllables. The townspeople didn't want anything to do with any of Dav's deputies, himself included, and knowing what he did about the history of the situation, he couldn't really blame them.

Around midmorning, John Henry went back to

the Collinses' boardinghouse to check on Iron Heart. He had looked in on the horse briefly before heading for the sheriff's office, but now he spent a few minutes going over Iron Heart's sleek hide with a curry comb, the two trail partners enjoying the companionship.

When he left the stable he didn't go into the house. Kate and old Jimpson probably wanted as little to do with him as everybody else in Chico, he thought.

Well, maybe not Kate. Not completely, anyway . . .

As he rounded the corner onto Main Street, he saw Carl Miller coming toward him along the boardwalk. Miller said, "Cobb! There you are. The sheriff sent me to find you."

"Does he need me to do something?" John Henry asked.

"He sure does. He's called in everybody. All the deputies."

That didn't sound good. John Henry frowned as he walked beside Miller toward the sheriff's office.

"You know what this is about?" he asked.

"You'll find out when you get there," Miller said.

That seemed to be Miller's final word on it, so John Henry didn't say anything else. A couple of minutes later, they reached the two-story stone building and went inside.

The sheriff's office was crowded with deputies. John Henry saw Steve Buckner and Aaron Kemp standing in front of Dav's desk. The sheriff was behind the desk, but on his feet rather than in the chair. He waved Miller and John Henry forward, and the other deputies standing around moved aside to let them through.

This was John Henry's first chance to see all of Dav's men at one time, in one place. They were an impressive group, but not in a good way. As a law officer back in Indian Territory, he had hunted down outlaws of all sorts—rustlers, whiskey runners, thieves, and murderers. Every man who wore a badge in Chico bore the same stamp of the badman. They were all shapes and sizes, but they had the same cold, hard eyes that had seen death on too many occasions.

"Here's Cobb, Sheriff," Miller said as he and John Henry came up to the big desk. "Reckon you can go ahead now."

Dav nodded and said, "Tell me what happened in the Buzzard's Nest, Cobb."

John Henry leaned his head toward Buckner and Kemp.

"I reckon these fellas have already told you, Sheriff," he said.

"I want to hear it from you," Dav insisted.

John Henry told him in short, brisk sentences. Dav appeared to be calm enough as he listened, but John Henry saw rage swirling around in the sheriff's eyes. Dav was furious that the miners had tried to set up an ambush for some of his men.

When John Henry was finished, Dav said, "Everybody who goes to the Buzzard's Nest knows that Buckner and Kemp stop in there nearly every night on their way to work. They were the targets of this attack. You just happened to be there with them, Cobb." Dav's lip curled in a sneer. "And it's a good thing for them you were, otherwise they probably would have gotten a good stomping."

Buckner and Kemp looked distinctly uncomfortable. John Henry supposed that Dav had given them a good chewing-out already.

Dav raised his voice and went on, "Let that be a lesson to all of you. Don't fall into the same routines. Don't ever forget that we're surrounded by enemies in this town. If you ever let your guard down enough that they can come after you, they might not stop until you're dead." He paused and drew in a deep breath. "At least, they might not unless they learn a good lesson today. A lesson so harsh that everybody in Chico will think twice before they ever dare to cross a duly appointed representative of the law again."

John Henry didn't like the sound of *that* at all.

Dav jerked a thumb toward the stairs leading to the cell block and ordered, "Bring them down."

"What about the Farnhams, Sheriff?" Miller asked.

Dav shook his head.

"It's already been decided what'll be done with them. They'll serve a week in jail for disturbing the peace, and we'll let it go at that. I want Spivey and the rest of those miners down here, though."

Several deputies drew their guns and went upstairs to fetch the prisoners. John Henry waited uneasily. The men came back down, herding Lou Spivey and the other miners along at gunpoint.

"Take them down to the well," Dav ordered. "If any of them try to make a break for it . . . kill them."

Spivey's rugged face was pale, but his eyes burned with anger. Surrounded by hardcases with drawn guns, though, there was nothing he could do except go along.

"Shouldn't the judge have something to do with this?" Miller asked.

"I've already spoken to Curwood," Dav said. "The trial was held in absentia. The judge levied two-hundred-dollar fines on each of the defendants, and he went along with my other suggestion, too."

Dav reached down and pulled open a drawer in his desk. His hand went into it and came out clutching a coiled bullwhip.

John Henry's emotions warred inside him. He'd been worried that Dav had something outrageous in mind, and the sight of the bullwhip confirmed that. Heavily outnumbered, and with the success of the mission that had brought him here at stake, it seemed that there was nothing he could do except stand by and let Dav do whatever he wanted.

But it was going to be hard. Lord, it was going to be hard.

"Arm yourselves with rifles and shotguns," Dav ordered the deputies who were still in the office. "Then follow me."

The deputies grabbed weapons from the racks

and fell in behind Dav as he left the office and
stalked out into the middle of the street. That
wasn't a very good defensive position, out in the
open like that, John Henry thought, but clearly
Dav wanted everybody in town to get a good look
at them.

John Henry knew Dav wasn't really afraid of
the townspeople, either, and probably with good
reason. The boardwalks had emptied in a hurry
as the prisoners were marched down to the
public well. John Henry saw faces peeking nervously from windows in nearly every building
they passed, but no one stepped out to confront
the group of crooked lawmen.

The miners stood in a group near the well,
covered by the deputies who had brought them
down here. Dav used the coiled bullwhip in his
hand to motion for John Henry and the others to
spread out and completely encircle the area around
the well.

"Tie Spivey to the one of the posts," Dav ordered,
indicating the thick posts that held up the cover
over the well.

"No!" Spivey yelled. "By God, Dav—"

One of the deputies standing near him drove
the butt of a rifle into the small of Spivey's back.
Spivey cried out in pain and stumbled forward.

Two more deputies grabbed his arms and forced
him toward the nearest post. Spivey struggled, but
he was still hurting from the blow to the back and
was no match for the deputies' strength.

John Henry knew what was coming, and the knowledge sickened him. He watched as the deputies forced Spivey up to the well and lifted his arms above his head. One of the men stood on the short wall around the well and used rawhide thongs to lash the miner's wrists together so they were looped around the post. The bonds were pulled so tight Spivey had to hold himself up on his toes to keep his weight from dragging down unbearably against his shoulder sockets. His face was pressed against the rough wood of the post.

Dav walked over to Spivey and leaned close to the burly miner.

"It was your idea to ambush my men in the Buzzard's Nest, wasn't it, Spivey?" Dav demanded. "You don't like the way I've tried to bring law and order to this town."

"You . . . you're just . . . a cheap crook!" Spivey gasped. "There's no . . . law here!"

"You're wrong," Dav said.

He reached up with his left hand while his right let the whip uncoil at his feet. The way it hissed and writhed reminded John Henry of a snake. Dav grasped the collar of Spivey's shirt and wrenched down with more power than he should have possessed in his slender body. The shirt ripped, baring Spivey's muscular back.

"This is the law in Chico!" Dav cried. "The law of the whip!"

Chapter Twenty-two

John Henry was standing about ten yards away from the well with a Winchester in his hand. It would be easy enough to raise the rifle to his shoulder and put a bullet through Dav's crazed brain before anyone could stop him.

But a heartbeat later he would be dead, too, more than likely, and then Dav's crew of killers would have free rein to do whatever they wanted in this town. They would loot it, certainly, and might well go on a spree of raping and killing as well. But as long as Dav was alive and had bigger plans than just taking over this particular settlement, he held the rest of them in check.

It was one of the hardest things John Henry had ever done, but he stood there unmoving while Dav backed away from Spivey, lifted his arm, and lashed out with cruel precision, laying the whip across the miner's back so that it left a bloody stripe behind it.

Spivey looked like he tried to hold it in, but he

let out a muffled cry of agony and his body surged against the post. Dav drew his arm back and struck again, leaving a second blood-oozing welt next to the first one.

Again and again the whip licked across Spivey's back in a savage caress. With each strike, Dav turned halfway around to get more power in the blows, so John Henry could see the sheriff's face in silhouette. Dav was sweating, and he seemed transported, caught up in the sheer joy of the pain he was inflicting.

More than ever, John Henry wanted to blow the son of a bitch's lights out.

Instead he stood there with all the stoicism ignorant people attributed to his father's race, while inside it was torturing him to witness this atrocity.

Dav delivered ten lashes to Spivey, and when he was finished, the miner's back was a bloody mess crisscrossed with crimson wounds. After a few lashes, Spivey had started screaming, but he'd passed out before Dav got to the end. Now he just hung there on the post, senseless and bleeding.

Finally Dav stepped back even more. He motioned with his free hand toward Spivey and barked, "Cut him down."

A couple of deputies held Spivey's arms while another man cut the thongs holding him to the post. Spivey would have dropped into the dirt of the street if the men hadn't supported him. They dragged him over to the closest boardwalk and lowered him facedown onto it. Flies instantly started buzzing around the gory ruin of Spivey's back.

Dav pointed the bullwhip's handle at one of the other miners and said, "That one."

The man began to curse and protest and then beg, but none of it did any good. He was tied to the post just as Spivey had been, and one of the deputies ripped the shirt from his back.

Dav had had enough personally, though. He handed the whip to Miller and said, "Five each for the others. Spivey was the ringleader."

Miller looked like he didn't relish the idea. He said, "Boss, do you really think—"

"Five each," Dav repeated, his voice hard as flint.

"Sure," Miller said with a sigh.

The next half hour was one of the longest John Henry had ever spent, as one by one the other five miners were strung up to the post and given five lashes by Miller. The deputy didn't strike with as much frenzied strength as Dav had, and the prisoners received only half as many lashes as Spivey had, but they still screamed and sagged against the post as their backs were bloodied.

Miller looked relieved when it was over. So did several of the other deputies. Hardcases they might be, but that didn't mean they were unmoved by what they had witnessed.

Dav, on the other hand, stood by smiling the whole time. When Miller was finished, he took the whip from the deputy and coiled it again.

"I want four men to stay here and keep an eye on the prisoners," the sheriff said.

"We ain't takin' 'em back to the jail?" Miller asked. He swept a hand toward the boardwalk where the miners lay moaning.

"No point in it. I've sent word to the owner of the Lucky Seven to come down here, pay their fines, and take them back to the mine. He ought to be here this afternoon. In the meantime, just leave them where they are."

Miller nodded and said, "Whatever you want, boss."

"What I want is for the citizens of this town to respect the law!"

Dav's voice rose as he spoke, and John Henry realized that he wasn't just responding to Miller's statement. Dav was addressing the whole town. Not everybody in Chico could hear him, of course, but enough people were standing inside open windows for his words to reach them. They would tell others, and those people would tell others . . .

Dav went on, "What I want is for everyone to understand that ambushing my men will not be tolerated! Attacking anybody who wears a badge will be punished swiftly and severely! These men got off easy! The next fools who try to stand up to the forces of the law might just wind up on the gallows!"

With that, Dav turned and strode toward the jail. His head was held high, and his hawklike profile was steady and calm. There wasn't an ounce of fear in the man, John Henry realized. Dav believed that he had the entire town cowed, and from the looks of things, he did.

Miller pointed out four deputies and told them to watch the prisoners until the owner of the Lucky Seven showed up to pay their fines and claim them. Then he told the other deputies to go on about their business.

John Henry wasn't sure what that was, so he approached Miller and asked, "Anything in particular I ought to be doing now?"

Miller shook his head.

"You're on patrol. That means you circulate through the town and maintain order."

"You don't really think anybody's going to get out of line after that display, do you, Deputy?" John Henry asked.

"Not if they've got a lick of sense in their heads," Miller said. "Because believe you me, Cobb, if Sam Dav says it'll be worse next time, you don't want to know what it's gonna be!"

Edgar Wellman stood at the window in the newspaper office for a long time before finally moving back to the desk. He had seen a lot of bad things in his life . . . hell, he had *done* a lot of bad things in his life . . . but he wasn't sure he had ever seen anything as horrifying as what had happened at the well.

The top of the desk was littered with sheets of paper. He had been rewriting the editorial Sheriff Dav had given him to print, struggling with the words. Dav might be a lot of things, but he wasn't really a writer. His constructions were awkward, his word choices eccentric, to say the least. Dav didn't really care how elegant the prose was, though; he just wanted his ideas put across to the readers.

Wellman sat down, picked up his pencil, and went back to work. He had trouble concentrating, though.

He kept hearing the screams and seeing the blood . . .

When the office door opened, he glanced up, then looked again as every muscle in his body stiffened. Sheriff Dav stood there, a cocky grin on his face as he leaned a shoulder against the doorjamb.

"I guess you saw what happened awhile ago, Edgar," Dav said.

"You mean the . . . the whippings?"

Dav straightened from his casual pose.

"I mean the law at work," he said. "What you saw, Mr. Editor, was the legal process doing its job."

"Doing it rather . . . harshly, wouldn't you say?"

Wellman would have called back the words when he saw the flicker of anger in Dav's eyes, but it was too late for that. And the next instant Dav chuckled and seemed genuinely amused, so Wellman supposed he hadn't overstepped too far. Not fatally, anyway.

"The law *is* harsh, Edgar," Dav said. "That's why it's the law. If it was easy, if there were no consequences, then nobody would bother to obey it, would they?"

"Those were the men who were involved in the brawl in the Buzzard's Nest last night?"

Dav took a step farther into the office.

"That was no common brawl," he snapped. "That was a deliberate attempt to ambush my men and injure them, maybe even kill them. Spivey and the others planned the whole thing, knowing that they would be breaking the law. I won't tolerate that. I *can't* tolerate that, not if I want to continue enforcing the law as it should be done."

"To your benefit, you mean."

"If it benefits me, it benefits the town in the long run, right? Because I protect the town."

Lord help us all, Wellman thought, because it sounded like Dav really believed the insanity he was spouting.

Dav came closer to the desk and went on, "The problem is, Chico's just not big enough for me, Edgar. I can do more. I can bring the law to the entire territory. New Mexico needs a man like me, a man who's not afraid to do what needs to be done to put things right."

Wellman looked down at the papers on his desk.

"You alluded to that in that editorial you gave me to rewrite," he said. "Are you saying that you have aspirations for higher office, Sheriff?"

"Would it be such a bad thing if I did?" Dav asked with a smile.

It would be utterly disastrous . . . but of course Wellman didn't dare say that. Instead he said, "It's an interesting idea." That ought to be vague enough to keep him out of trouble, he told himself.

"I can't do it all by myself, though," Dav said. "I need help, Edgar. I need a voice to rally the people behind me."

The people of Chico would never rally behind him, Wellman thought. Not after the bloody spectacle they had witnessed today. They all knew Samuel Dav for what he really was.

A madman.

But . . . The thought stirred in Wellman's mind. Chico was a small town. People in other parts of the territory might hear rumors about the whippings, but as long as they hadn't seen it with their own eyes, they would harbor doubts. And where doubts existed, a skillful editorialist and reporter could work his way in and magnify those doubts. For the most part, people believed whatever someone they considered smarter than themselves told them to believe.

And most people believed that journalists were smarter than they were.

"You want me to build you up, spread the word about what a dynamic, effective law enforcement officer you are," Wellman said.

Dav pointed a finger at him and said, "Now you're getting the idea. I need a reputation, and a clever newspaperman can help me spread that reputation."

"Of course," Wellman mused as he leaned back in his chair. Even though he was still horrified by what he had seen, his thoughts were falling back into the familiar cunning patterns. "A front page story in the *Star*, to go along with the editorial, could be very effective. Not so much for local readers, mind you—"

"But if you could get those papers into the hands of readers in Santa Fe and Albuquerque and all the other towns in the territory . . ."

"The fame of Samuel Dav would spread quickly," Wellman agreed.

Dav slapped a hand down on the desk, the report making Wellman jump a little.

"Now you're talking, Edgar! People love a man who comes out of nowhere to change things, to give them hope."

"But if they know the truth—"

"The truth is what we tell them it is," Dav cut in. "People want to believe. Tell them you'll keep them safe, tell them you'll take care of them, and they'll fall all over themselves to believe you."

Wellman knew the sheriff was right. He had seen too much of humanity not to be cynical about it. Manipulating people was the easiest thing in the world. Just tell them what they want to hear, and the biggest lie in the world would become the truth in their minds.

"How about it, Edgar?" Dav went on. "You and I

together, we could run this whole territory. All you've got to do is throw in with me. Not out of fear, mind you. But because I need a newspaperman like you."

And now Dav was telling him what *he* wanted to hear, Wellman thought. The bad part about it was . . . it was working.

Wellman stood up and nodded.

"I'm with you, Sheriff," he said.

Chapter Twenty-three

After the flurry of action that had accompanied John Henry's arrival in Chico, things actually settled down for a couple of days. The town was peaceful. Maybe because everybody was too scared to be any other way right now, but still . . . peaceful.

Then the first edition of the Chico *Star* to be printed in a couple of months hit the streets.

John Henry was sitting at the counter in Abernathy's Café when one of the townsmen came in holding a folded newspaper. He slapped it down and said to the counter man, "Did you ever see the likes of that, Harley?"

"What is that, the newspaper?" Harley asked. "I didn't think it was bein' published anymore."

"First edition in a while, but Wellman says it's back to stay." The townsman stabbed a finger down on the paper. "Look what else he says."

The newspaper was turned so that it was upside-down to John Henry, but he didn't have any trouble reading that way. At the top of the page was a boxed editorial, and the headline on it read SHERIFF STANDS UP FOR LAW AND ORDER.

"Hell, that's—"

The counter man stopped short in whatever he'd been about to say. Probably something like "*loco*" or "crazy," John Henry thought as the man glanced toward him nervously. As long as he had a deputy's badge pinned to his shirt, nobody in Chico was going to talk too freely around him.

He held out a hand and asked, "Can I take a look at that?"

The man who had brought in the paper handed it over without hesitation, saying, "Sure, Deputy, you keep it as long as you want. Just plain keep it. I don't need it."

"Thanks," John Henry said dryly. He unfolded the paper so that he could take in the whole front page. The editorial was what interested him the most:

Sheriff Stands Up for Law and Order

Earlier this week, the citizens of Chico bore witness to a stirring example of law enforcement, as Sheriff Samuel Dav, capably assisted by his deputies, dealt swiftly, efficiently, and fairly with a group of ruffians who brutally attacked several of the sheriff's men the previous night. In the sort of speedy trial to which our justice system aspires but seldom attains, Judge Jonathan Curwood found the defendants guilty, assessed fines on them for their crimes, and sentenced them as well to a bout of corporal punishment the likes of which would teach them the lesson that crime does not pay. Sheriff Dav, in a gesture of mercy, prevailed upon the judge to lessen that punishment somewhat for some of the conspirators.

This is yet another demonstration of how the sheriff tempers his devotion to the law with his concern for his fellow man. In the opinion of this newspaper, there is no finer gentleman in the entirety of the territory than Samuel Dav. His conduct in the office of sheriff is a sterling example of his exceptional qualities. Consider how Sheriff Dav and his deputies have dealt with Chico's lawless elements, suppressing them so that the town's streets are once more safe and the citizens can walk them without fear.

Unfortunately for us here in Chico, the fame of such an outstanding lawman has spread quickly, and it seems inevitable that higher duties will soon be calling to Samuel Dav, as a man with his high moral standing will be summoned to the greater good. We can be thankful that we had his services for as long as we did, but we will have to be gracious and let him answer that summons.

New Mexico Territory needs Samuel Dav.

John Henry managed not to let out a whistle of admiration at the sheer gall of the editorial. He had a glimmering now of what Dav's bigger plan was. Dav figured on running for higher office. Even governor, maybe. This was the first step on that road. John Henry wondered if copies of this newspaper were already being sent out across the territory. It wouldn't surprise him one bit if that were the case.

The rest of the front page consisted of an announcement that the *Star* would once again be published on a regular weekly schedule and a couple of local news stories, both of which managed to work in mentions of what a fine, upstanding lawman Samuel Dav was. John Henry carefully kept his face expressionless as he read them.

When he was finished he folded the paper and set it on the counter again.

"I'll leave that there," he said. "I'm sure other folks will want to read it."

"People all over town are reading it already, Deputy," said the man who had brought the paper into the café. "Wellman practically blanketed the streets with it."

That didn't surprise John Henry. He had a hunch that the editor had printed so many copies at Dav's order. Obviously, Wellman was working with Dav now, either out of fear or because he had decided it would be to his benefit.

There were always people who found it easier to go along with evil rather than to fight it.

John Henry finished his coffee and left the café. As he walked along the street he saw a number of Chico's citizens reading the newspaper. When he passed they all glanced at him, then looked away quickly, trying to hide what they were feeling. They weren't very good at it, though.

Dav might have finally overplayed his hand by causing that editorial to be printed, John Henry thought.

Because in the eyes of every citizen he passed, outrage smoldered, along with the beginnings of something that might be determination.

Lucinda Hammond was a long time answering the knock on the door, long enough that Edgar Wellman began to worry she wasn't going to respond to the summons. Finally, though, the door swung open and Lucinda stood there, standing straighter than Wellman had seen her in recent weeks. He wondered for a second what had stiffened her spine, but then he saw the anger in her eyes and the newspaper in her hand and knew the answer to that question.

"Lucinda," he said quickly, "I can explain—"

"Go away, Edgar." Her voice was flat and hard, like a piece of flint. "I don't want to talk to you. I'm not interested in your explanations."

She stepped back and started to swing the door shut. Wellman said, "But, Lucinda, please! I did it for you."

That stopped her, probably because on the surface it was such an outrageous claim. She stared at him for a second, then said, "You aligned yourself with that monster, with the man who murdered my husband right in front of my eyes, and you have the audacity to say that you did it for me?"

"I did," Wellman insisted. "If you'll just hear me out, I'm sure I can make you understand."

For a moment she still looked like she was about to slam the door in his face, but then she opened it wider again and said, "I'll listen to you. But I'm not going to believe you."

"Perhaps you will," Wellman said as he stepped into the foyer and took off his hat. "I was only thinking of you."

Lucinda folded her arms across her chest and glared at him. She wore a dark blue dress and her hair was brushed. Wellman thought she looked lovely.

"I'm not going to ask you into the parlor, and I'm not going to offer you anything to drink," she said coldly. "If you have anything to say to me, Edgar, I'd advise you to get on with it before I run out of patience. And I warn you, my patience is in very short supply right now."

Wellman gestured at the paper she held and asked, "Who brought that to you?"

"It doesn't matter. One of my friends. I still have a few in this town, you know."

"I know, because I'm one of them."

She looked like she no longer believed that.

When she didn't say anything, Wellman knew she was waiting for him to go on, so he said,

"Sheriff Dav came to see me the other day, after the . . . after what happened at the well."

"After he took a bullwhip to those men and beat them within an inch of their lives, that's what you mean," Lucinda snapped.

"Now to be fair, the sheriff himself only gave lashes to Lou Spivey—"

He stopped short at the contemptuous look on her face.

"I know, I know," Wellman hurried on. "He was responsible for the whole thing. But he came to see me afterward and talked to me about publishing the paper again."

"Did he threaten you at gunpoint? Did he say that he was going to kill you unless you printed exactly what he wanted?"

For a second, Wellman considered lying and telling Lucinda that was what had happened. But he was afraid that she would see right through him. She was an intelligent, discerning woman, and if she caught him in a lie, she would never trust him again. She might not anyway, but he hoped he could talk her into considering the possibility.

"He didn't actually threaten me, although he made it quite clear that I would regret it if I didn't go along with what he wanted. Earlier, even before that happened, he had given me some notes for an editorial he wanted me to write."

"The editorial that appeared in today's paper?" Lucinda asked.

Wellman nodded.

"I had no choice, but I wasn't motivated by fear, Lucinda. I did it because I realized that this was the best way I could help you."

"Help me?" she said, her voice trembling slightly from the depth of the emotion she obviously felt. "Help me how? By celebrating the actions of the man who made me a widow?"

Wellman drew in a deep breath and asked, "May I be blunt?"

"Please do," she said, scorn dripping from her tone.

"Our sheriff has designs on you, Lucinda. He wants you for himself. As your friend, I felt that I ought to do everything in my power to prevent that unacceptable circumstance from ever occurring."

She stared at him, clearly surprised by what she had just heard. After several seconds, she said, "You're throwing your support behind Dav in order to save me from him?"

"That's right. He's an ambitious man, to say the least. He yearns for more power and a higher office." Wellman shrugged. "What better way to get him out of Chico and out of our lives than to help him get what he wants?"

It was a logical argument. Wellman had gone over it enough times in his head that he was even starting to believe it a little himself. At the time he had come to his agreement with Dav, he had been motivated by a mixture of fear and his own ambition. But if he had stopped to think about it, he argued, there might have been some concern for Lucinda's well-being mixed in there, too.

Time dragged by as Wellman waited for her to respond. Seconds seemed like hours. Finally, Lucinda said, "I don't know whether to believe you or not, Edgar. Even if you are telling the truth, I wish you hadn't done this." She brandished the folded newspaper. "I can take care of myself. I don't want to do anything to further this scoundrel's ambitions."

"That wasn't my motive, I assure you. It was secondary to making sure that he leaves you alone."

"You should let me worry about myself."

He smiled and said, "I would if I could. Unfortunately, I'm powerless in the face of my own friendship for you."

He almost said "affection" instead of "friendship." But that would be going too far, he'd realized at the last second. It was too soon for that.

He had planted the seed, though, and he would have to be content with that for now. He could tell by looking at Lucinda that she wasn't as angry as she had been when she came to the door. That was progress.

"I suppose I can't fault you for being my friend. I hope you won't write any more editorials like this, though."

"I can't make any promises," he said. "I want the sheriff gone from our town, and I'll do whatever I can to accomplish that."

Of course, when Dav went to Santa Fe, Wellman intended to go with him. A journalist who had the ear of the new territorial governor would have no trouble getting a position on one of the newspapers in the capital.

Lucinda didn't have to know anything about that until the time came, though, and Wellman still harbored hopes of convincing *her* to go with *him*.

"I can understand wanting Dav gone," Lucinda said. "I've thought about little else these past few weeks. I think our preferred methods of going about it are different, though."

"You mean—"

"I'm mean if it was up to me, I'd blow his evil reptilian brains out."

Chapter Twenty-four

The air of tension that gripped Chico grew even stronger following the appearance of the newspaper. It was like the feeling when a storm was about to break, that electrically charged potential for devastating violence.

Several times each day, John Henry caught townspeople looking at him with hate in their eyes and knew that only the threat of the gun on his hip prevented them from taking revenge on him for all the harm that had been done to them, even though he hadn't taken part in any of it.

The badge he wore was enough to make him a target, all by itself.

He was confident that he could catch Dav alone sometime and take the sheriff prisoner. Dav seemed to trust him. He might even be able to nab several of the deputies as well, capturing them one or two at a time and locking them up in the jail without the others knowing.

It would be well-nigh impossible, though, for him to get all of them that way. And once the others discovered what he was doing, they would storm the jail, which he wouldn't be able to defend on his own. They would overrun the place and kill him.

Or he had could grab Dav and make a run for Santa Fe, but that would leave the rest of those gun-wolves loose to do whatever they wanted in Chico. Either that or they would come after him like a pack of real wolves. Neither option appealed to John Henry.

What he needed was an army.

Not the cavalry, though. If a troop of soldiers showed up, it could lead to a pitched battle in which innocent people would be hurt. What he needed were allies who could blend in until the time came to strike, so they could take the deputies by surprise . . .

Those thoughts were stirring around in his head as he walked toward the Collinses' boardinghouse several nights after the whipping of the miners and the publication of the *Star*. There were people in Chico he could trust, he told himself, but the trick would be getting them to trust him. To them he was an outlaw and a gunfighter named John Cobb who was pretending to be a lawman, no better than the rest of the gang that had taken over the town. He had to convince them somehow that the opposite of that situation was really true.

It wasn't going to be easy. Even Kate Collins, who

had shown signs now and then of warming up to him early on, had been cold as ice toward him the past few days. A sullen silence reigned in the boardinghouse whenever he was around.

His hand moved closer to the butt of his gun as he spotted two figures coming toward him in the dusk. He relaxed a little when he recognized them as his fellow deputies Steve Buckner and Aaron Kemp.

"Howdy, fellas," John Henry greeted them. "Headed downtown for your shifts?"

"That's right," Buckner said. "You missed supper, Cobb. Miss Kate wasn't happy with you."

"Miss Kate hasn't been happy with any of us for quite a while now," John Henry pointed out.

Buckner let out a rueful chuckle.

"You ain't lyin' about that," he said. "She's like everybody else in this town: plumb mad as an old wet hen at us." Buckner paused and then surprised John Henry by adding, "Can't say as I really blame 'em, either."

"Steve," Kemp said in a warning tone.

"Blast it, I can't help it," Buckner said. "What the sheriff done to Spivey and those other miners . . . Well, that was rough, Aaron, mighty damn rough, and you know it."

That note of dissatisfaction was something John Henry hadn't heard from any of the deputies until now. He supposed that some of them were afraid of Dav, too, at least to a certain extent, just like the townspeople. Greed had probably drawn them all here to pin on badges and pretend to be real lawmen, but they might have gotten in deeper than they really expected.

That possibility might be something he could use in the future, John Henry thought. The *near* future, he amended.

Because the situation here in Chico was intolerable and couldn't be allowed to go on for much longer.

Kemp said, "You flap your gums too much and you're gonna get us in trouble."

"You think Cobb's gonna go runnin' to the sheriff tellin' tales?" Buckner demanded. "I don't think so, not after the way he sided us in that fight in the Buzzard's Nest. We're *compadres* now, ain't that right, Cobb?"

John Henry suddenly wondered if this was a trick of some sort, a test of his loyalty to Dav. He said in a flat voice, "I mind my own business. That goes both ways."

"Sure, sure." Buckner chuckled again. "Hell, I'm just spoutin' words to hear myself talk. That's a bad habit with fellas like me who're in love with the sound of their own voices."

Kemp's taciturn grunt indicated that he agreed with that much, anyway.

John Henry bid the two of them good night and walked on toward the boardinghouse. He didn't know how many of the deputies had been rubbed the wrong way by what Dav had done with the miners. For all he knew, Buckner might be the only one. It was nearly impossible to tell how Kemp felt about anything. Still, the conversation had been interesting for a number of potential reasons, and he filed it away in his mind.

The gloom had thickened by the time he approached the boardinghouse. He swung wide to go around the house and pay a visit to Iron Heart in the stable out back, to make sure the horse was getting along all right. As soon as he got a chance, he needed to take Iron Heart out for a run. The big steed needed to stretch his legs.

John Henry paused, going stock-still, as he once again noticed two figures in the gloom. This pair was slipping along the side of the stable as if they were up to no good. He was in the thick shadow of a tree, practically unnoticeable, so he stayed where he was and watched as the two forms disappeared into the stable. The light had faded so much he hadn't been able to tell anything about them, not even if they were male or female.

He was confident they were male, though. A couple of women wouldn't have any reason to be out skulking around like that.

He supposed it was possible they were horse thieves. Sliding his Colt noiselessly from its holster, he started forward again. His natural stealth allowed him to approach the barn without making anything other than the tiniest of sounds.

When he got closer he heard the murmur of voices coming from inside the stable. It sounded like more than two men talking in there. It seemed like they were trying to keep their voices down, but the discussion was so animated that was difficult.

"—do something now," one man was saying as John Henry approached near enough to make out the words. "This can't go on any longer."

"People will die," another man said. John Henry wasn't sure, but he thought the voice belonged to old Jimpson Collins, Kate's grandfather.

"People are already dying," the first man shot back. "What happened to Sid Harney? What about Eddie McCoy, or Fritz Dumars, or Theo Larchmont? We don't know, do we, because they all disappeared after they tried to stand up to Dav and his gang!"

A third man added, "I tell you one thing . . . those fellas all left families behind. They'd have come back to their wives and kids if they could. That means they're all dead."

"And a dozen or more besides," the first man went on. "That's why we have to do something to get rid of Dav now, before he murders anybody else. Good Lord, we all know he shot down Milton Hammond in cold blood, right in front of Lucinda! He's never even bothered to deny that."

Several more men spoke up, confirming John Henry's impression that there was a whole group inside the stable. He wasn't the least bit surprised by what he was hearing. Any time a tyrant took control, resistance against his ironhanded rule would rise sooner or later. No dictator could hold on to power forever. That was just the way of the world.

"Hold on, hold on," one of the men said. "I don't like Dav any more than the rest of you, but you're all forgetting something: we elected him. He won that election fair and square. If we go against him, then *we're* breaking the law!"

"Maybe the election wasn't all that fair," another man insisted. "He lied to us about what he intended to do when he got in office. We thought we were electin' a decent lawman, not somebody who'd come in and change everything for the worse. Anyway, the only reason we elected him was because he got that bank robbery loot back, and I'm not sure but what that whole thing was a put-up deal!"

That brought a chorus of agreement from several men, with one of them saying, "I bet some of the varmints who held up the bank are wearin' deputy badges right now!"

John Henry suspected the same thing was true. Clearly, Dav had had dark plans right from the beginning.

Unforeseen circumstances had given him an opportunity here, John Henry mused as he continued listening to the men argue about what, if anything, they ought to do. If he walked in there among them, they might scatter at the sight of him, or they might attack him, thinking he was spying on them for the sheriff.

But if he could get them to listen to him, if he could convince them of who he really was and that he was on their side, he might be able to swear them to secrecy and lay the groundwork for a plan to oust Dav and his gunmen from power.

With his characteristic decisiveness, John Henry made up his mind. It was worth a try. He slid his Colt back into its holster. If he showed himself with a gun in his hand, the men would panic and make his job that much harder, no doubt about that.

He took a deep breath and was about to step out of the shadows into the stable when he heard the faint scrape of boot leather on the ground behind him. Instinct made him twist around to meet the potential threat.

He was too late. He wasn't the only one around here who could be stealthy. He caught a glimpse of an arm rising and falling, and then something smashed into his head with enough force to knock him off his feet and send him spiraling down into an even deeper darkness.

Chapter Twenty-five

Consciousness crept slowly back into John Henry's brain, bringing with it pain and a dim awareness of his surroundings. As he began to gather his wits about him, he realized that he was slightly surprised to still be alive. Given the depth of the hatred the citizens of Chico felt toward the sheriff's men, the group gathered in the stable might well have killed him while he was out cold and helpless.

Something nudged his shoulder. He felt warm breath against his face. Whatever it was bumped him again.

His eyelids flickered open. At first he couldn't see anything. The shadows around him were thick and impenetrable.

Then his vision began to adjust. He made out a faint glow and after a moment figured out that it was starlight filtering through cracks between boards. He was inside a building. The mingled smells of straw, manure, and horseflesh told him it was probably the stable behind the Collinses' boardinghouse.

A huge, dark shape loomed over him. It bent down toward him and nudged his shoulder again. John Henry reached up and felt the soft nose of his horse.

"Iron Heart . . ." he murmured.

The horse nickered softly, clearly pleased that John Henry had regained consciousness. Iron Heart's presence confirmed John Henry's speculation about where he was.

When the horse bent down again, John Henry looped his arm around Iron Heart's neck and used that grip to help him stand up. He was a little unsteady on his feet after being clouted like that. His head spun and threatened to steal his balance from him.

After a moment, though, things settled down and he was able to stand up without hanging on to Iron Heart. He looked around.

The inside of the stable was dark. He had been knocked out early in the evening, but it was well after nightfall now, he thought. He had been unconscious for a while.

As he leaned against the side of Iron Heart's stall, he checked the holster at his side. Empty, of course. They had taken his gun. It would have been too much to hope for that they hadn't.

He reached up and carefully explored the side of his head where the blow had landed. He found a good-sized lump that was sticky where it had oozed blood. He hadn't seen what sort of bludgeon his attacker used, but he would have been willing to bet it was a gun butt.

He was lucky his head wasn't busted wide open or stove in, he told himself. But why was he still alive? Once the conspirators had him in their power, why hadn't they gone ahead and killed him?

If they'd done that, they would have had a body to dispose of, he reasoned. Maybe they didn't want to take a chance on his corpse being found and Dav going on a rampage that would leave significant numbers of the townspeople dead.

Or maybe they'd just drawn the line at killing him in cold blood. John Henry wanted to think that was a possibility.

He was puzzled, though, by the fact that they had left him not only alive but apparently unguarded. Surely whoever had knocked him out had realized that he was eavesdropping on the meeting. They believed him to be one of Dav's deputies, so they would expect him to go running to the sheriff to reveal the conspiracy as soon as he regained consciousness.

It was more than he could figure out right now. His brain was still too fuzzy. He needed to get out of here, needed a chance to gather his wits more. He wasn't sure it would be a good idea to go into the boardinghouse, though.

John Henry felt around on the stall gate until he

located the latch. He opened it and swung the gate out wide enough for him to leave the stall.

"See you later, pard," he muttered to Iron Heart as he closed the gate and fastened it.

The unmistakable, distinctly menacing sound of somebody cocking both barrels of a shotgun made him stiffen.

"Maybe you will, and maybe you won't," rumbled a familiar voice. "That all depends on what you do next."

So they hadn't left him unguarded after all.

John Henry lowered the hand he had used to latch the gate but otherwise didn't move. The man with the shotgun had probably been lurking here in the darkness for quite a while, and there was a good chance his eyes were more adjusted to the shadows than John Henry's were.

"Take it easy, *amigo*," he said quietly. "Some of those scatterguns have hair triggers."

"This one doesn't. If I splatter your guts all over this barn, it'll be on purpose."

John Henry had placed the voice now. He said, "You don't want to do that, Mr. Farnham."

"You know who I am?"

"Peabody Farnham, the blacksmith," John Henry said.

"Then you'll know I just got out of jail earlier today. Me and my boy spent a week in there partially because of you, mister. I'm not inclined to be overly fond of you right now. There's only one reason you're not in worse shape than you already are."

"What's that?" John Henry asked, genuinely curious.

"Because I had a lot of time to think while we were locked up, and I'm convinced my son, Nate, would be dead right now if it wasn't for you."

That took John Henry by surprise. He said, "How do you figure that?"

"I went over it and over it in my head," Farnham said. "When Nate charged at the two of you, Miller was about to kill him. I saw him reaching for his gun. But then you bulled into him and knocked him down before he could draw."

"I was just trying to get in Nate's way," John Henry said.

"I don't think so. You were getting in *Miller's* way so he wouldn't gun down my boy. Damned if I can figure out why, though, Cobb. I know your reputation. You're a badman, a killer. What'd you do, take pity on a dummy for a second?"

"That's not the way it was," John Henry replied before he could stop himself or frame the sort of callous answer that the real John Cobb might have given.

After a few seconds, Farnham said, "I didn't really think so. That's why I convinced the fellas who were in here with me a while ago not to cut your throat. I wanted a chance to talk to you first. To thank you, I guess. As bad as the last week was, at least my son is still alive, and so am I."

"What happened after that?"

"With the meeting, you mean? It broke up in a

hurry. Catching one of the men you're plotting against spying on you will do that."

"Who was it that hit me?" John Henry asked.

"I'm not sure I should tell you that."

"As long as you've got that shotgun, I'm not in any position to make trouble for anybody, now am I?"

"I suppose not," Farnham admitted. "And since you won't be leaving here tonight unless I'm convinced we can trust you, I guess it won't do any harm to tell you it was Alvin Turnage."

"Turnage?" John Henry repeated, surprised. "The bank teller?"

Farnham chuckled in the darkness and said, "You wouldn't think it to look at him, but Alvin rode with Jeb Stuart's cavalry during the war. Did plenty of scouting for the Rebs, too. He's as tough a man as you'll find in Chico, outside of the sheriff and his gang of hardcases."

"That's good to know," John Henry said. He wasn't completely shocked by the revelation about Turnage. Plenty of men had performed heroically during the war and then gone on to lead quiet, peaceful lives once the great conflict was over.

Men such as that would make good allies if and when the showdown with Dav came.

"So after he knocked me out, somebody dragged me in here?" John Henry went on.

"I did."

"I think I remember hearing your voice earlier. And Jimpson's. I didn't recognize the others."

"Then you can't retaliate against them, can you?"

"I don't plan on retaliating against anybody," John Henry said. "You don't know the full story of what's going on here, Farnham."

"Then why don't you tell me?" the blacksmith suggested. "Convince me that I shouldn't kill you. If I did, that would cut down the odds by one when we finally strike back against Dav."

"That's what you're planning to do? Stage an uprising against the sheriff?"

"You heard it for yourself, didn't you? He's going to just keep on killing, keep milking this town for everything it's worth, and use it as a stepping-stone to even greater power. Unless somebody stops him. And who's that going to be if it's not us?"

John Henry said, "The law."

"Law?" Farnham repeated. A harsh laugh came from him. "What law? Dav is the law in Chico. Duly elected, as he likes to brag. And with that weasel of a newspaperman blowing his horn, the whole territory's going to know about it soon."

"Dav's not the only law in the territory," John Henry insisted. "Not hardly. The federal marshals have jurisdiction here, too."

"Federal marshals, huh? You happen to know where we could find us one of those?"

"As a matter of fact," John Henry said, "I do."

Chapter Twenty-six

"I don't believe it," Farnham insisted a few minutes later.

"It's the truth," John Henry said.

"Then where's your badge? All I've ever seen you wearing is that tin star Dav pinned on you."

"You don't think he would have hired me if he knew I was really a deputy United States marshal named John Henry Sixkiller instead of a killer and gunfighter named Cobb, do you?"

Farnham had come closer, emerging from the shadows at the edge of the barn, and John Henry's eyes had gotten more accustomed to the darkness. John Henry could see the massive blacksmith now, standing a few feet away with the shotgun still pointed at him. A few rays of starlight that came through cracks between the boards even gleamed off the weapon's twin barrels.

"And you say Governor Wallace sent you here?" Farnham asked.

"That's right. He sent in some men before, but none of them ever came back."

Farnham grunted and said, "That's not surprising. Any strangers who showed up in town and acted too nosy disappeared in a hurry. Dav's men probably took them up in the San Juans somewhere, shot them in the head, and dumped the bodies in a ravine. That's likely what would have happened to you if you hadn't come up with the idea of pretending to be that fella Cobb and got yourself hired."

"From the sound of that, you've decided to believe me," John Henry said, smiling even though it was too dark in the stable for Farnham to see the expression.

"Let's just say I'm not completely convinced you're a lying son of a bitch anymore. I'll have to see some proof before I'll believe it, though."

"My badge and bona fides are hidden in my gear in the house," John Henry pointed out. "We can go take a look at them."

"We're not going anywhere. I want you right here in this barn where there's nowhere for you to run and not enough room to try any tricks. Open that gate and back up into the stall with your horse."

"You plan on locking me up like you were locked up?"

"It's not exactly the same thing," Farnham

rumbled. "But if you're in there with that gate between the two of us, you can't get to me before I can pull the triggers on this greener."

John Henry did what the blacksmith told him to do, opening the gate and stepping back into the stall with Iron Heart. He planned to cooperate as much as possible. He had taken a big risk by revealing the truth to Farnham, and now he had convince the man they were really allies. There was no turning back.

Once John Henry was in the stall with the gate closed, Farnham scraped a match into life and held the flame to the wick of a lantern hanging from a nail. After being in near-total darkness for so long, the sudden glare was a little blinding to John Henry. He squinted against it and saw that Farnham was having the same reaction.

The blacksmith had the shotgun in his right hand. He used his left to unhook the lantern's handle and carry it over to the doors, which were closed almost all the way. There was just a big enough gap for Farnham to stick his foot in it and drag one of the doors open.

Then he held the lantern up and waved it back and forth in an obvious signal to someone in the house.

"You were supposed to let them know when I came to, so you could all decide what to do with me," John Henry guessed.

"That's right," Farnham said. "And don't go thinking it's decided already. Just because you've got me leaning your way doesn't mean I can't be outvoted."

He hung the lantern back on the nail and stood near the stall, holding the shotgun with both hands again and keeping the barrels pointed in John Henry's general direction.

It didn't take long for those waiting in the house to respond. John Henry heard footsteps outside.

Kate Collins was the first one to hurry into the barn, which took John Henry by surprise. He hadn't known that she was in on the planned uprising against Dav. Her grandfather followed her, and then Alvin Turnage and a couple of other townsmen. John Henry recalled seeing them around the settlement, but he didn't know their names.

He felt another shock when he saw Kate clutching something in her hand and realized it was the leather folder that contained his deputy U.S. marshal's badge and his identification papers. She held it up and said to Farnham, "I was about to come out here anyway when I saw your signal, Peabody. Look at what I found when I searched his belongings!"

"Wouldn't be something that says this fella is really a federal star packer, would it?" Farnham asked.

"How did you know?" Kate's gaze darted toward John Henry in the stall. "Did he already tell you?"

"That's what he said. I didn't know whether to believe him or not, though."

Jimpson said, "The badge and the papers look

real enough to me. Good Lord, we nearly killed a U.S. marshal! We'd have wound up at the end of a hangrope for sure!"

"We didn't know who he was," Kate said. "We couldn't have been held responsible." She came over to the stall and looked over the gate at John Henry. "Why didn't you tell us who you really are?"

"I can answer that," Turnage said before John Henry could reply. "How would he have known who to trust? Any of us could be working secretly for the sheriff. And if he'd simply ridden into town and announced his identity, Dav's men would have gunned him down right away. Isn't that right, Marshal Sixkiller?"

"That's pretty much the size of it," John Henry agreed. "I figured on working against Dav from the inside." He paused, then added, "And I'm not real happy about having my gear gone through like that, but I don't suppose there's anything I can do about it."

One of the other men said, "Well, now what do we do?"

With a shrewd expression on her face, Kate said, "It seems that we have an unexpected ally. Can we *really* trust you?"

"You can," John Henry assured her.

"What did you think he would say?" Turnage asked. "That's exactly what he'd want you to believe if he planned to betray us to Dav."

"All I can do is tell you how things are," John Henry said. "I can't force anybody to believe me."

The other townsman said, "He was there when they whipped Spivey and the rest of those men from the Lucky Seven. I saw him with my own eyes. He didn't make a move to stop that hellish thing."

"What do you think I should have done?" John Henry asked with a trace of irritation in his voice. "Sure, I could have gunned down Dav. But then the rest of the deputies would have killed me, and you folks wouldn't be any better off. There's a good chance you'd be *worse* off."

"He's right about that," Turnage muttered. "Some of those deputies aren't much better than mad dogs. Dav keeps them reined in a little . . . until it suits his purposes to unleash them."

"And he saved my boy Nate's life," Farnham added. "I'm convinced of it, and I don't think the real John Cobb would've done something like that. Not from what I've heard of him." Farnham pointed a thick finger at John Henry. "That means this fella is somebody besides who he's pretending to be, and it seems likely to me that he's telling the truth about being a marshal."

Kate came over to John Henry and held out the leather folder.

"I'm sorry about going through your things," she said as he took the folder from her. "I was look-ing for guns more than anything else. We wanted to make sure you were disarmed until we figured out what to do with you. And Peabody said he wasn't sure you were really who you claimed to be, so I thought I might find some letters or something else that would tell us for sure."

"That's all right," he told her. He slipped the folder into his pocket. "You didn't want to take any chances, and when you're in the sort of fix that you folks are, of course you're a mite desperate." John Henry looked around at the people gathered in the stable. "You're planning some sort of attack on Dav and his men, aren't you?"

They exchanged glances. This was it: they had to decide whether to trust him or not.

After a moment, Turnage said, "That's right. We've got a dozen men lined up. We figure that if we all strike at the same time and take Dav and the deputies by surprise, we have a chance to get the upper hand on them."

"You also have a good chance of getting killed," John Henry said. "Dav's men are all top gunhands. You'll be outnumbered, too. Any chance you have will be a small one."

"Not all of the deputies are on duty at the same time," Farnham pointed out. "If we can kill or capture the ones who are, then the odds would be better against the others."

John Henry thought about that for a moment, then said, "Turn that around, and you'll have an even better chance."

"You mean take care of the ones who are off duty first?" Turnage asked. "That might work."

That was a variation on the same plan John Henry had considered, but he had discarded the idea because he knew he couldn't carry it out by himself. But now, if he had the help of the townspeople . . .

"And the first step," he said, "is to take the jail."

Chapter Twenty-seven

They stayed in the barn for another half hour, making plans. More men had been there earlier, before Turnage had discovered John Henry eavesdropping on the meeting, but the ones who had remained were the leaders. They could pass along any decisions to the others who were involved.

"Make sure that everyone is trustworthy," John Henry stressed. "All it would take to ruin everything and put everyone's life at risk would be for someone to sell you out to the sheriff."

"As far as I can see, you're the weakest link in the chain when it comes to being trustworthy, Marshal," Turnage said. "Everyone else has known each other for years. You're not much more than a stranger to us . . . and until just a little while ago, we all thought that you worked for our bitterest enemy."

"That's a good point," John Henry admitted. "I know you're putting your faith in me. As far as

I'm concerned, that's one more reason not to let you down."

The plan was plenty dangerous, but it had at least a chance of working, John Henry thought. The deputies' living quarters were scattered across the settlement. Four of them, including John Henry, lived here at the Collinses' boardinghouse. One of them, a man named Axminster, was asleep inside the house while the discussion was going on in the stable, in fact. Others had rooms in the hotel or upstairs at the Buzzard's Nest, and three of them had moved into an abandoned house, taking it over.

"We'll need to know who's on duty and who's asleep," John Henry explained. "If we can grab the men who are off duty and take them prisoner, we won't have to worry about them when we make our move against the others."

"The middle of the night is the best time to strike," Turnage said. "That's always been true in war. Take the enemy by surprise."

"And this is a war," John Henry agreed, "just on a smaller scale. If we can grab half the deputies and lock them up in the jail, we'll have a place to fall back if we need to, as well as some bargaining chips."

Farnham said, "Dav won't bargain. I don't reckon he really gives a damn about the lives of his men, not when it comes to whether his plans succeed or fail, anyway."

"You're probably right about that," John Henry said, "but not all of Dav's men are quite as ambitious or fanatical as he is. Even with Dav ordering them on, some of them might think twice about attacking the jail if it meant putting their friends' lives in danger."

"What about Dav himself?" Kate asked. "Does anybody know where he spends his nights?"

"From what I can tell, he moves around a lot. I guess he's like any tyrant and figures that sooner or later somebody will try to fight back. He doesn't want to fall into any routines that they might use against him."

Turnage said, "If we could lay our hands on Dav right at the start, that would certainly improve our chances."

John Henry nodded.

"That would be a stroke of luck," he said. "But it may not be possible. We'll have to wait and see. Tomorrow I'll see what I can find out and start trying to pin down where everybody is at what times."

They had done all the planning they could for now, so the group dispersed. Turnage, Farnham, and the other two townsmen headed for their homes, while John Henry, Kate, and old Jimpson Collins went into the boardinghouse.

Jimpson clumped up the rear stairs that led from the kitchen to the second floor. Kate paused in the shadowy room and turned to John Henry.

"You'd better not be playing us for fools," she whispered with a note of fierceness in her voice. "If you are, I . . . I'll never forgive you."

"You know the truth now, Kate," he told her. "I give you my word on that."

"And I'll give you my word . . . if you betray us, I'll do my best to kill you myself."

"You sound like you mean that," John Henry said.

"You'd better believe that I do," Kate said.

Ever since he had come to Chico, John Henry had taken special note of the comings and goings of Sheriff Dav and the deputies, figuring that the more he knew about their habits, the better. Over the next few days he increased that scrutiny even more, until he knew when each man was on duty and when he wasn't, and where they spent their time when they weren't working.

Not surprisingly, the only one whose movements he really couldn't predict was Samuel Dav himself. The sheriff was an extremely cautious man. He could pop up anywhere, any time. John Henry recalled how the baker, Wilhelm Heinsdorf, had claimed that Dav was some sort of supernatural being. John Henry could almost believe that. The man was a phantom, as hard to grab as the air.

Without his crew of gun-wolves, though, Dav would be no real threat, so first things first, John Henry reasoned. He and the leaders of the uprising met in the stable behind the Collinses' boardinghouse each night and put together their plan of assault.

Alvin Turnage would strike first, capturing Fred Axminster at the boardinghouse. Once Axminster was tied and gagged, Turnage would go to the blacksmith shop and join forces with Peabody Farnham and four other men. The six of them would proceed to the hotel, where they would grab the four deputies who would be there.

Meanwhile, five more men would go after the three deputies who would be sleeping in rooms on the second floor of the Buzzard's Nest. Speed, stealth, and surprise would be essential to the success of both missions.

While that was going on, John Henry would take care of his part of the job: capturing the jail. Gil Hobart would be there, possibly with one or two deputies. If everything went as it was supposed to, the townsmen would bring their prisoners to the jail to be locked up. Once eight or nine of the deputies were behind bars, the odds would be a lot closer to even.

There was plenty that could go wrong with the plan, John Henry knew. He fully expected that before it was over, something *would* go wrong. Men might well die. But the alternative was letting Dav's brutal rule over the town continue, and no one was willing to accept that.

The next night, the group of "revolutionaries" would make their move.

* * *

John Henry and the others had all left the stable and gone their separate ways after finalizing their plans. The night was quiet and dark. The only sound inside the barn was the occasional stamp of a hoof or the swish of a horse's tail.

No one was around to see the shadow that suddenly stole along the outside of the stable's rear wall. The man had been concealed there in the thickest darkness, where he stood almost no chance of being spotted, and had waited in complete silence with his ear pressed to a tiny crack between the boards, listening to the low-voiced discussion inside.

Nor was this the first night he had spied on the plotters inside the barn. He knew every bit of their plans.

As he moved away from the stable, he stuck to the shadows as much as possible. He didn't want to be spotted back there. That could ruin everything.

He couldn't avoid the moonlight entirely, though, and as he crossed quickly through a patch of it, for a second the silvery glow illuminated his features, casting shadows and throwing his features into stark relief.

Then Deputy Steve Buckner was out of the moonlight and continued hurrying through the night, away from the boardinghouse.

Chapter Twenty-eight

John Henry had always been blessed with cool nerves, so he was calm the next day and able to carry on with his normal routine as if that night wouldn't likely bring with it powder smoke and flaming death.

His day's patrol went peacefully. He went into both the bank and the blacksmith shop, and when Alvin Turnage and Peabody Farnham looked at him, their expressions were stony, as if they still considered him one of Sheriff Dav's gun-wolves and weren't aware of his true identity. That was exactly how they needed to regard him for now, John Henry thought.

Despite his steady demeanor, the day seemed to drag, and John Henry was glad when the sun sank behind the San Juans. He went back to the office, where Carl Miller was sitting at the desk. Dav himself hadn't been around much the past few days, or at least he wasn't showing himself.

"Everything's quiet," John Henry reported.

Miller nodded and said, "That's what I'm hearin' from the other fellas." A frown creased the deputy's forehead. "Somethin's not right, though."

John Henry was careful not to show the alarm he felt. Had Miller somehow tumbled onto the fact that an uprising was in the works?

"Thought I heard some thunder rumblin' up over the mountains awhile back," Miller went on. "Could be we'll get a storm tonight." He rubbed a hand on the back of his neck. "I always get this funny feelin' back here when there's fixin' to be a storm."

"You could be right," John Henry said. He had seen a few clouds gathering to the west, as well, but they hadn't closed in and blotted out the sun before it set. If a storm was indeed on the way, it would probably still be several hours before it got there.

That might be a good thing, he mused. Some thunder and rain would help him and his allies conceal what they were doing.

And under the circumstances, he would take any stroke of luck he could get.

"I guess you're on your way back to the boardin' house," Miller went on.

"That's right. Miss Collins doesn't like it when people are late for supper."

"Well, I wouldn't want to make any gal as pretty as Kate Collins mad at me," Miller said with a grin. "Of course, Steve Buckner's got his eye on her, too.

You boys aren't gonna wind up in a shootin' scrape over her, are you?"

"No chance of that," John Henry assured him. He changed the subject and risked asking, "Say, where's the sheriff these days? I've hardly seen him around lately."

Miller grunted. He didn't seem suspicious about the question as he said, "He's been spendin' a lot of time with that newspaperman. Wouldn't surprise me if they were hatchin' plans for the boss to become an even bigger boss."

"Me, neither," John Henry said. "If that were to happen, you reckon we'd go along with him, wherever he went?"

"I wouldn't count on it. You can be an even bigger outlaw in politics, but you've got to be slicker about it."

John Henry thought that was probably one of the truest statements he had ever heard. Wisdom sometimes popped up in unlikely places.

He left the office and returned to the boarding-house. Miller had been right about the thunder. John Henry heard a low rumble from the direction of the mountains as he walked along the street.

He got to the house just as Kate was setting the last of the food on the table in the dining room. She gave him a brief glare in keeping with how she treated anybody who bent one of her rules. John Henry smiled to himself, secure in the knowledge that they were allies in the effort to end Samuel Dav's rule over the settlement.

Buckner was quieter than usual during the meal. That was a little troubling but didn't have to mean anything, John Henry told himself. After supper, Buckner and Kemp set off for downtown to start their shifts on patrol. Kemp had been as taciturn as ever while they were eating.

Before the night was over, he might be swapping lead with both of them, John Henry thought. That disturbed him more than it should have. He certainly didn't have any fondness for men who would work for Dav, but he had seen Buckner and Kemp quite a bit during the past two weeks, and it was only normal to feel at least a bit of familiarity with them.

Seeing your enemy as a human being with thoughts and emotions could be damned inconvenient, John Henry mused. But there was nothing that could be done about it now.

He went upstairs at the same time as Fred Axminster and gave the other deputy a polite nod as they each went to their rooms. Once he was in his room, John Henry settled down to wait. He took out his watch, opened it, and set it on the bedside table.

Midnight was the time they were going to start their plan in motion, and it couldn't come too soon to suit him.

The house was dark and quiet when John Henry slipped out of his room a few minutes before midnight. He knew that Kate and her grandfather would be awake. He doubted if they had slept any during the evening. They were probably as keyed up with anticipation as he was. By morning Chico would be free again . . .

Or else any resistance would be smashed so thoroughly that Dav could finish looting the town without any opposition at all.

John Henry paused as he saw that Axminster's door was open. He drew his gun and approached cautiously. Axminster usually snored loudly, and now no sound came from inside the room. John Henry stopped short of the door and gave a low whistle.

A similar whistle answered him from inside. John Henry whispered, "Turnage?"

"Yes," the bank teller replied. "I've got him."

John Henry stepped into the doorway, gun leveled in case this was some sort of trick on Axminster's part. Then a match flared to life, and as John Henry's eyes narrowed against the glare, he saw Axminster sprawled facedown on the bed. The deputy had a bloody lump on the back of his head, and John Henry guessed it came from the butt of the gun Turnage held as the teller stood next to the bed.

"He was so sound asleep he never heard me sneak in," Turnage whispered.

"You didn't kill him, did you?"

"No, he's breathing. I'm going to tie and gag

him, and then Nate Farnham is supposed to come and help me take him to the jail."

"Can Nate handle that?" John Henry asked.

"Don't worry," Turnage said. "He'll do whatever his father tells him to do, or die trying."

John Henry nodded. The first step of the plan was almost complete. They wouldn't have to worry about Axminster now.

He left Turnage binding the deputy's hands and catfooted to the stairs. He went down them in silence, making one quick stop in the kitchen when he reached the ground floor, before letting himself out the front door and heading for the sheriff's office and jail.

The storm over the mountains had moved closer. The thunder was louder now, and John Henry saw streaks of lightning clawing across the sky like skeletal fingers. Gusts of cool wind prowled through the streets, whipping up little spirals of dust here and there.

The businesses along Main Street were all dark except for the Buzzard's Nest, and as John Henry looked over the batwings he could see the swamper sweeping up already as a couple of drinkers lingered at the bar. The saloon was busy until well after midnight on Saturday night, but during the week like this, when everybody had to be up early for work the next morning, it usually closed down not much after this.

John Henry ducked into alleys whenever he saw one of the deputies strolling along the boardwalks.

Using caution and stealth, he made his way to the sheriff's office. When he got there he tried the door, only to find it locked.

That was an obstacle, but not a major one and he was prepared for it. He knocked on the thick wooden door. It had a small, square peephole in it that could be opened, and a moment later Gil Hobart looked out at him and asked in that distinctive voice, "Who's there?"

"It's John Cobb, Gil," John Henry replied. "Let me in."

"You ain't on duty tonight," Hobart replied. "I ain't supposed to let nobody in unless it's the sheriff or one of the deputies that's on duty."

"I know that. But I was able to sneak a piece of Kate Collins's apple pie out of the kitchen tonight, and I thought you might want it."

He held up the saucer with the slab of pie on it that he had brought from the boardinghouse. Sometime in the past, Gil Hobart had sampled Kate's pie, and John Henry had heard him proclaim on numerous occasions that it was the best pie Hobart had ever eaten.

Even though the peephole, John Henry could hear Hobart licking his lips in anticipation. The jailer said, "You ain't gonna tell the sheriff about this, are you, Cobb?"

"And get in trouble myself? I don't think so."

"Hang on a minute. Lemme get the keys."

Hobart was back at the door in less than a

minute. John Henry heard a key rattle in the lock, and then the door swung open.

"Hurry up," Hobart said. "Come on in."

John Henry went into the office. Hobart swung the door closed behind him but didn't lock it. John Henry took the saucer over to the desk and set it down.

"Dig in, Gil," he told Hobart with a smile.

Hobart came over to the desk and opened a drawer to dig out a fork. There were several utensils in there that were used by the deputies whenever meals on trays were brought over from Abernathy's Café. John Henry eased behind him as Hobart cut off a big bite of the pie and stuffed it in his mouth. He rested his right hand on the butt of his Colt and got ready to reach down with his left and pluck Hobart's revolver from its holster.

Before John Henry could make that move, the office door opened again. Steve Buckner stepped into the room, leveled the gun in his hand at John Henry, and said, "Don't do it, Cobb, or whatever the hell your name is."

Chapter Twenty-nine

John Henry didn't try to draw. Fast with a gun though he might be, he couldn't outdraw a revolver that was already pointed right at him.

"Wha'n'th'hell you doin', Steve?" Hobart asked thickly around the mouthful of pie.

"Keepin' you from bein' coldcocked on the head by this lyin' son of a gun, Gil," Buckner replied. "He's a deputy United States marshal."

Hobart twisted his head to look back over his shoulder at John Henry. He swallowed the pie and said, "Really? A federal star packer?"

"I believe Steve's mixed up," John Henry said, keeping himself cool and composed. "I don't think John Cobb ever carried a badge for Uncle Sam."

"I reckon he sure as hell didn't," Buckner snapped, "but you ain't John Cobb. I never did catch your name when I was listenin' in on those little get-togethers in the stable behind the boardin' house, mister, but I know who you are and why you're here."

John Henry didn't have any idea how Buckner had tumbled to what was going on, but that didn't matter now. The whole plan depended on him taking control of the jail. If he failed, then in a short time his newfound allies would begin showing up with their captives, only to be taken prisoner—or killed—themselves.

"I don't know what you think you heard, Buckner," he said, stalling for time while he tried to figure out his next move, "but you got it all wrong, that's for sure."

"Yeah, Steve," Hobart put in. "I don't think a real lawman would bring me pie."

"Damn it, Gil, forget about the pie! Stand up and move away from him! If he pulls iron on me, you don't want to get caught in the crossfire."

Hobart started to get to his feet. John Henry knew he had run out of time. Hobart being so close to him was the only thing keeping Buckner from squeezing the trigger. Once the jailer was clear of him, he wouldn't have a chance to do anything except make a desperate grab for his gun and get himself killed. If he was going to make a play that might actually work, it had to be now.

As Hobart got to his feet, he picked up the saucer, unwilling to leave his pie behind. John Henry suddenly put his hand under the saucer and shoved it up, smashing the pie into Hobart's face. That took the jailer by surprise and made him reel back a step. John Henry darted behind him. Across the room, Buckner let out a startled curse but didn't fire.

John Henry reached around and plucked the saucer, with remnants of pie clinging to it, from Hobart's fingers and sent it spinning across the room, straight at Buckner's face.

Buckner ducked instinctively but the saucer clipped him on the head anyway, shattering. John Henry had charged right behind it. He tackled Buckner around the waist and drove him back against the doorjamb. John Henry reached up with his left hand and closed it around the six-gun's cylinder so it couldn't turn and Buckner couldn't fire.

One thing John Henry had stressed with the townspeople who were staging the uprising was that they had to strike quietly. A bunch of gunshots would rouse the town and draw more attention from the other deputies than they could handle. He didn't intend to let Buckner get a shot off if he could help it.

The deputy's head struck hard against the door-jamb, but the impact failed to knock him out. He fought back, slamming a punch to the side of John Henry's head that sent the federal lawman's hat flying. John Henry shrugged off the punishment and hooked his right fist into Buckner's belly. Buckner gasped and tried to double over, but John Henry was crowding him too close for that.

John Henry grabbed the wrist of Buckner's gun

hand and forced it down, at the same time bringing up his knee. Buckner's hand hit John Henry's knee and the fingers relaxed their grip on the gun. John Henry wrenched the weapon away from the deputy and smashed it across Buckner's face. The blow twisted Buckner's head to the side and made him go limp.

Bunching his fingers in Buckner's shirtfront, John Henry pivoted and slung him across the room toward the desk, where Gil Hobart was stumbling around pawing at his eyes. He was still half-blinded from getting apple pie shoved in his face.

John Henry wasn't sure how Kate Collins would feel about her pie being used as a weapon. That thought flickered across his mind in the time it took him to flip Buckner's gun around and level it at the jailer.

"Don't try anything, Gil," he warned as he kicked the door closed so that no one passing by on the street could see what was happening. "I've got you covered."

Hobart finished wiping the sticky pie out of his eyes and stared in disbelief across the room.

"Cobb?" he asked. "You . . . you're really what Steve said?"

"Afraid so," John Henry replied. "Reach across with your left hand and take your gun out, slow and careful-like. Put it on the desk."

"Take it easy," Hobart said as he followed John Henry's orders and set the gun on the desk. "I ain't no gunslinger, and I don't have any hankerin' to get shot, neither."

John Henry nodded toward the stairs and asked, "Is the cell block unlocked?"

"Yeah. No prisoners up there now."

John Henry circled to the side and kept Buckner's gun pointed at the jailer. He used the barrel to gesture toward Buckner and said, "Come over here and pick him up. You're going to take him up the stairs, and both of you are going into one of the cells."

"You're lockin' us up?"

"That's the idea."

Hobart shook his head ponderously.

"It ain't gonna work. One of the other deputies will just come along and let us out when we start yellin' for help."

John Henry considered this and then nodded.

"Good point," he admitted. "You'll tie and gag Buckner and put him one cell, and then I'll lock you in another one."

"There still won't be anything stoppin' me from yellin'."

"Well . . . I could just kill you," John Henry said. "That would keep you quiet."

"Or . . . I could cooperate and let you tie and gag me, too," Hobart suggested.

"That's what I'd rather do. You don't seem like that bad an *hombre*, Gil. You've just got poor taste in bosses."

"You came here to put the sheriff out of business, is that it?"

"That's it," John Henry said.

Hobart drew in a deep breath, then let it out in a sigh. He nodded.

"I reckon that's fine by me. I ain't sayin' I never pulled anything crooked in my life, but some of the things I've seen since comin' here to Chico . . . well, I just didn't cotton to 'em, that's all. Only reason I stuck was because I just had to take care of the jail and didn't have to be out there makin' life miserable for folks. I'll play along with you, Cobb."

"Sixkiller," John Henry said. "That's my real name, John Henry Sixkiller."

Hobart regarded him for a moment, then nodded.

"It suits you," he said. "Just don't kill *me*, 'cause I ain't gonna give you no trouble."

He picked up the still senseless Buckner and slung the deputy over his shoulder. John Henry switched Buckner's gun to his left hand and drew his own Colt as he followed Hobart up the stairs to the cell block. While John Henry kept him covered, Hobart lowered Buckner onto the bunk in one of the cells, then tied his hands behind his back and stuffed a bandana in his mouth to serve as a gag.

John Henry was careful about approaching the big jailer, still wary of a trick, but Hobart kept his word and cooperated. He let John Henry tie his hands and gag him.

"When all this is over, I'll remember how you helped me out like this, Gil," John Henry promised. "That might make some difference in how the law looks at things."

With that taken care of, the jail was in John Henry's hands. He hurried downstairs to wait for the others to show up with their prisoners. He'd been listening for gunshots, but the settlement remained quiet, as if nothing were going on tonight.

That couldn't be any further from the truth, John Henry thought. At least, he hoped that was the case and that the rest of the operation was going as planned.

Barely a minute after he'd come back downstairs, a soft tap sounded on the door. John Henry blew out the lamp and went over to look out the peephole. Pieces of broken saucer crunched under his boots as he approached the door.

"It's us, Marshal," Alvin Turnage said before John Henry could ask who was out there. Turnage was showing a lot of confidence that John Henry had been successful in capturing the jail.

That confidence wasn't misplaced. John Henry swung the door open and saw Turnage's slender form beside the massive, hulking shape of Nate Farnham. Nate had Fred Axminster cradled in his arms like a baby.

Axminster had regained consciousness. He jerked his head around and made muffled noises through the gag in his mouth, but that was all he could do. Nate's arms might as well have been iron bands strapped around him.

The newcomers moved quietly into the office, and as John Henry closed the door behind them, Turnage asked, "Did everything go as planned?"

"So far," John Henry replied. "As far as I know, anyway. I don't know what's happening at the hotel."

"Nate and I are on our way to the blacksmith shop to join up with Peabody and the others," Turnage said, "as soon as we put Deputy Axminster in one of the cells."

"Take him on up, Nate," John Henry said, but the young man hesitated.

"You're our friend now, right?" he asked as he frowned suspiciously at John Henry.

"That's right, Nate," Turnage said. "This man is our friend."

Nate nodded and said, "All right, then." He carried Axminster up the stairs as if the deputy only weighed as much as a puppy or a kitten. Axminster had about as much chance of getting loose as a puppy or a kitten would have, too.

Turnage followed them up the stairs to make sure Axminster was locked up securely. John Henry waited by the door in the darkened office in case any of his coconspirators showed up with more prisoners.

Turnage and Nate came down and slipped out to rendezvous with Nate's father and the other men waiting at the blacksmith shop. John Henry wanted to go with them. Even though he had picked the job of staying here at the jail for this part of the operation because it was the key to everything, not being in the middle of the action chafed at him.

Soon enough, he told himself. Soon enough the time for stealth would be over, and they could take the fight to the rest of the enemy.

Somewhere out there was Samuel Dav, John Henry thought.

And every instinct in his body told him that the two of them would be facing each other with guns in their hands before the night was over.

Chapter Thirty

Only one lamp was burning in the newspaper office. Edgar Wellman leaned back in the chair behind the desk and watched Dav reading the sheets of paper the sheriff held in his hand. He felt some justifiable anxiety as he waited to see if Dav liked what he had written.

Finally Dav nodded and set the sheaf of papers back on the desk.

"Not bad," he said. "The stories make it sound like I'm responsible for everything good that happens in this part of the territory, whether I really had anything to do with it or not, and they completely ignore the more . . . problematical aspects of the situation."

"That's what you wanted, isn't it?" Wellman asked.

"Exactly," Dav said with another nod. "And you can get these stories printed in newspapers scattered all over the territory?"

"I think so. It may take awhile, but I guarantee you, Sheriff, within six months nearly everyone in New Mexico will have heard of the gallant fighting lawman named Samuel Dav."

That put a pleased smile on Dav's face.

"Good. When it comes time for the president to appoint a new territorial governor, I want my name to be the first one that comes to mind."

Wellman frowned and said, "Why would the president need to appoint a new governor? I thought General Wallace was doing a good job."

Dav waved off the question.

"Never mind about that," he said. "Maybe you'd better get started working on the first speech I'll be making once I take office. I know it'll be awhile yet, but it doesn't hurt to be prepared."

Wellman was about to ask more questions when he decided it might be wise not to press Dav on the issue. Instead he said, "I didn't know you wanted me to write your political speeches for you, too."

"I've been impressed with your work, Edgar. You're good at what you do."

Praise such as that had always pleased Wellman. He found that it wasn't quite so flattering when it came from the likes of Dav. However, he had thrown his lot in with the sheriff, and it would be dangerous to try to back out now.

So he just nodded and said, "Thank you. I appreciate that, Sheriff."

"Call me Sam," Dav replied. "We're going to be partners now, after all."

Wellman knew better than to believe that. Dav didn't have any partners, only people who followed his orders out of greed or fear or both. But if Dav wanted to pretend otherwise, that was fine with Wellman.

"All right, Sam," he said.

Dav stood up.

"Make sure you put something in that speech about how I'm going to crack down on lawlessness from one end of the territory to the other. There aren't going to be gangs of crooks preying on the people of New Mexico anymore."

If Dav got his way, that would be true, thought Wellman.

There would only be *one* gang of crooks preying on the citizens, and its headquarters would be in the territorial governor's office.

Dav left the newspaper office. Wellman gathered up the papers and aligned them in a neat stack on his desk. He blew out the lamp and went into his living quarters at the rear of the building.

The window was open back there to let in a little fresh air, and as Wellman was feeling in his pocket for a match to light the lamp beside his bed, he heard the low mutter of voices from somewhere outside. He left the match where it was, and in a mixture of caution and a journalist's curiosity, he moved closer to the window.

The curtains were closed over it, muffling the sound. He parted them slightly and put his ear to the gap. There shouldn't have been anyone skulking

around in the alley at this time of night, and he
wanted to know who was out there and what they
were up to.

"—waiting for us at the jail," Wellman heard.
The man's voice was familiar, and after a couple
of seconds the newspaperman placed it. The voice
belonged to Alvin Turnage, one of the tellers at
the bank.

Something was different, though. Turnage's
tone was crisp and hard, as if he were accustomed
to giving orders. That didn't make any sense. The
man was about as mild mannered as he could be.

Wellman caught part of another sentence.

"—go after the other deputies, right?"

That question came in a rumbling tone that un-
mistakably belonged to Peabody Farnham, the
blacksmith. Turnage and Farnham . . . and something about the deputies? That didn't make any
sense.

But Wellman's journalistic instincts were starting
to kick in now. His gut told him that something was
going on in Chico tonight, something big and important and probably dangerous. His first thought
was to go find Sheriff Dav or some of the deputies
and warn them.

If he did that, though, he wouldn't be able to
see how the story was going to play out. And the
story was everything, wasn't it? He couldn't very
well report the news if he was helping to make it,
could he?

The men who'd been behind the newspaper

office had gone on now. Wellman pushed the curtains aside and noiselessly raised the window more, so he could lean through it and look along the alley. It was plenty dark back here, but he could make out the shapes of half a dozen men dragging some limp forms. They were headed for the jail, Turnage had said. Wellman's pulse began to race as he recalled that.

The townspeople were fighting back at last, Wellman realized. They were staging a coup, an uprising against Dav's tyrannical rule. But even if they had managed to capture a few of the deputies, they wouldn't stand any chance against the rest of the sheriff's cold-blooded killer crew. Would they?

Wellman didn't know the answer to that, but he knew one thing.

He was going to find out.

The odds against the groups of townies being able to capture the off-duty deputies and bring them to the jail without being discovered were astronomical, John Henry knew. He wasn't really expecting it to happen. But the more of Dav's men who could be taken out of the fight at the start, the better. It was a matter of making the odds not quite so overwhelming.

Still, when Turnage, the Farnhams, and several other men arrived at the jail with four prisoners, John Henry began to hope maybe the plan would work without any hitches after all.

"Any problems?" he asked Turnage as Peabody and Nate hauled the bound, gagged, and unconscious deputies up the stairs to the cell block.

Turnage shook his head.

"No, we got in the back door of the Buzzard's Nest without any trouble. There was one moment when I was worried, when one of the girls who works there discovered us, but she didn't give the alarm. She just looked at us and turned away. She probably has grudges of her own against the sheriff's men."

"More than likely," John Henry agreed.

"We took them one by one, knocked them out, and tied them up. They weren't any match for Peabody and Nate. Not many men would be."

"I can testify to that," John Henry said, recalling his own run-in with the blacksmith and his son.

Creases appeared on the bank teller's forehead as he asked, "What about the men who were going to the hotel?"

John Henry could only shake his head and say, "I haven't seen or heard anything from them. But maybe that's good. There hasn't been any shooting or yelling from over there."

"The old idea that no news is good news, eh? I wish I could believe that."

So did John Henry.

"Do you want us to go see if we can find out what's holding them up?" Turnage went on.

John Henry considered the idea for a moment, then shook his head.

"No, you and the others are going to fort up here for the time being," he said. "Nobody's going back out there until we're all together again."

Turnage looked like he might want to argue the point, but before he could another knock sounded on the office door. John Henry motioned for Turnage to stay where he was. He drew his gun as he approached the door.

"Who's out there?" he called softly.

"Kate Collins," came the reply.

John Henry stiffened in surprise. Kate and her grandfather were supposed to stay at the boarding-house tonight, well out of the line of fire. Jimpson was too old to be right in the middle of a gun battle, and Kate was . . . well, Kate was a woman, and although John Henry knew she might argue that such an attitude was unfair, he couldn't help the way he felt about such things.

He checked through the peephole to make sure none of the deputies had brought them here as prisoners in an effort to gain entry to the jail. Kate and Jimpson were alone. He unlocked the door and swung it open.

"Get inside quick," he told them. "What are you—"

Before he could finish asking them what they were doing there, a burst of gunshots rang out, shattering the night's stillness, and John Henry could tell that they came from the direction of the hotel.

Chapter Thirty-one

Well, so much for everything going off without a hitch, John Henry thought bitterly.

But that reaction lasted only a split second. He wasn't the sort to stand around brooding when action needed to be taken.

"Get in here!" he told Kate and Jimpson. "Alvin, hold the jail!"

"I'm coming with you," Turnage said as Kate and her grandfather hurried into the building.

"No, you're not. I need a good man to take over here." John Henry added over his shoulder, "Lock the door behind me!"

He didn't take the time to see if Turnage followed his orders. Instead he ran toward the hotel, gun in hand.

After that initial volley, a crashing silence had fallen over Chico again. The silence didn't last long. Before John Henry could reach the hotel, more shots roared. Not all together now, but in an irregular pattern, as if men were firing at each other from behind cover.

As John Henry cut across the street and approached the hotel, lightning flickered and thunder boomed like cannon fire. The storm had held off all evening, but now it appeared that it was about to break.

The flash from the electrical display in the heavens lit up the street and the boardwalks for a second, and during that time John Henry spotted another man running toward the hotel. He recognized the stocky form of Deputy Aaron Kemp.

Kemp saw him, too, and yelled, "Cobb! Do you know what's goin' on? What's all that shooting?"

Kemp didn't know yet that a small-scale revolution was taking place in Chico tonight, nor did he know John Henry's true identity. He could put that to use, John Henry thought.

He paused as he and Kemp both reached the front of the hotel at the same time.

"The shots came from inside," John Henry said. "We'd better find out what's happening."

"Have you seen Steve?"

"No," John Henry lied. "Maybe he's inside."

Concern for his friend made Kemp turn toward the hotel's double doors. As he did so, John Henry stepped behind him and struck. The gun in his hand chopped down in a hard, swift stroke and thudded against the back of Kemp's head.

Kemp never saw the blow coming. He grunted and fell to his knees, then pitched forward onto his face, out cold. John Henry reached down, grabbed the collar of Kemp's shirt, and dragged him to the end of the boardwalk and into the dark mouth of the alley beside the hotel.

John Henry would have liked to take Kemp back to the jail and lock him up, since that would put him out of the fight permanently, but there was no time for that. The gun battle was still going on inside the hotel. Innocent people might be dying. John Henry would just have to hope that Kemp would remain unconscious for a while.

He ran down the alley, figuring it might be better to use the rear stairs. Pausing at the side door, he waited for a second, then jerked it open and went through in a rush. No bursts of muzzle flame split the gloom in the rear hallway.

The stairs were to John Henry's right. He could tell from the way the reports echoed in the stairwell that the shots were coming from the second floor. He went up, taking the stairs two or three at a time.

Stopping at the top of the staircase, he went to a knee and took off his hat to peer around the corner into the upper corridor. At the far end of the hall were the main stairs that led down into the lobby. A man lay there on the landing, facedown. John Henry's mouth tightened into a grim line as he spotted the pool of blood spreading around the man's head.

He couldn't see the dead man's face, but the man's clothes told John Henry that he was one of the townspeople, not a deputy. That meant one of his allies had already been killed.

Another man was down at the landing, lying behind a small table he had overturned. He fired over the top of it at an open door about halfway along the corridor. At least two men were inside the room that went with that door, leaning out to throw lead at the man who had taken cover behind the table.

The angle was bad on both sides, but the two men inside the hotel room had the advantage of superior firepower. Eventually they would shoot that table to pieces. It wouldn't stop their bullets much longer.

John Henry thought furiously. The room where the deputies were holed up was on the front side of the hotel. A narrow balcony ran along there. John Henry figured that represented his best chance to get the drop on them.

He put his hat on and stood up, then ducked around the corner from the rear stairs and lowered his shoulder, ramming it against the closest door. With a splintering of wood, the door burst open. Light from the hall spilled into the room and revealed an elderly couple sitting up in bed, arms around each other, eyes wide with terror.

"Sorry, folks," John Henry told them as he ran across the room to the window. "Just stay hunkered down and you'll be all right."

He hoped that was true. He thrust up the sash and stepped over the sill onto the balcony.

He had counted the doors, so he knew how many windows he had to pass to reach the room he wanted. Even if he hadn't, he would have known where he needed to go because of the muzzle flashes he saw through the window. The men in the room weren't paying any attention to what was going on behind them, so they had no idea he was right outside.

He tried the window, but it wouldn't go up. Locked! That left him only one way in.

The balcony was only a couple of feet wide, more for decoration than anything else. John Henry drew back as much as he could. As he did so, another cannon volley of thunder shook the settlement, accompanied by a blinding flash of lightning. John Henry felt the first fat drop of rain hit his face as he launched himself at the window as hard as he could.

With a crash of shattering glass, he smashed through it and fell toward the floor inside the room. Sharp edges clawed at him, but he ignored the pain. He caught himself on his left hand as the two men in the room whirled toward him in surprise. Another lightning flash from outside revealed their faces. John Henry recognized them as two of Dav's deputies who'd been sleeping here in the hotel, just as he expected.

Then their guns began to roar again and his Colt blasted back at them, as the muzzle flashes competed with the lightning to see which could be the most garish and eye-searing.

Whether the deputies had recognized him or not, they must have taken him for an enemy. Bullets plowed into the floor next to John Henry and whined through the air above his head. His revolver bucked in his hand as he triggered four swift shots.

The slugs hammered into the two gunmen and drove them backward. One of the men hit the wall of the hotel room and started to slide down on it, leaving a bloody smear on the wallpaper from the wounds in his back where John Henry's bullets had come out.

The other deputy toppled through the open door, landing half in and half out of the room. He twitched as the man down at the landing shot him again and drove a slug into his body.

John Henry scrambled to his feet and approached the two fallen men carefully, keeping his gun leveled in case he needed to use it again. He still had one round in the cylinder.

Both deputies were dead, though, so John Henry took advantage of the chance to dump the empty cartridges and thumb in fresh rounds from the loops on his shell belt. He filled all six chambers this time, instead of leaving an empty one for the Colt's hammer to rest on as he usually did. Before this night was over he would probably need every shot he could get.

The man in the hallway had stopped shooting. John Henry called, "Hold your fire! I'm coming out."

"Who's there?" the man shouted back.

"Marshal Sixkiller."

He stepped into the corridor and saw the man at the landing climbing painfully to his feet. Blood stained the man's shirt on the side.

"How badly are you hit?" John Henry asked as he hurried down the hall.

The man shook his head and said, "It's just a crease, I think. Hurts like blazes, though."

"They'll do that," John Henry agreed. He was able to get a better look at the dead townsman now and recognized him as the baker, Wilhelm Heinsdorf. That was a damned shame, John Henry thought . . . but it was a damned shame any innocent people had to die to free Chico from the evil grip of Samuel Dav.

"What happened?"

"One of the deputies woke up just at the wrong time and grabbed a gun, started blazing away at us just as we were about to grab them," the townie replied. "Heinsdorf and I tried to fight back. The others turned tail and ran." Scorn was obvious in his voice.

"Not everybody's cut out for a gunfight," John Henry said. "Were there only two deputies?"

"Yeah, I don't know where the others who have rooms here are."

"Let's get back to the jail. We may be in for a siege now."

And it might be too late for them to reach that sanctuary, John Henry thought, but he didn't see any point in saying it until he knew for sure what the situation was. One thing was certain: at least some of the other deputies would have heard the gunfire and would know that something was happening on this stormy night. They would be primed for trouble.

"What do we do about Wilhelm?" the other man asked.

"Leave him here," John Henry said. "There's nothing else we can do right now."

With guns drawn, the two of them hurried down the stairs. The hotel lobby was deserted. Most likely everybody else in the place had the covers pulled over their heads . . . if they weren't cowering underneath the beds.

John Henry turned out the lamps, plunging the lobby into darkness. He didn't want the two of them to be silhouetted against the light when they went out. As they paused at the door, John Henry said, "Make for the jail as fast as you can."

Then he turned the knob, threw the door open, and plunged out into the night.

Chapter Thirty-two

Edgar Wellman pulled his hat down tighter on his head as a gust of wind brushed against his face. He hurried along the alley toward the sheriff's office and jail, and as he reached it and started up the narrow passage between it and the building next to it, lightning flashed. In that split second of illumination, he spotted Deputy Cobb running across the street, away from the jail toward the hotel.

Moments earlier, Wellman had heard shots and thought they were coming from the direction of the hotel, although he couldn't be sure about that.

Wherever they came from, though, they were a clear indication that hell was breaking loose in Chico tonight.

Wellman had a strong hunch that whatever happened, it would center around the jail, so that was why he had come here. He wanted to witness these momentous events firsthand so he could write about them later. Maybe that meant he had become a real journalist. That was for someone else to decide. He just wanted to get the story.

He waited there at the corner of the jail and watched as Cobb met someone on the boardwalk in front of the hotel. Wellman wasn't sure, but he thought the other man was one of the deputies. But a moment later he frowned in confusion as he saw Cobb pistol-whip the man and apparently knock him out. Cobb dragged the limp form into the alley next to the hotel, disappearing into the darkness and not coming back out.

Muzzle flashes lit up one of the windows on the hotel's second floor. At least, Wellman thought that was what he was seeing, not reflections of the lightning that split the night sky every few seconds. Muffled gunshots came from inside the hotel.

Movement on the balcony caught Wellman's eye. Someone had climbed out a window and was making his way along the balcony to another window . . .

A moment later, Wellman heard the crash of glass as the window shattered, and then more shots blasted.

None of it made any sense to the newspaperman, but he kept watching anyway. This was fascinating.

Rain started to fall, big, fat drops splattering here and there, the sort of sporadic rain that comes before a downpour. A couple of minutes later, several men ran along the street toward the hotel, their attention no doubt drawn by the shooting. Wellman thought they were some of Dav's deputies.

Should he call out to them, tell them what was going on, at least as much of it as he could guess?

No, Wellman decided.

And then a second after that, the front door of the hotel flew open and two men charged out onto the boardwalk with guns in their hands.

John Henry saw several things right away when he and the townsman left the hotel. The rain was falling a little harder now, but the drops were still scattered.

And there were three well-armed men charging up the street toward them.

In the near-constant flicker of lightning, John Henry recognized them as three of Sheriff Dav's men. They hadn't drawn their guns yet, so he swung his Colt toward them and called, "Hold it right there!"

As the deputies slowed, one of them exclaimed, "Cobb, what are you—"

The man beside him yelled, "The hell with that! Nobody throws down on me!"

He clawed his revolver from its holster.

John Henry recognized the man who had gone for his gun as Hoffman, one of the deputies he had clashed with at the pass east of the settlement. Hoffman had probably been waiting for a chance to even the score with the man he knew as John Cobb, so he wasn't going to pass up this opportunity.

It was a foolish move, though, because John Henry's gun was already drawn. The Colt roared and bucked against his palm as he put a bullet in Hoffman's chest. The deputy went backward as if he'd been slapped by a giant hand.

At John Henry's side, the townie opened up on the other two. They reacted with the swift, deadly instincts of professional gunmen, weaving away from each other so they'd be harder to hit as they drew their guns. Flame gouted from the muzzles.

John Henry felt as much as heard a bullet whip past his ear. At the same time, the townsman grunted and staggered. His gun blasted again, and fate must have guided the shot. One of the remaining deputies doubled over as the slug punched into his guts.

John Henry triggered twice more and sent the third deputy spinning off his feet. He turned and grabbed the arm of the wounded man who had fought at his side, steadying him.

"Come on," John Henry urged. "Let's get you to the jail."

But as they turned in that direction, more shots exploded. These came from the other direction. Bullets pounded into the street, kicking up clods of dirt and geysers of dust. The shots struck between John Henry and the jail, so he had to turn back, helping the wounded man with him.

From the corner of his eye he caught glimpses

of the shadowy forms firing at them. They had to be more of Dav's men, and if they had seen the gunfight moments earlier they would know that "Cobb" had turned on them. That was why they were spraying lead at John Henry and the man stumbling along beside him.

John Henry started back toward the hotel but realized a second later that he and his companion couldn't get there. Bullets shattered the front windows. The two men were bracketed now, with leaden death both behind them and in front of them. The only bit of cover was a wagon parked in front of the building next to the hotel. John Henry veered toward it, still urging the wounded man to keep up with him.

They reached the wagon and crouched between it and the boardwalk. Bullets thudded into the vehicle's thick sideboards. The wagon wasn't going to protect them for long. They were still too exposed. But it was better than nothing, John Henry thought as he snapped a shot over the wagon's seat, aiming at a muzzle flash half a block away.

He bent down again as a bullet hummed over his head. The townsman was leaning against one of the wagon wheels, but he was beginning to slump. His strength deserted him, and he fell to the ground. The wheel was all that held him up.

John Henry knelt beside him and asked, "How bad are you hit?"

"P-pretty bad," the man replied. His voice was

tight with pain. "A couple of bullets . . . went through me. I feel all . . . loose inside."

"You'll be all right," John Henry said. "I'll get you to the jail. Some of our other men are holed up there, and they'll take care of you."

"You can't . . . do that. We're . . . pinned down here."

John Henry didn't want to admit it, but the man was right. And taking cover behind the wagon would give them only a momentary respite. In a matter of minutes, some of the deputies would circle around so they could get a better shot.

"You can make a run for it . . . if I cover you," the townie went on. "I just need to . . . borrow some bullets. Then I can . . . keep them off of you long enough . . . for you to make it to the jail."

"You can't—" John Henry began.

"What I can't do . . . is live more than another few minutes." In the silvery flicker of lightning, John Henry saw the strained smile on the man's face. "Let me spend 'em . . . trying to kill some of those bastards."

John Henry couldn't refuse that request. He took the man's gun and filled the cylinder with cartridges from his own belt, then pressed it back into his hand. John Henry still had Buckner's gun tucked into his waistband, so he gave it to the townsman, too.

"When I stand up . . . and start shooting . . . you light a shuck for the jail," the man said.

"All right," John Henry said. "It's a hell of a thing you're doing, *amigo*."

"Just make sure . . . you kill Dav before the night's over."

"I'll do my best," John Henry promised.

"Gimme a hand . . . standing up."

John Henry grasped the man's arm and steadied him. The man gathered his strength and then straightened from his position on the ground. He let out a yell and thrust his arms to the sides so that he could fire in both directions. He continued shouting in defiance as the guns roared and spouted flame.

John Henry burst from behind the wagon and sprinted toward the jail. He didn't look back, but he heard the man's shout chopped off abruptly to a gurgle. Both guns continued to explode, though.

Bullets sang past John Henry and chewed up the ground around his racing feet, but providence and the covering fire from the dying townie shielded him. He hoped that somebody in the jail saw him coming and recognized him.

As he bounded onto the boardwalk, the door of the marshal's office flew open. John Henry left his feet in a dive that carried him into the building. He felt a slug pluck at his coat as he flew through the air.

Then he was inside and the door slammed behind him as he hit the floor. He heard the bar drop across it. The jail was dark except for the backflashes as several men fired from rifle slits cut into the thick stone walls. This place had been built for defense. The windows were all barred and had shutters over them that could be closed from inside. That had been done already.

They would have a chance to see how well the building would hold up to an attack, John Henry thought as he got to his feet.

"Marshal Sixkiller," Turnage said in the darkness. "Are you there?"

"I'm here," John Henry said.

"Were you hit?"

John Henry took a second to assess his condition. Sometimes in the heat of battle, a man might be wounded and not even notice it at the time. But in this case he was able to say, "No, I'm all right. Looks like they all missed, although I've got luck to thank for that. It certainly wasn't for lack of trying on their part."

"The man who came with you from the hotel . . . he didn't make it. We saw him go down after he gave you a chance to make a run for it. It looked like . . . they shot him to pieces."

"He was hit bad and dying already," John Henry explained. "Otherwise I never would have left him there."

"Who was he?"

The question made John Henry draw in a sharp breath. He had never even known the man's name.

"A good friend and a brave man," he said. "That's all I know."

Sometimes that had to be enough.

Chapter Thirty-three

As the gunfire continued both inside and outside the jail, John Henry asked, "Has anybody been hit in here?"

"Not so far," Turnage replied. "We've been lucky, too."

John Henry added things up in his head.

"We have eight men in here, counting Jimpson," he said. "There are five deputies locked up in the cell block, six if you count Hobart, two dead in the hotel and three in the street . . . although I can't be absolutely sure about the three in the street. Even if they're not dead, they ought to be hit bad enough that they're out of the fight."

"That should leave Dav with just ten deputies," Turnage said. "Eight against ten, and the eight are in a place that was built to be defended. Those aren't bad odds, Marshal."

"No, they're not," John Henry agreed. "But you need to add Dav himself to the mix, and throw in the fact that those deputies are professional killers, most of them. We still have our work cut out for us."

John Henry didn't know where Kate was, so he was a little surprised when she spoke up right next to him.

"I can use a rifle," she said. "So there are nine of us to hold the jail."

"I don't know if that's a good idea. In fact, if there was any way to get you out of here without exposing you to their fire, I would."

"You'd have a fight on your hands if you tried," she snapped. "This is my town, too, Marshal. And I'll be damned if I won't stand up and try to help take it back."

John Henry knew there was no point in arguing about it. They were all stuck in here for the time being, Kate included.

And there were bigger worries as well, because while the jail was plenty sturdy, sooner or later those inside it would run out of ammunition, not to mention food and water.

"What's the situation on supplies?" he asked. "Does anybody know?"

Turnage said, "I have no idea. Should we make an inventory? We'll need light for that."

John Henry fished a lucifer from his pocket and snapped it to life with his thumbnail.

"No point in standing around in the dark now," he said with a faint smile as he squinted against the light. "We're already under siege, and I don't expect that to change anytime soon."

He lit the lamp on the sheriff's desk, and as the yellow glow welled up and filled the room, he took a look around. The men who stood at the rifle slits, firing out into the night, had taken their weapons from the racks on the wall. John Henry opened a cabinet next to the gun racks and found a dozen boxes of ammunition. They weren't going to run out of firepower anytime soon.

Food and water were a different story. He found some canned peaches on a shelf in the small storeroom behind the office, along with a couple of bottles of whiskey. That was it for provisions. The peaches would last less than a day, and John Henry figured it wouldn't be a good idea for any of them to be sampling the rotgut. They would need to keep their wits about them.

"How long do you think we can hold out?" Peabody Farnham asked.

"Until morning, for sure," John Henry replied. "Probably on up into the day."

"But not indefinitely," Turnage said.

John Henry shook his head and said, "No, not indefinitely."

"And there's no help on the way, is there?"

"No. Governor Wallace sent me here alone. If you're thinking that if I don't get in touch with him by a certain time, he'll send in the army . . . that's not going to happen."

"Our plan was to take the fight to them," Turnage went on, his voice growing bleak now. "Out there in the open, where we had a chance to move around, we might have been able to make a fight of it. Stuck in here, all we can do is wait for them to starve us out."

John Henry's brain was working furiously. He said, "That's true, Alvin, unless we can come up with a way to turn things around so that the odds are on our side."

"I don't think that's possible."

"Almost anything is possible," John Henry said. "Sometimes it's just not easy. But I may have an idea . . ."

Edgar Wellman had hunkered down behind a rain barrel while the gun battle was going on in the street. A stray bullet could kill a man just as dead as one aimed straight at him.

One thing was certain, he told himself in the aftermath of the shooting, once the man he had known as Deputy John Cobb retreated into the jail. "Cobb" wasn't who he'd said he was. Wellman couldn't help but wonder if he wasn't another of those undercover investigators sent in by the governor.

If that was the case, the man had lasted longer than the others. He had even persuaded the townspeople to stage some sort of uprising against Dav. But from the looks of things, the man's string had played out tonight. He and his allies were trapped inside the jail.

The ringing of boot heels against boardwalk planks caught Wellman's attention. Since the shooting seemed to be over except for some desultory sniping between the jail's defenders and the deputies who had taken cover across the street, he shook the rainwater from his hat and stood up. A quick look around the corner revealed the tall, lean, predatory figure of Sheriff Samuel Dav striding along the boardwalk toward him.

"Sheriff!" Wellman called softly.

Dav's reaction was instantaneous. He stopped short and drew his gun with blinding speed. Wellman ducked back and yelped, "Hold your fire! Don't shoot, Sheriff. It's me, Edgar Wellman."

"Wellman," Dav said curtly. "What are you doing here?"

The newspaperman risked poking his head around the corner again. Dav had lowered his gun but hadn't put it away.

"I'm a journalist, Sheriff," Wellman said. "And there's a big story going on in Chico tonight. It's my duty to witness it and report on it."

Dav let out a contemptuous snort that told Wellman all he needed to know about the sheriff's true opinion of him. Dav had been using him . . . and Wellman had been content to let himself be used.

"Come on out of that alley," Dav said. "Nobody's going to bother shooting at you."

Wellman stepped up onto the boardwalk. He

was glad to be out of the rain, which was falling at a steadier rate now.

"Do you know what's going on here?" Dav demanded. "There are dead men lying in the street, and they look like some of my deputies."

"They are some of your deputies," Wellman said. "Cobb and another man gunned them down a little while ago."

Most of the time Dav was unflappable, but that news prompted a startled exclamation from him.

"Cobb? Are you sure?"

"The lightning was bright enough for me to get a good look. It was Cobb, all right, although I'd wager that's not really his name, Sheriff. I think he was just pretending to be a notorious gunfighter when he came here . . . although he does seem to handle a Colt with considerable skill."

"He must be an outside lawman of some sort," Dav muttered.

"That would be my guess as well."

"Do you know where the rest of my deputies are?"

Wellman remembered what he had seen from the window of his living quarters behind the newspaper office and said, "I think some of them may have been captured and locked up inside the jail. That's where Cobb—we might as well call him that for now—and his friends are holed up. They were trying to stage a coup against you tonight, Sheriff."

"They can't do that," Dav grated. "I'm the legally

elected sheriff in these parts. If they attack me and my men, that makes them outlaws!"

"It appears they're willing to risk that," Wellman said. "I'm sure they thought that if they could remove you from power, they could appeal to the territorial governor for clemency later on."

"And Wallace probably would have granted it to them," Dav said. "Well, they'll never get the chance. I'll have their hides, each and every one of them. How dare they try to stage a violent insurrection, and then insult me even more by taking refuge in my jail!"

Dav's reaction didn't surprise Wellman. The sheriff was mad. Clearly he believed that he had the right to run roughshod over anyone who opposed him. He believed it was his destiny to rule over first Chico and then eventually the entire territory.

And fanatical though he might be, Dav had a chance to make that fever dream come true, Wellman thought. All it took was telling people what they wanted to hear, even though most of it was lies.

That and crushing any real opposition into bloody ruins, no matter what it took. That was what Dav had to do tonight. He had to make sure this uprising was put down in swift, brutal, ruthless fashion. He had to teach a harsh lesson to anyone who dared to oppose him.

And he had to kill the man who'd pretended to

be John Cobb. That might be the most important thing of all.

"Stay here out of the way, where you won't get hurt," Dav went on. "When this is over, you'll have to write about how one of my own men betrayed me and tried to help outlaws take over my town. It'll make people admire me even more when they read about how I stopped that lawless horde from prevailing."

Wellman swallowed and said, "Of course, Sheriff." Staying out of harm's way was one of the things he did best. "That jail is awfully solid. How are you going to get them out of there?"

"Let me worry about that," Dav snapped. He stepped out into the rain and hurried across the street well short of where the shooting was going on. From there he could work his way up to where his deputies had taken cover and find out exactly how the situation stood.

Wellman had no idea what Dav's plan might be, but he knew he was very glad he wasn't the man who had pretended to be John Cobb. The sheriff would want vengeance on that man more than any of the others.

And Samuel Dav's vengeance, Wellman was certain, would be a terrible thing to behold.

Chapter Thirty-four

John Henry got the ring of keys from the desk, went upstairs, and let himself into the cell block. By now all the prisoners had regained consciousness, but they were still tied and gagged, so all they could do when they saw him was writhe around on the bunks and shout muffled curses at him through the gags.

He hadn't brought a lamp or lantern with him, but once the cell block door was open, enough light came from downstairs for him to see the window at the end of the corridor between the cells. It wasn't barred, but when he examined it more closely he saw that it had been nailed shut.

That problem could be dealt with. He went back downstairs and found a hammer in the storeroom.

"Need a hand with something?" Farnham asked. Irregularly spaced shots continued from the men posted at the loopholes.

"You might be better at this than I am," John Henry admitted. "Come on."

Kate intercepted them on the way to the stairs and asked, "What are you doing?"

"Peabody's just giving me a hand with something," John Henry said.

Farnham said, "You can keep an eye on Nate for me for a few minutes, can't you, Miss Kate?"

"Of course," she said, "but if there's some other way I can help—"

"There's not," John Henry assured her. "Not right now, anyway."

She didn't look convinced of that, but she didn't say anything else. As John Henry and Farnham went on up the stairs, Kate walked over to where Nate Farnham sat in one of the armchairs with an anxious look on his face and rested a comforting hand on his massive shoulder.

"Can you pull those nails?" John Henry asked the blacksmith when they reached the window.

A grin stretched across Farnham's bearded face.

"You bet I can," he said. "Let me see that hammer."

He took the tool from John Henry. The nail heads had been bent over. Farnham straightened them without much trouble, then caught one of them with the hammer's claw. The muscles in his arms and shoulders bunched and he let out a small grunt of effort. The nail made a tiny screeching sound as it pulled free of the wood.

Farnham made short work of the other nails, tossing each of them aside as he pulled them loose.

"The window ought to open now," Farnham said when he was finished. "Looks like it might have been painted shut, too, but that won't be a problem."

He handed the hammer to John Henry, got hold of the window, and forced it up. Cool air rushed in, bringing splatters of rain with it.

"I don't see what good this does us, though," Farnham added.

John Henry leaned over and stuck his head out the window, twisting his neck so he could look up at the roof. Rainwater ran in his eyes. He had to blink several times to clear his vision.

The building's roof was flat. The edge of it was about four feet above the top of the window. If he stood on the sill, he would just about be able to reach it.

There was a good-sized gap on one side of the jail, but the building on the other side, which was also two stories, was only about eight feet away. That wasn't an easy jump, but John Henry figured he could make it. Once he was on the roof of the other building, he could find a way down to the ground, and then he would be loose in Chico to wreak havoc on Dav's forces and even the odds. They wouldn't be expecting him, and that element of surprise would come in handy.

"I think I know what you're fixing to do," Farnham said when John Henry pulled his head back inside the window. "You'd better take somebody with you. I'll come."

"No offense, Peabody, but I don't think you're

really built for clambering around on top of buildings. Besides, Nate would worry himself sick."

Farnham sighed and said, "That's true, he would. But maybe one of the other fellas could go. Mr. Turnage, maybe."

"I need him to stay here, too, to take charge of things while I'm gone."

Although John Henry didn't say it, the main reason he didn't want anyone to come with him was because he didn't want to be responsible for their safety. He could move faster and more efficiently if he only had to worry about getting himself killed.

Not wanting anything to hinder him, he took off his hat and coat. Earlier, he had reloaded his Colt and filled all the loops in his shell belt from one of the ammunition boxes in the cabinet. As he got ready to climb onto the windowsill, Farnham stopped him by saying, "You're not going back downstairs before you leave?"

"You can tell the others where I've gone."

"Miss Kate's liable to be unhappy about you risking your neck without saying good-bye to her first."

"I think you're wrong about that," John Henry said. "It's not like she has any special feelings for me."

"Hmmph," Farnham said, making it clear that he thought John Henry was wrong.

John Henry didn't have the time to ponder that now. He threw a leg over the sill, then swung his other leg so that he was sitting in the window. He got a good grip and pulled himself up until he was standing on the sill. It was slippery from the rain, so he had to be careful.

He braced himself with his left hand and reached up with his right. His fingers came up just short of the rooftop. He stretched as much as he could but still couldn't grasp the edge of the roof.

"Blast it," he said as he lowered his arm and bent slightly to talk to Farnham through the open window. "I'm not quite tall enough."

"How much more do you need?" the blacksmith asked.

"Three or four inches."

"We can do that," Farnham said. "Move a little."

John Henry did so, and Farnham put his arms out the window and laced his fingers together to form a stirrup.

"Put a foot in there," he told John Henry. "I won't drop you."

John Henry lifted his left foot from the sill and placed it in Farnham's cupped hands. He started to ask Farnham if he was sure he could hold his weight, but then he remembered how effortlessly the blacksmith had carried those captured deputies up the stairs. He tightened his grip of his left hand on the top of the window and said, "All right."

"Up you go," said Farnham as he lifted.

John Henry felt himself rising, almost as if by magic. His right hand closed over the edge of the roof. As soon as that grip was secure, he let go of the window with his left hand and reached up with it, too. He heaved with his arms and Farnham lifted, and John Henry went up and over the short wall around the rooftop.

He lay there for a moment with the rain falling on him. The leading edge of the storm had moved on, so that the lightning was now in the distance to the east and the rumble of thunder was like the sound of distant drums instead of cannon fire, but the rain was still steady. That made the night very dark, and since John Henry's trousers and shirt were dark as well, he hoped that would help him blend into the shadows. That was one reason he had left his lighter-colored hat inside the jail.

The sound of voices somewhere nearby made him roll quickly onto his belly and reach down to his holster. He drew the Colt and waited.

The voices came from the roof of the next building, he realized, the same building he had intended to leap over to once he gained the roof of the jail. It seemed that somebody else had had the same idea, only in reverse.

But not exactly the same idea, he saw as a couple of men appeared, their shapes dim and shadowy in the rain. They were carrying something. They extended it across the gap between buildings, and as they set it down with a clatter, John Henry knew it had to be a ladder. They were going to use it as a bridge.

That wasn't a bad idea, he thought as he lay there motionless. With the ladder there, he wouldn't have to risk making the jump in the rain.

All he had to do was deal with the two deputies who were about to cross over to the jail. He wasn't sure what they intended to do once they got here, since as far as Dav knew the second-floor window on the back of the building was still nailed shut from the inside.

Maybe he had better wait for a minute, John Henry decided, and the deputies would reveal their plan.

One of them said, "Hold on to that damn ladder," and started across, crawling on hands and knees almost as if the ladder were upright and he was climbing it. The other man braced the ladder so it wouldn't slip.

When the first deputy reached the roof, he stood up and turned back toward his partner.

"Throw it across," he called, "but make sure it's a good throw."

The second deputy picked up something from the roof where he stood, held it cradled in both hands, and then carefully tossed it across the gap. The first deputy reached out and gathered it in, clutching it tightly against his body.

"I don't see how you're gonna light the fuse in this rain," the second deputy said.

"The stovepipe's got a cover on it. All I have to do is hold the dynamite under that, light the fuse, and drop these sticks right down the pipe. They'll blow the stove to pieces and cut down everybody in the office."

"That'll make a hell of a mess out of the office, too."

"Yeah, well, it's the sheriff's idea, so I reckon he's willing to make a mess to teach those bastards a lesson."

"How's he gonna teach 'em anything if they're blowed up?"

"Well . . . it'll teach the rest of the town, I guess."

The man carrying the dynamite turned toward the spot where the stovepipe stuck up a foot or so from the rooftop.

John Henry's blood had turned cold in his veins as he listened to the conversation. These men were about to carry out mass murder. Kate, her grandfather, Alvin Turnage, Nate Farnham, everybody who was in the sheriff's office would die. John Henry might have to give up the advantage of surprise as far as the rest of the gunmen went, but he had to stop that bomb from going off.

He surged to his feet, leveled his gun at the deputy who was about twenty feet away, and shouted, "Drop that dynamite, mister!"

Chapter Thirty-five

Instead of following the order, the man whirled around to face John Henry and grabbed desperately for the gun in his holster. John Henry pulled the trigger, aiming to wound the man in the leg and knock his feet out from under him.

But the hand holding the dynamite was swinging around, too, and just as John Henry's bullet ripped through the air, the bundle of explosive cylinders intercepted the slug's path.

The bullet must have struck one of the blasting caps attached to a twisted-together length of fuse, because it detonated with a sharp *crack*.

The boom that followed instantly was like the biggest clap of thunder John Henry had ever heard, and the ball of fire was brighter than any flash of lightning.

The force of the explosion threw John Henry backward. He sailed through the air and slammed down on the rooftop, skidding across it. He might have slid right off the building if the little wall around the edge hadn't stopped him. As it was, he was stunned, unable to make his muscles respond to any of the desperate commands his brain was sending them. He was completely deaf as well and couldn't hear anything except a gigantic ringing in his ears that threatened to drive him mad.

He felt splinters spray against his face as a bullet struck the wall near him. That made him aware that somebody was shooting at him, probably the man who'd been left on the roof of the other building.

He knew he didn't have to worry about the man who'd been holding the dynamite. There wouldn't be anything left of that *hombre*.

John Henry tried again to move, and this time he was able to. He rolled onto his side and struggled to lift his gun. The explosion had half-blinded him as well as deafened him, but as he blinked rapidly he was able to spot some muzzle flashes from the other roof. He thrust the Colt toward them and triggered three shots as fast as he could manage to squeeze the trigger.

He couldn't tell if he'd hit anything, but the shots from the other building stopped, which told him he had either wounded the man over there or at least forced him to flee. He rolled on over, onto his belly, and pushed himself to hands and knees, pausing there to shake his head groggily.

His brain began to clear, along with his eyesight. He still couldn't hear anything except the ringing.

He hoped his hearing wasn't gone permanently, but he couldn't worry about that right now.

John Henry struggled to his feet and looked around. The ladder was gone, dislodged from its position by the blast. The roof had collapsed where the man had been standing when the dynamite went off, leaving a gaping hole with ragged, splintered edges. The hole was a good ten feet wide, and when John Henry stumbled closer to it, he found himself looking down into the cell block. The deputy who'd been in the cell directly underneath the explosion was dead, turned into a gory mess by the debris that had come crashing down on him.

The muffled sound of shots was the first indication John Henry had that his hearing was starting to come back to him. His step was a little steadier as he moved over to the front of the building. Dav's men had renewed their frontal assault on the jail. Muzzle flashes flickered like fireflies from the building across the street where they had forted up.

If he could get behind them, he could turn the tables, he thought. The ladder might be gone, but he could still make the jump across to the other building.

But as he turned in that direction, more men appeared up there and opened fire on him, forcing him to dive to the roof. The other deputy must have gotten away, he thought, and spread the word that he was up here trying to escape the trap that the jail had become.

That deadly volley of gunfire continued to rip across the roof. If he stood up, he'd be drilled in a split second. That left him with only one option. He kept his head down and crawled over to the hole in the roof.

Holstering his gun, John Henry turned around and maneuvered backward until his legs were dangling over the opening. He slid the rest of the way into the hole, hanging by his hands for a second before he let go and dropped into the wrecked cell. One foot slipped in a puddle of blood that had leaked from the dead prisoner.

The blast had buckled the door of this cell so that it was partially open. John Henry grasped the bars and forced it back enough for him to slip through the opening.

Across the aisle, Steve Buckner had finally worked his gag loose enough that he could talk.

"Damn it, Cobb—" he began.

"Sixkiller," John Henry interrupted. "My name's John Henry Sixkiller."

"I don't give a damn what your name is," Buckner said. "Untie me and give me a gun."

"So you can shoot me? I'm not that *loco*, Buckner."

"No, blast it! I'll help you. Dav's bound to have you outnumbered, and you can use every gun you can get!"

With the death of the deputy on the roof, John Henry figured the odds were about even, at least as far as the numbers went. He said, "Why would you turn on the sheriff that way?"

Buckner glared at him from the cell, then said, "Because I know Kate's here. Dav'll wipe out the whole bunch of you, includin' her, and I can't let that happen." He sighed. "Anyway, I may be a hardcase, but Dav's like some sort of crazy *lobo* wolf! When he whipped that fella the way he did, I knew I couldn't keep backin' his play for much longer."

Buckner sounded sincere, John Henry thought, but it might all be a ruse to strike at the jail's defenders from within.

"Listen, I don't blame you for not believin' me," Buckner went on. "But it's the truth, Cobb . . . I mean, Sixkiller. What are you, anyway?"

"Deputy U.S. marshal," John Henry answered curtly.

"Well, I can't say as I'm surprised. You put up a pretty good front, but I always thought you weren't quite as low-down as the rest of us. Turn me loose and give me a gun and I'll try to make up for some of what I done while workin' for Dav."

Alvin Turnage came up the stairs, poking a rifle barrel in front of him, and reached the cell block in time to hear Buckner's plea. The bank teller asked, "Marshal, are you all right?"

"Shaken up a little," John Henry admitted. "But I reckon I'll be fine."

"What in the world happened up there?" Turnage asked as he glanced toward the hole in the roof.

"One of Dav's men was going to drop a bundle of dynamite down the stovepipe and blow everybody to kingdom come," John Henry answered. "I stopped him. Not quite the way I intended, but . . ."

"Good Lord," Turnage muttered. "The dynamite . . . ?"

"Yeah. And then before I could get off the roof, more of Dav's men showed up and pinned me down. All I could do was drop down through that hole."

"So we're still stuck here."

"That's about the size of it," John Henry agreed.

Buckner spoke up again, saying, "I can help you—"

"Shut up," Turnage snapped. "Why should we trust the likes of you?"

"Because I love Kate Collins!" Buckner burst out. "And if Dav has his way, he'll wipe out everybody in here, includin' her. That business with the dynamite is proof enough of that! I'll do whatever I have to to save Kate, and when it's all over you can lock me up again. I'll take what's comin' to me."

"He sounds like he's telling the truth," John Henry said.

Turnage frowned.

"Maybe so, but he's been one of Dav's men all along—"

"All I was interested in was the loot," Buckner

said. "I know, that makes me a sorry son of a bitch. But I never killed nobody for him. Dav had an inner circle, Miller and a few others, who took care of all of that. I'd testify to it in court, too."

John Henry and Turnage looked at each for a moment, and then Turnage shrugged.

"I trust your judgment, Marshal," he said.

John Henry came to a decision and nodded.

"Get the keys and a Winchester," he told Turnage, adding, "And tell everybody what we're doing. We don't want any of them getting trigger-happy when they see that Buckner's loose."

As Turnage went downstairs, John Henry looked at Buckner and went on, "I'll be keeping an eye on you. First time it even looks like you're thinking about double-crossing us, I aim to put a bullet in your head."

"You don't have to worry about that," Buckner said. "I want to settle Dav's hash as much as you do. I figure that's my only chance with Kate."

"We'll see," John Henry said. He didn't care one way or the other about Buckner's would-be romance with Kate Collins. Right now all that mattered was keeping these people alive and figuring out some way to defeat Dav.

Turnage came back with the keys and one of the rifles. As he handed them to John Henry, he said, "Peabody thinks you've lost your mind. So do I, if I'm being honest."

"Buckner knows that if he tries anything, I'll shoot

him," John Henry said as he unlocked Buckner's cell. He went inside and untied the deputy's bonds.

Buckner stood up shakily from the bunk and rubbed his wrists to get some feeling back in his hands.

"You won't be sorry about this, Sixkiller," he said.

"I'd better not be, because you'll be dead if I am."

"How about you stop threatenin' me and give me a gun?"

John Henry handed him the Winchester and said, "Somebody's got to guard this hole in the roof to make sure Dav doesn't send some of his men through it. I think that's a good job for you."

"All right." Buckner's eyes narrowed. "What's to stop me from climbin' out and gettin' away?"

"If you're telling the truth about how you feel about Kate, you won't do that," John Henry said. "You'll stay here and do everything you can to protect her."

"Now you're startin' to understand," Buckner said with a nod. He paused, then went on, "You know Dav will try something else, don't you? He won't have the patience to try starvin' you out."

"That's what I figured," John Henry said. "Now it's just a matter of waiting to see what he comes up with next."

Chapter Thirty-six

Wellman thought that Dav might burst a vein when Carl Miller told them what had happened on the roof of the jail. The sheriff's face turned bright red with rage.

"Is there anybody in this damned town who can do anything right except me?" Dav roared.

"It was just a bad break, boss," Miller said.

Especially for the deputy who'd been holding the bundle of dynamite, Wellman thought. There wouldn't be enough of that poor bastard left to scrape up with a spoon.

The three men were in the back room of the hardware store, directly across the street from the jail. Dav had made this his temporary headquarters, since he was displaced from the sheriff's office. Four deputies were in the front of the store, kneeling at the windows they had knocked out with their rifle barrels and taking occasional potshots at the jail. The flurry of renewed firing that had followed the explosion had tapered off again.

The other three deputies were positioned around the jail to act as snipers if any of the defenders holed up in there tried to sneak out.

"What do we do now?" Miller asked. "There's a hole in the roof. Reckon we could get some men through there and catch 'em in a cross fire?"

Dav expressed his contempt for that idea with a slashing gesture.

"We don't have enough men for that," he said. "We'd have to split our force, and then we wouldn't have enough to carry the battle on either front."

"Well . . . there's always waitin' 'em out," Miller suggested. "You know they don't have much to eat or drink in there, Sheriff. We can keep 'em pinned down for a day or two, and they'll start gettin' mighty hungry and thirsty."

Dav's mouth twisted in a sneer.

"We could do that," he said, "but we're not going to. That wouldn't be enough to show the rest of the townspeople that they'd better not ever try anything like this again."

A short time earlier, Wellman had been horrified as he listened to Dav and Miller hatching the plan to drop dynamite down the stovepipe and blow up the jail. He was only one man, though. There was nothing he could do to stop them.

So he wasn't surprised when Dav continued to be obsessed with the idea of teaching the citizens of Chico a lesson. Dav was morally outraged, as odd as that term sounded when applied to him, that anyone would dare to oppose him.

Dav appeared to have reached a decision. He said, "Carl, I want you to go out there under a flag of truce and ask for a parley."

"A parley about what?" Miller wanted to know. "We've got 'em trapped in there. They can't get out. They're beat."

"Tell them they have until eight o'clock in the morning to surrender."

Miller shook his head and said, "They won't do it."

"I don't care about that. Just tell them."

"Why eight o'clock?" Miller wanted to know.

"Because the sun will be up by then, and everybody will be able to see what happens next."

Somehow, that was the most ominous-sounding thing he had heard so far, Wellman thought.

"All right," Miller said with a shrug of his beefy shoulder. "I'll tell 'em that eight o'clock's the deadline. Do I tell 'em what happens if they don't surrender by then?"

Dav smiled and said, "No, they'll find out then along with everyone else." He turned toward the hardware store's rear door and motioned to Wellman. "Come on, Edgar, you're going with me."

His tone made it clear that he wouldn't put up with any argument. Wellman followed him out into the rainy night, wondering if the sheriff just wanted him along so that later on he could write about what was happening . . . or if Dav had some other, more sinister use for him this time.

Once John Henry reached a decision, he didn't spend a lot of time brooding about it. He had placed his trust in Steve Buckner, and he left it at that. If Buckner betrayed his trust, he would deal with that when the time came.

For now, he checked to see how everyone downstairs was doing. Amazingly, the jail's defenders had suffered no injuries. A few bullets had come through the loopholes in the wall, but they hadn't hit anyone. Wilhelm Heinsdorf and the man who had died in the street were the only casualties the townspeople had suffered so far.

Kate came up to John Henry and asked, "Is it true? Did you really turn Steve Buckner loose and give him a gun?"

"It's true," John Henry admitted.

"Why would you do that? He works for Sheriff Dav."

Obviously, Turnage hadn't gone into detail about the reason that had prompted Buckner's change of heart, John Henry thought. John Henry didn't think he ought to, either. That was something for Buckner and Kate to work out . . . if they survived this night.

He was saved from having to answer Kate's question by one of the townsmen posted at the loopholes, who turned his head and called, "Somebody just came out of the hardware store holdin' a white flag! I think it's Deputy Miller."

John Henry went over to the wall and motioned the man aside. He put his eye to the little opening and saw that the townie was right. Carl Miller stood on the boardwalk in front of the hardware store, holding a lantern in one hand and a piece of board with a white rag tied to it in the other. Miller looked distinctly nervous as he stepped down into the street and walked forward slowly.

The deputy had good reason to be nervous. It would have been easy for the men in the jail to shoot him while he was out in the open like this. They were all basically decent individuals, though, so it would have seemed too much like murder to gun Miller down under these circumstances.

"What do we do, Marshal?" one of the men asked.

"It's probably a trick," Peabody Farnham said. "Don't trust him, Marshal."

"I don't intend to, but I need to find out what he wants," John Henry said. He went to one of the windows and lifted the bar off the shutters. Opening one side slightly, so that he could see the deputy through the narrow crack, he called, "That's far enough, Miller!"

Miller came to a stop. Still looking nervous, he asked, "Is that you, Cobb?"

There was no point now in keeping his real identity a secret. John Henry replied, "That's Sixkiller. Deputy United States Marshal Sixkiller."

"Well . . . all right. I got a message for you, Marshal, from Sheriff Dav."

"Dav's no longer the sheriff in this town. I've removed him from office and declared martial law."

John Henry knew he didn't actually have the authority to do that, but on the other hand, he wanted Miller and the rest of Dav's men to know that they risked the wrath of the federal government by continuing to support the sheriff.

Miller frowned, maybe thinking about that very thing, and then said, "That's between you and the sheriff, mister. All I'm doin' is deliverin' a message. You got until eight o'clock in the mornin' to come out of there and surrender."

"What happens if we don't?"

"Never you mind about that. You'd better do it, that's all."

Miller sounded a little tentative, John Henry thought. Maybe he didn't actually know what Dav intended to do if the townspeople didn't surrender by eight o'clock.

John Henry knew what would happen if they *did* surrender. Dav was *loco* enough that he might line them all up and have them shot—or something even worse.

"You've delivered your message, Miller," John Henry called. "Tell Dav nobody's coming out."

"That's up to you," Miller said as he began backing away. "Just remember, I got this white flag. We still got us a truce."

John Henry turned, took the rifle from the man

standing next to him, thrust the barrel through the loophole, and drew a quick bead. He pressed the trigger and the Winchester cracked. Dirt spurted from the ground ten feet in front of Miller, who dropped both the lantern and the white flag and whirled around to make a frantic dash for the door of the hardware store. The deputies inside the building opened fire to cover his retreat.

"Maybe I shouldn't have done that," John Henry said as he gave the rifle back to the man who'd been using it, "but I just couldn't stomach any more of him."

"What do you reckon is going to happen at eight o'clock?" Farnham asked.

"Nothing good," John Henry said.

The rain had slacked off to an intermittent drizzle as Wellman walked toward the Hammond mansion with Dav. He had to hurry to keep up with the sheriff's long-legged strides.

"Where are we going, Samuel?" Wellman asked. The answer to that question was fairly obvious, but he hoped Dav would explain what he had in mind. The closer they came to Lucinda's house, the more worried Wellman was.

"I'm going to get some leverage," Dav replied, "and you're going to help me, Edgar."

"What . . . what do you want me to do?"

"I doubt if Mrs. Hammond would open the door for me at this time of night . . . but she will for you."

Wellman started to hang back.

"I'm not sure I want to be any part of this," he said, knowing that he was risking his life by arguing with Dav. "Lucinda is my friend—"

"Exactly," Dav cut in. "So I know you want to look out for her best interests."

"That's true, I do," Wellman said worriedly.

"So you can either help me, or I'll kick her door down and whatever happens after that will be on your head, not mine."

That wasn't what anybody would call a subtle threat, thought Wellman, but he supposed the time for subtlety was long gone. Everything boiled down now to survival . . . for him, for Lucinda, for the very town itself.

Because Wellman was coming to understand that Samuel Dav might burn the whole settlement to the ground rather than allow its citizens to get away with defying him.

"All right," he said with a sigh. "Just tell me what you want me to do."

Chapter Thirty-seven

Lights were burning inside the Hammond mansion. That came as no surprise to Wellman. With all the shooting going on in town, not to mention the huge explosion on the roof of the jail, probably everyone in Chico was awake tonight except the youngest children and perhaps the very old and hard of hearing. The houses might be dark, and certainly no one was going to venture out unless they had to, but people would be awake, holding each other in the dark and trying not to tremble in fear.

Not Lucinda Hammond, though. She wasn't the sort to cower in the shadows.

A brass lion's-head knocker was set in the middle of the big front door. Tentatively, Wellman took hold of it, drew in a deep breath, and then rapped sharply. There was no response, so after a moment he knocked again.

This time Lucinda asked from the other side of the door, "Who's out there?"

"It's me, Lucinda," the newspaperman said. "Edgar Wellman."

Dav was standing to the side of the door where Lucinda couldn't see him if she looked out. Wellman was sick inside, feeling as if he were betraying her. Which was exactly what he was doing, he told himself. He still didn't know what Dav was going to do, but if he hurt her, Wellman made a vow that he would kill Dav himself.

It was an empty, hollow promise. He always ran away from trouble. He didn't charge right into it, head-on.

The door opened, swinging back to reveal Lucinda standing there in a silk dressing gown. She had a shotgun in her hands. At the sight of the rain-soaked newspaperman standing on her front porch, her eyes widened.

"Good Lord, Edgar, you look like a wet dog!" she exclaimed as she lowered the shotgun and took a step toward him. That brought her over the threshold of the doorway.

Wellman couldn't take it anymore. Something snapped inside him. Without thinking about what he was doing, he cried, "Lucinda, get back inside! Dav—"

That was as far as he got before Dav sprang out of the shadows, striking like a big cat. The gun in his hand smashed into Wellman's head. The blow knocked Wellman to the side and made him fall to his knees.

Lucinda gasped and tried to raise the shotgun, but Dav grabbed the barrels and wrenched the weapon aside, tearing it loose from her grip. He slung it into the yard and then clamped his hand around her upper left arm to jerk her completely out of the house and onto the porch.

"You're coming with me, my dear," he said.

Lucinda screamed and struggled, but she was no match for the sheriff's almost supernatural strength. He dragged her toward the porch steps.

Wellman's head was spinning crazily from the clout it had taken, but he hadn't passed out. He knew what was going on, and he struggled to his feet again.

"Let her go!" he yelled as he tried to get hold of Dav. His efforts were feeble. Dav laughed as he pulled free. His grip on Lucinda never loosened as he kicked Wellman in the belly and sent the news-paperman sprawling backward.

Lucinda didn't cry and beg. She fought and shouted oaths that Wellman, in his current pain-racked state, was vaguely surprised that she even knew.

"You might as well stop fighting," Dav snapped. "You're coming with me, Lucinda, and if those friends of yours want to save your life, they'll give themselves up."

A hostage! Wellman thought. Dav was going to

use her as a hostage. He would threaten to kill her unless the townspeople in the jail surrendered.

And Wellman didn't doubt for a second that Dav would follow through on that threat if they defied him. Dav had lusted after Lucinda Hammond for a long time, but there were plenty of women in the world and he would give her up if that was what it took to get what he really wanted.

Power. Dominance. To be the ruler of all he surveyed.

That son of a bitch.

Wellman found the strength to pull himself to his feet. He stumbled down the steps. Dav had almost reached the gate in the fence around the mansion's front yard. Wellman lurched toward the long shape that lay in the grass and reached down to pick it up. He lifted the shotgun and stumbled after Dav and Lucinda.

"Let her go!" he cried again. "Let her go or I'll kill you, Dav!"

The sheriff must have heard something in Wellman's voice that alarmed him. Still holding tightly to Lucinda, he twisted around and brought up the gun in his other hand. Wellman realized, too late, that his threat was an empty one. He couldn't use the shotgun. At this range, if he cut loose with it he would kill Lucinda, too.

Dav didn't have any such qualms. The gun in his hand roared once and then again as flame gouted from its muzzle. Wellman felt the bullets strike him like hammer blows, driving him backward. The shotgun slipped from his fingers and thudded to the soggy ground. Wellman's balance deserted him. He went down, landing in the grass with his arms outflung at his sides.

"Looks like I'll have to find some other scribbler to write stories about me," Dav commented with a laugh. "Well, he wasn't all that good at it anyway."

For the first time tonight, Lucinda began to cry. Wellman heard Dav's scornful words, and then her sobs. She was crying for *him*, he realized with a shock. She was crying because Dav had killed him. Somehow that made the horrible pain in his chest a little easier to bear.

He clung to that thought as the rain beaded and trickled down his face and darkness crept in from all around him.

John Henry stayed on the move, even though there weren't really all that many places to go in the sheriff's office and jail. But he circulated among the defenders, talking to them and trying to keep their spirits up, and he went upstairs to the cell block fairly often to check on Buckner, too.

During one of those visits, while Buckner sat on a three-legged stool with the rifle across his knees, he asked, "Have you seen Aaron tonight?"

"Kemp? I ran into him earlier, just as all this was getting started."

"I reckon he's dead, then," Buckner said grimly.

John Henry shook his head.

"He wasn't the last time I saw him. I knocked him out and dragged him into an alley. Didn't see any reason to kill him. Not then, anyway."

"What about later?"

"I've traded shots with several of Dav's men," John Henry answered honestly. "I didn't recognize any of them as Kemp, but the light wasn't that good most of the time."

Buckner sighed.

"Aaron ain't a bad sort, you know. He's like me . . . He got used to takin' the easy road. That meant breakin' the law sometimes. Once you've done that, it's hard to get back on the other side. But he never shot anybody who didn't have it comin'. I'm talkin' about gents who were a lot worse than we were. I don't expect a lawdog like you to see it this way, Sixkiller, but all owlhoots ain't the same."

"I know that," John Henry admitted. "But it's not up to me to decide such things. My job's just to bring 'em in and let the courts sort things out."

"And if they don't want to be brought in?"

John Henry shrugged and said, "My authority extends to the use of force."

"Which is law talk for shootin' 'em."

John Henry shrugged again.

"Sooner or later, everybody's got to make up their mind which side they're on."

"Well, I won't ask you not to shoot Aaron if it comes down to that," Buckner said. "I don't reckon that'd be right."

"I appreciate that."

"Which ain't the same thing as sayin' that *I'll* shoot him. I just hope I'll never have to make that choice."

John Henry changed the subject by saying, "Any sign of trouble up here?"

"Not a bit. Haven't heard anything goin' on up there on the roof." Buckner paused. "You know, you ought to turn Gil Hobart loose, too. He'd help you, like I am."

"I'll think about it," John Henry said. He had already considered the possibility of freeing the former jailer in return for a promise that Hobart would fight on their side. Right now it didn't seem to be necessary, though, as the standoff continued.

The hours of the night dragged by. Men yawned from time to time, but no one was really in any danger of dozing off. The defenders were all too keyed up to sleep. They knew it was possible, even likely, that these were their last hours on earth. Going through something like that did a lot to clear a man's mind of any clutter.

Finally, gray light began to filter through the cracks around the window shutters. Dawn was approaching. John Henry used a knife to open the cans of peaches in the storeroom and passed them around. It wasn't much of a breakfast, but it was better than nothing. They had coffee, but no water with which to brew it.

John Henry blew out the lamps as the light from outside grew brighter. While he was doing that, Kate came over to him and said, "It'll be eight o'clock in less than an hour. Dav's deadline."

"You think we ought to surrender?" John Henry asked.

Kate laughed and shook her head.

"I'd rather die fighting than be lined up in front of a firing squad or whipped to death."

"He wouldn't do that to you."

"He was willing to blow me up along with the rest," she pointed out. Her voice took on a bitter edge as she went on, "But you're probably right. I'm sure the sheriff would have some other, more suitable punishment in mind for me."

John Henry didn't want to add to her worries, but he figured she was right about that.

There was still a can of peaches on the desk. He picked it up and handed it to her.

"Why don't you take this up to Buckner?" he suggested.

"You think so?" she asked.

"Wouldn't hurt."

Kate nodded, took the peaches, and went up the stairs. Maybe Buckner would work up the courage to tell her why he had changed sides. Maybe not. That wasn't really any of his business, John Henry told himself.

A short time later, he took out his watch and opened it. His instincts were telling him time was up, and he saw that they were right. The watch's hands had just ticked over to eight o'clock.

"Somethin's happenin' across the street!" one of the men at the loopholes called excitedly.

John Henry went to a window and unfastened the shutters. He pulled one side back enough to look out. Turnage and Peabody Farnham were beside him. The rest of the defenders crowded to the other window.

John Henry saw men moving around behind the false front of the hardware store, but he couldn't tell what they were doing.

"Should we take some potshots at them?" one of the men asked.

"Hold on," John Henry said. "I want to see what Dav is up to."

He frowned as he heard some heavy thudding sounds. A moment later he figured out what they were as the men on the roof put their shoulders against the false front and heaved. They had been knocking loose the supports that held the false front in place, John Henry thought.

With a squealing of nails, it came free and toppled forward, crashing down on the awning over the boardwalk in front of the store. The awning sagged under the weight but didn't collapse.

That left the deputies on top of the building exposed, but John Henry called, "Hold your fire!"

before the defenders inside the jail could open
up on them. Dav's men scurried back away from
the edge.

"What in the world are they doing?" Turnage
asked.

A second later they all got the answer to that
question as something rose into sight on the roof
of the hardware store, lifted by several of Dav's
men. Two thick beams had been nailed and lashed
together to form a crude cross.

And hanging from it, bound by her wrists and
ankles, was the figure of a woman.

Chapter Thirty-eight

"Oh my God!" Turnage said in a voice thick with horror. "That's Lucinda Hammond! That bastard! That unholy bastard!"

"The widow of the man Dav gunned down awhile back?" John Henry asked.

"That's right." Turnage leaned forward intently. "Can you tell if she's still alive?"

"I think so," John Henry said. "Yes, she just moved her head. She's alive."

"Thank God for that, anyway," Farnham muttered.

Dav's men scuttled back away from the cross, which remained upright. They must have nailed together some sort of frame that would hold it up, John Henry thought.

A shout came from across the street.

"Hello, the jail! You hear me in there?"

"That's Dav," Turnage grated.

John Henry opened the shutter a little wider and called, "We hear you!"

"Take a good look at Mrs. Hammond! If you don't come out and surrender, I'll leave her hanging up there for as long as it takes! You think she'll make it through the day? I don't! She's already having trouble breathing!"

"He's not giving us any choice," Turnage said. "We can't let that poor woman hang there and die."

"If we surrender, he'll kill us all," Farnham said. He looked over his shoulder at his son. "I can't do that."

"We have to go out sometime," another man argued. "Might as well make a fight of it. And maybe he'll spare Miz Hammond if we do."

The animated discussion went back and forth, but John Henry didn't take part in it. As far as he could see, both roads facing them led ultimately to death.

So he was doing his best to find a third trail, one that might not wind up with all the defenders dying.

Dav shouted again from across the street, saying, "It's up to you! But the sun's going to be mighty hot before the day's over!"

Lucinda Hammond lifted her head and cried, "Don't listen to him! Don't give up! Don't let him make you—"

From somewhere behind her, the black snake of a bullwhip struck, curling around to lash across her legs, which were left mostly bare because the dressing gown she wore sagged away from them. She screamed in pain.

Several of the men inside the sheriff's office started toward the door. John Henry didn't blame them for reacting that way, but he snapped, "Hold it! Nobody's going out there yet."

"This is unbearable," Turnage said. "I'm sorry, Marshal, but he's won. We can't allow him to torture her."

"We're not going to," John Henry promised. "Hold everybody together, Alvin. I'm counting on you."

"All right," Turnage said with obvious reluctance. "What are you going to do?"

"Take the fight to Dav," John Henry said. He hurried to the storeroom and found a bucket, then carried it and one of the Winchesters up the stairs to the cell block. He was aware of Turnage, Farnham, and the other men watching him curiously, but he didn't take the time to explain his hastily formed plan.

When he reached the corridor between the cells, he found Buckner and Kate standing there. An unmistakable tension existed between them, hanging in the air so thickly it was almost like a physical presence.

"What's goin' on down there?" Buckner asked. "We heard some yellin'."

"Dav's using Mrs. Hammond as a hostage to try to lure us out."

Kate's eyes widened. She exclaimed, "Oh dear Lord! That poor woman. What's he done?"

Quickly, John Henry sketched in the details.

"I did the right thing by changin' sides," Buckner said. "Dav's gone plumb *loco*."

"He always was," Kate said. "He just hid it from everyone until after he was elected. Then he set out to destroy us."

John Henry said, "He's not going to get away with it." He handed Buckner the keys. "If you're sure we can trust him, turn Hobart loose. He can cover us."

"Where are we goin'?" Buckner asked, his eyes narrowing.

"Out there," John Henry said. "After Dav."

"He's probably got riflemen posted around the jail, waitin' for us to make a break."

"That's why we're going to make it more difficult for them."

John Henry went into the cell that Buckner had occupied and started ripping up the bedding. He tore pieces off the mattress, too, and stuffed them into the bucket along with the torn-up sheet and blanket.

When he had filled the bucket, he doused the contents with coal oil from a can of the foul-smelling stuff that sat in a corner, where it could be used to fill the lamps. Then he went into the wrecked cell, avoiding the mangled body of the deputy who had been killed in the collapse of the roof, and found some broken pieces of board long enough for him to lean them in the hole in the roof. They formed a makeshift ramp.

"What in the world?" Kate asked.

"Hand me that bucket," John Henry told her.

She did so. Buckner and Hobart came up behind her, looking equally puzzled.

John Henry climbed up the boards until he could reach up and set the bucket on the roof at the edge of the jagged hole. He got a match from his pocket and struck it, then dropped it into the oil-soaked bedding. Flames shot up immediately, followed by thick gouts of gray smoke.

The morning breeze caught the smoke and began spreading it across the roof.

John Henry turned his head to look down at the others.

"Buckner, you're coming with me. Hobart, you follow us as far as the roof, and when Dav's men start shooting at us, you give us some covering fire. When we're clear, throw the bucket off the roof so it doesn't catch the building on fire."

"Where are we headed?" Buckner asked.

"We'll have to jump to the building next door. The building on the other side of it is only one story. If we make it to the roof of that one, we can get to the ground from there. Then we go after Dav. Simple as that."

"Yeah, simple," Buckner said. "Also downright crazy."

"Well, I never figured on living forever," John

Henry said. He pulled an extra Colt from his waistband and tossed it down to Buckner. "You coming?"

"Right behind you," the former deputy said. He turned and handed his rifle to Hobart. "You with us, Gil?"

"Damn right," the gravelly voiced jailer said.

John Henry scrambled up through the hole on the roof. The smoke from the bucket wasn't thick enough to hide him completely, but it had to be obscuring the vision of the riflemen posted around the jail. Shots began to crack as the men opened fire.

John Henry broke into a crouching run. Buckner pulled himself through the hole and lunged after him. Hobart emerged from the opening a couple of seconds later and stretched out on the roof. He began firing through the smoke as well, aiming at the sounds of the other shots.

The edge of the roof came up pretty quickly. John Henry had his Colt in his hand, because he didn't want to risk it falling out of his holster. He leaped into the air, planted a foot on the low wall around the edge of the building, and launched himself into space with all the power he could muster behind the jump.

The breathtaking sensation of flying through the air rushed through him, but it lasted only a second before he landed at the edge of the other roof and threw himself forward. He heard yelling and figured Buckner must have let out a shout when he made his jump. An instant later Buckner hit the roof, too, and rolled forward.

Bullets whined over their heads.

Hobart's rifle continued to crack, though, and John Henry heard a man let out a howl of pain somewhere not far away. One of Hobart's shots must have scored.

The smoke was drifting over this building as well. Buckner coughed and said, "You all right, Marshal?"

"Yeah," John Henry replied. "Let's go."

They gathered themselves, sprang up, and sprinted for the far edge of the building. This jump was easier, except for the fact that the roof of the next building along the street was slanted instead of flat. When they leaped across the gap and sprawled on it, they began to roll toward the edge.

John Henry used his toes to stop himself, then holstered his gun and slid down the rest of the way. He and Buckner hung side by side from the eaves and then dropped to the alley floor.

It felt pretty good to have solid ground under his feet again, John Henry thought.

He drew his gun and said, "All right, we'll circle around and see if we can get to the hardware store."

"I'm with you, Marshal," Buckner said. "This is gonna save me some prison time, right?"

"Maybe," John Henry said with a quick grin. "If you live through it."

With guns up and ready, they hurried along the alley and around the rear corner of the building.

The shooting continued from the top of the jail as Hobart attempted to pick off some of the deputies.

John Henry and Buckner ran along the narrow side street on which they found themselves. They had to get well away from the jail before they cut back over and tried to cross Main Street.

Dav or someone on his side must have figured out what they were trying to do and moved to cut them off, because suddenly two deputies came running around the corner of a building ahead of them. The men skidded to a halt and opened fire.

John Henry crouched and fired twice, and so did Buckner. One of the deputies doubled over and collapsed. The other one ran for cover, dragging a bloodstained and bullet-creased leg behind him.

"He's liable to get back and tell Dav where we are," Buckner said.

"Dav's probably got that figured out by now anyway," John Henry replied. "One way or another, we'll have to fight our way through to him."

"If we can kill him, that'll end this fight," Buckner said. "The rest of the bunch will cut their losses and run."

"That's what I'm counting on," John Henry said with a grim nod.

When they had covered several blocks without running into any more opposition, John Henry led the way along another alley back to Main Street. The deputies in the hardware store and the townspeople inside the jail were still shooting at each other. John Henry paused at the corner and looked around, checking for any lurking bushwhackers.

"All we can do is make a run for it," he told Buckner. "The men holed up in the hardware store won't have a very good angle to shoot at us."

"That don't mean they can't hit us."

"No, it doesn't. But we're over here and we need to be over there."

Buckner grinned and said, "I'm not arguin' with you, Marshal. I'm ready to go whenever you say the word."

John Henry paused a moment longer.

"Did you get anything worked out with Kate?" he asked.

"Well, she didn't slap my face when I told her how I feel, so I'm takin' that as a good sign. She said we'd talk about it later, when all this is over."

"I reckon that's one more good reason to stay alive," John Henry said.

With that, he burst out into the street at a dead run.

Chapter Thirty-nine

Buckner was right behind him. As bullets began to come their direction, John Henry zigzagged to throw off the aim of Dav's men. Of course, he knew there was a chance he would run right into the path of a slug, but that was a chance he had to take.

The closer they came to the other side of the street, the worse the angle for the men in the hardware store. But there were still riflemen on top of some of the buildings behind them, and John Henry was reminded of that fact when a bullet whined past his right ear and kicked up dust in the street in front of him.

That seemed like the widest street he had ever crossed, even though he knew it really wasn't. Having bullets flying around his head tended to alter a fella's perceptions. But at long last he and Buckner pounded into an alley and ducked behind some water barrels, safe for the moment.

Buckner wheezed as he tried to catch his breath.

"I ain't . . . used to . . . runnin' like that," he said. "I was always taught . . . any chore you can't do from horseback . . . ain't worth doin'."

"You wouldn't have made much of a farmer, then," John Henry said, remembering his father and many of the men he had known back in Indian Territory.

"No, sir, I . . . sure wouldn't have."

After a minute or two, they were ready to move again. As they began working their way along the back of the buildings on this side of the street, using whatever cover they could find, Buckner asked, "How many men you reckon Dav's got left?"

"Eight or nine altogether. Maybe one or two less than that."

"You've really whittled 'em down."

"That was the idea."

"If you'd asked me yesterday whether I thought anybody could break Dav's hold on this town, I'd have said no," Bucker said. "I'd have said hell, no, and anybody would be a fool to try. Danged if it ain't startin' to look like you might pull it off."

"I've had plenty of help," John Henry said. "And at least two good men have died. I don't want their deaths to be for nothing."

"If Dav comes out on top, a lot more folks will die."

"I know. And I'll do everything I can to stop that from happening."

They were getting close to the hardware store now. John Henry checked every alley before they crossed the mouth of it, just in case any of the deputies were waiting to bushwhack them. They had just gone past one of those alley mouths when John Henry heard a faint splashing sound. There had been a rain barrel in that alley, he recalled.

And from the sound of it, somebody had been hidden in that barrel. He whirled and brought up his gun, and so did Buckner.

"Hold it!" a voice ordered.

They found themselves facing Aaron Kemp, who stood in the rain barrel with water streaming down from his face and clothes. His Colt was leveled at them, but their guns were pointed at him.

No one pulled the trigger. Not yet.

"Steve!" Kemp exclaimed. "What are you doin' with this . . . this turncoat?"

"Take it easy, Aaron," Buckner urged. "We don't have to do this. That was mighty smart of you, hidin' in that rain barrel like that, though."

"You didn't answer my question. Have you changed sides?"

Buckner drew in a deep breath and said, "Yeah . . . yeah, I have. You know good and well that Dav's the craziest *hombre* we ever crossed trails with, *amigo*. I mean, good Lord, he's got poor Miz Hammond tied up there on a cross! No man in his right mind would do somethin' like that."

"We told the man we'd back his play," Kemp said stubbornly. "I don't like goin' back on my word, Steve."

"Neither do I, but sometimes things change.

When we rode in here, we didn't know the job was gonna turn out the way it has."

Kemp's eyes narrowed.

"This is about that girl, isn't it?" he asked. "Kate Collins?"

"She's in the jail with the others," Buckner said. "Dav's already tried to kill her once. If he wins, it'll go bad for her, Aaron. Mighty bad."

Kemp scowled for a second, then his face twisted in a grimace.

"Damn it, I can't throw down on a man I rode with as long as I have with you," he said. He lowered his gun. "But I'm not going to turn traitor, either. You two go on and do what you have to do. I'm heading for the stable to get my horse and ride away from here."

"That's the smart thing to do," John Henry said.

"I didn't ask for your opinion, Cobb, or whatever the hell your name is. And I'm sure as blazes not doing this for you."

Buckner said, "You go on, Aaron. We'll cross trails later."

Kemp shook his head.

"Not if I have anything to say about it. We're not pards anymore, Steve. That's the way it's gotta be."

Kemp climbed out of the barrel, shook himself off, and trotted away along the alley without looking back. Buckner watched him go with an expression of regret on his face.

"At least the two of you didn't have to shoot each other," John Henry pointed out.

"Yeah, there's that to be thankful for." Buckner jerked his head toward the hardware store. "Come on."

As they approached it, John Henry made sure all the chambers in his Colt's cylinder were full. There might not be time for reloading.

"Day's liable to have a lookout posted at the back door," Buckner warned. "Maybe you better let me go first."

"Because anybody who's been in the hardware store all night won't know that you're on our side now," John Henry mused. "That's pretty smart. You wouldn't be thinking of a last-minute double-cross, would you?"

"If I wanted to kill you, Marshal, I've had plenty of chances before now," Buckner pointed out.

"That's right." John Henry drew back behind the corner of the building. "Go ahead."

Buckner nodded and trotted toward the rear door of the hardware store. When he reached it, he banged a fist on it.

"Open up in there!" he called. "It's Buckner!"

One of the deputies jerked the door open and peered out with a surprised expression on his face.

"Steve!" he said. "Where the hell have you been? We figured those damn townies must've killed you."

The deputies in the hardware store must not have gotten a good enough look at Buckner as he dashed across the street with John Henry to recognize him. John Henry had thought that was probably the case, but it was nice to have the hunch confirmed.

"No, I'm here, come to help you boys," Buckner said. "Step out here and gimme a hand. I got somethin' that'll turn the tide for us."

The deputy came out of the store, asking, "What—"

That was as far as he got before Buckner's free hand shot out, grabbed his shirtfront, and jerked him off his feet. Buckner's gun rose and fell, and the deputy sprawled on the ground, out cold.

John Henry quickly rejoined Buckner and said, "There's no way of knowing how many are in there."

"Not without goin' in," Buckner agreed. The two men looked at each other, nodded, and charged through the door.

Four men knelt at the front windows, firing at the jail. As John Henry and Buckner came up behind them, John Henry called in a loud, commanding voice, "Drop your guns! Elevate, in the name of the law!"

Even though they were taken completely by surprise, the crooked deputies weren't going to give up without a fight. They whirled around, the rifles in their hands spitting flame.

A sack of flour on a shelf near John Henry's head exploded as a bullet struck it, sending a white cloud into the air. John Henry returned the fire and saw one of the rifleman go over backward, the Winchester flying from his hands as he collapsed over the front windowsill and hung there awkwardly.

Beside John Henry, Buckner's gun was roaring as well. He staggered but stayed on his feet as he drove a slug into the chest of another deputy.

John Henry felt the hot breath of a bullet against his cheek as he triggered again and again. Another deputy dropped his gun and clapped his hands to his suddenly crimson-spouting throat as he reeled to the side. He pitched to the floor as his lifeblood continued to gurgle out.

Buckner downed the last of the deputies with a sizzling slug into the man's belly. Silence seemed to echo in the room as the shooting abruptly ended.

"That leaves Dav," John Henry said.

"I ain't seen Carl Miller, either," Buckner said. "He's probably up on the roof with the sheriff."

"I guess we can call on them to give up," John Henry suggested. "They can't hope to win now."

Buckner shook his head.

"You do that and he'll kill Miz Hammond just for spite, if he ain't already. We got to get up there."

John Henry knew Buckner was right. He looked around and said, "Let's find a ladder."

The shooting from the jail across the street had stopped. The defenders might have heard six-guns going off and figured out that he and Buckner had reached their goal, John Henry thought. He stepped to the window so they could see him and waved to let them know that he and Buckner were all right.

"There ain't no ladder in here!" Buckner said. "I don't know how we're gonna get up there."

"How about some rope?"

Buckner grabbed a coiled lasso from a stack of them.

"We got that."

"Come on."

They hurried out into the rear alley. John Henry had done a bit of cowboying back in Indian Territory. He formed a loop in the rope and looked for some place to throw it. He didn't see any projections that would support their weight, though.

They had fought their way this far, he thought desperately, and yet they couldn't get to Dav and Miller and save Lucinda Hammond!

Suddenly Dav shouted, "Damn you, Cobb! I know you're down there somewhere! Show yourself, or I'll kill the woman right now!"

John Henry knew the crazed sheriff meant it. He glanced over at Buckner and said, "I'll go out in the street and try to draw him up to the front of the building where you can get a shot at him."

"He'll gun you down," Buckner protested.

"Maybe, but not if you get him first."

Buckner clearly didn't like the plan, but he said, "All right, we'll give it a try. I don't know what else we can do."

With the lasso still in his hand, John Henry hurried along the passage next to the building.

Buckner followed him. When they had reached the edge of the street, John Henry called, "Dav! I'm here, Dav!"

"Get out there in the street where I can see you!" Dav shouted back.

John Henry had spotted something that made him alter his plan. He tapped Buckner on the shoulder and pointed to one of the posts that held up the awning over the boardwalk. It had cracked when the false front fell on the awning, and it was bent in the middle now.

"Tie the rope around that post and pull," John Henry whispered. "When it breaks, the awning will collapse and let that false front fall on down at an angle. Maybe I can run up it to the roof."

"Without Dav and Miller shootin' you on the way?"

John Henry smiled faintly and said, "I'm counting on them being surprised enough to give me a few seconds."

"Might as well," Buckner said. "It's no crazier than anything else we've done."

John Henry noticed blood on the former deputy's shirt.

"Are you all right?" he asked.

"Just got a little crease back there. I'll be fine."

John Henry didn't know if Buckner was telling the truth, but there wasn't time to check on the wound now.

While Buckner hurried to the cracked post and began tying the rope around it, John Henry sidled out into the street, calling, "Here I am, Dav!" He still had his gun in his hand.

"Tell the people in the jail to hold their fire, or I'll shoot the woman!"

John Henry turned his head and shouted at the jail, "Turnage! Farnham! You heard him! Everybody stay out of this! It's between me and the sheriff now!"

That ought to appeal to Dav's vanity and sense of the dramatic, John Henry thought. And he was willing to take his chance in a showdown with the crooked lawman.

Dav came to the front of the building where John Henry could see him. The bullwhip still dangled from his hand. Miller stepped up behind him, holding a revolver that was aimed at Lucinda Hammond. Lucinda seemed to have passed out. Her head drooped forward and her hair hung in front of her face.

"Who are you?" Dav demanded as he glared down at John Henry.

"Deputy U.S. Marshal John Henry Sixkiller. I was sent here to put a stop to your reign of terror, Dav."

That brought a laugh from Dav.

"My so-called reign of terror is just starting, Sixkiller. I'll be running this whole territory before I'm through. And then—" He stopped short and shook his head. "But there's no need to waste time explaining everything to you. You're going to be dead in less than a minute."

John Henry glanced at Buckner, who had opened the doors of the hardware store and retreated inside. He gave a tiny nod, and Buckner heaved on the rope.

Cracked or not, the post didn't budge.

Buckner heaved again, still with no result. Obviously, the post wasn't damaged as much as John Henry had thought it was.

Then, as John Henry tried to keep the amazement off his face, two huge shapes loomed up behind Buckner, who got out of the way in a hurry as Peabody and Nate Farnham strode past him. They must have seen what he and Buckner were trying to do, gotten out of the jail somehow, and circled around to come in the back of the hardware store. They didn't bother with the rope. Instead they stepped out onto the boardwalk, wrapped their arms around the post, and put their massive muscles to work like a pair of father and son Samsons.

The post didn't stand a chance.

It broke all the way with a sharp crack, and more splintering sounded as the awning collapsed and the false front lying on top of it tipped down toward the ground. John Henry hoped the Farnhams had been able to throw themselves backward, out of the way of the falling debris. He lunged forward, breaking into a run that carried him swiftly toward the toppling false front.

It landed at an angle, its top wedged against the ground. John Henry bounded onto it, his momentum carrying him up the steep angle. Something popped loudly, but it wasn't a gun. Dav lashed at him with the bullwhip. He felt the sharp sting as it cracked against his shoulder but kept coming. The next strike caught him on the wrist and made him drop his gun.

But he was close enough now to tackle Dav. The sheriff yelled in surprise and alarm as he toppled forward. He and John Henry rolled back down the inclined false front, slugging at each other.

They hit the street in a welter of dust. Dav was still trying to use the bullwhip on him, but John Henry thrust up his arm and let the braided strand coil around it. He slammed a punch into Dav's face with his other fist, then flipped the slack in the whip around the sheriff's neck. John Henry caught hold of the whip with his other hand and twisted, tightening the loop that encircled Dav's throat.

Dav kicked and flailed, but John Henry didn't let off on the pressure. At this moment there was no mercy in John Henry Sixkiller. He hung on as Dav's struggles grew more and more frantic. Not only were Dav's grandiose dreams slipping away from him, but so was his life and he had to know that.

Wilhelm Heinsdorf had thought that Dav was some sort of supernatural monster, a creature of the darkness that could not be killed. But Samuel Dav was a human being. Terribly flawed, but still a human being.

Anything human could die.

And so he did, on this clear morning, under a blue sky washed clean by the storm of the night before. John Henry felt Dav's muscles go slack, so, too, the man's purple face and protruding tongue and eyes.

But he didn't let go of the whip for another couple of minutes, just to be sure.

John Henry's head was swimming. So much had happened, and now as he eased his hold on the whip, reaction set in. He was barely aware of what was going on as strong hands gripped him and lifted him to his feet. He looked up and saw several men cutting Lucinda Hammond loose from the cross. Peabody Farnham held him up and rumbled, "Are you all right, Marshal?"

"Yeah," John Henry rasped. "Miller?"

"Dead," Farnham said. "He tried to get away when he saw you choking the life out of Dav. That fella Buckner stopped him."

"If you want a real sheriff for a change," John Henry said, "you might do worse than Buckner."

"He worked for Dav!"

"A man can change. I reckon Buckner's proved that." John Henry looked around. "What about the other deputies? Were any of them left alive?"

"Only the ones locked up in the jail. It's all over, Marshal. You've saved the town."

"We saved the town," John Henry said. "All of us together."

Alvin Turnage hurried toward them, a sheaf of

papers in his hand. He was clearly excited about something, but the first thing he asked was, "Marshal, are you all right?"

"I'll live," John Henry said. "What's that you've got there?"

"Something I found in a locked box in Dav's desk," Turnage said. "And you need to take a look at it."

What John Henry really wanted to do right now was wash down some breakfast with a few cups of coffee and then sleep for about a week. But he took the documents from Turnage and forced himself to concentrate on them. As he realized what he was looking at, he knew that Peabody Farnham had been wrong a few moments earlier.

This wasn't over yet.

Chapter Forty

Three days later, John Henry walked into the Palace of the Governors in Santa Fe and asked to see Governor Lew Wallace.

The governor's aide, Filipe Montoya, stared up at him in obvious surprise.

"Señor Sixkiller," he said. "You have returned."

"I know," John Henry said with a grin. "Pretty far-fetched, isn't it?"

Montoya stood up from his desk and said, "I'll take you to see the governor right now. I know he'll be anxious to hear what you have to say."

Wallace was writing again when Montoya showed John Henry into the office.

"Still putting that fella Ben-Hur through his paces?" John Henry asked as he took off his hat and held it in his left hand.

"A chariot race, in fact." Wallace set his pen aside and stood up to offer John Henry his hand. "Do you have a report for me, Marshal Sixkiller?"

"I do," John Henry said.

Wallace nodded and said, "That'll be all, Filipe."

"Actually," John Henry said, "I'd like for Señor Montoya to stay, if that's all right with you, Governor."

"Me?" Montoya said in evident surprise. "But why?"

"Because you play an important part in this, *señor.*" John Henry dropped his hat in a chair and used his left hand to reach into his coat. He brought out a folded sheaf of papers and set them on Wallace's desk. "There's my report, along with some other documents, Governor. Samuel Dav is dead, along with a number of the gunmen he hired as deputies. The other so-called deputies are locked up in Chico's jail. It's undergoing some repairs, but it's still sturdy enough to hold those varmints."

Wallace looked astonished. He said, "I didn't expect you to go in there and . . . and clean up the whole town, Marshal!"

"Then why'd you send me?" John Henry asked in a genuinely puzzled voice.

A bark of laughter came from Wallace.

"Why indeed?" he said. "It's just rare to find a man who performs his job so efficiently these days. Congratulations, sir."

"Well, that's not quite all of it," John Henry said. "There's still Señor Montoya's part."

Montoya shook his head and said, "I have no

part in this. I'm confused, Governor. I don't know what this man is talking about."

"I'm talking about the plan you hatched with Dav to take over the territory," John Henry said, a hard edge coming into his voice. "You were going to build him up and get him appointed territorial governor, but you'd be the real power behind him, pulling his strings. I could read between the lines of what you wrote to Dav, even if he couldn't. He'd convinced himself that he would be running things and you'd just be helping him. But it would have been the other way around."

"That's insane!" Montoya said.

"And very confusing," Wallace said. "Why in the world would this Samuel Dav be appointed territorial governor? I'm not planning on stepping down from the post anytime soon."

John Henry smiled and said, "Oh, they were going to assassinate you, Governor. And then, once they were running things, they were going to let the Mexican army come in here and take over. They were going to sell the whole territory back to Mexico. It would have been just about the biggest act of land piracy in history."

Wide-eyed, Montoya jabbed a finger at John Henry and exclaimed, "He's *loco*! None of that is true, Governor! It . . . it's the ravings of a madman!"

"It's all right there in the papers, in your writing, *señor*," John Henry said mildly. "You expected Dav to destroy them, but he didn't. Maybe he was a mite suspicious of you after all and wanted something to hold over your head if he needed to. Anyway, I guess we should leave the governor to look them over." John Henry paused. "I expect he'll recognize your hand, Montoya."

The aide's face contorted with hatred. His hand dived under his coat and came out with a small, nickel-plated pistol. He had to know that he couldn't talk his way out of all the evidence against him, but at least he could shoot the man who had ruined his plans.

But John Henry was already moving, stepping forward swiftly. His left hand caught Montoya's wrist and wrenched it aside as the aide fired. The gun went off with a little *crack*, but the bullet thudded harmlessly into the thick adobe wall.

The next second, John Henry's right fist crashed into Montoya's jaw. The punch slewed Montoya's head to the side. His eyes rolled up in their sockets and he collapsed, out cold. John Henry took the gun out of his hand, just in case.

Placing the pistol on the desk next to the papers, John Henry said, "I guess that's one more bit of proof, Governor, but it wasn't really necessary. There's plenty there to put Montoya behind bars for a long, long time."

Wallace looked shaken. He passed a hand over his face and said, "Good Lord, I . . . I never suspected. Filipe always seemed like a loyal friend."

"Maybe he was once. But people can change."

He thought about Steve Buckner and Edgar Wellman. Buckner had risked his life to put things right in Chico, and Wellman had sacrificed his trying to save Lucinda Hammond. John Henry had heard about that from Lucinda while she was recovering from the ordeal she had gone through.

Yes, people could change . . . but thankfully, that went both ways.

And although Samuel Dav had done a great deal of damage in Chico, both physical and emotional, most of that damage could be repaired. The town would survive and flourish, John Henry thought.

He reached for his hat.

"You're leaving?" Wallace asked.

"Job's done."

"There's that other business I mentioned when you were here before, down in Lincoln County . . ."

"I'm sorry, Governor," John Henry said with a smile and a shake of his head. "I'm going home."

TURN THE PAGE FOR AN EXCITING PREVIEW

THE GREATEST WESTERN WRITER
OF THE 21ST CENTURY

It's Springtime in Wyoming. Preacher is on the move, joining a trail drive led by freewheeling adventurer Wiley Courtland. Wiley has good horses to deliver to the American Fur Company at Fort Gifford. An Indian war party, led by the cunning and ruthless Red Knife, has other plans.

Furiously fighting their way to safety, the horse traders make it to Fort Gifford, where the beautiful wife of the fort's commander makes a raid of her own, with the help of Preacher's newfound buddy Wiley. While jealousy erupts, Red Knife and his bloodthirsty legion of warriors come galloping over the horizon—and lay siege to the fort. Before help can come, an act of treachery opens the gates to a massacre . . .

Only one man survives the carnage. From the smoke and blood, he emerges, clinging to his life and loaded for bear. On his own—the way he likes it—Preacher begins his war of revenge . . .

PREACHER'S MASSACRE
by William W. Johnstone
with J. A. Johnstone

Coming in January 2013
Wherever Pinnacle Books are sold!

Chapter One

Springtime in the Rocky Mountains was mighty pretty, thought Preacher, but not so much when some varmints were trying to kill you.

Which was what was happening now. It was hard to appreciate the beauties of nature when you were stretched out behind a log with a handful of bloodthirsty savages closing in on you.

He sure wished he could get to his pistols. He had four of them, all double-shotted and heavily charged, and if he could get to them he would be able to cut a wide, bloody swath through the warriors who had jumped him first thing this morning, just as the sun was coming up.

He had gone down to the creek to get some water for the coffeepot. Normally he would have tucked a couple of the flintlock pistols behind the broad leather belt cinched around his waist, but he hadn't put the belt on yet this morning.

It was a greenhorn mistake, and that bothered

Preacher as much or more than the fact that he might die in the next few minutes. He'd always figured on dying, but he didn't like the idea of it happening because he'd done something foolish or careless. He had spent most of the past twenty-five years in these mountains, dealing with the frontier's dangers on a daily basis, and he should have known better.

"You're gettin' old, Preacher," he said aloud. "And you're gonna have to be mighty lucky to keep on gettin' any older."

Of course, he was fortunate that the first arrow to come flying out of the trees hadn't killed him. If he hadn't twisted and bent down at just the right time to fill the coffeepot, the arrow would have buried itself between his shoulder blades instead of slicing a little gash in the side of his neck as it went past him. When he felt that, he'd reacted instantly by launching into a dive that carried him behind a fallen tree at the edge of the stream.

More arrows had whipped through the air above him. Others thudded into the log. He got a good enough look at them to tell that they were Blackfoot arrows.

That eliminated any chance of talking his way out of this. The Blackfeet hated him with a special passion stronger than any of the other tribes. He had killed many of their warriors over the years, often by slipping into the sleeping villages and cutting throats. Some of the Indians called him Ghost Killer because of his ability to get in and out of their camps without being seen and leaving death in his wake.

Once, many, many years earlier, when he was just beginning to get the reputation that still followed him, the Blackfeet had captured him. They had tied him to a stake, and come morning they would have lit a fire at his feet and burned him to death. He was powerless to do anything except talk.

So talk he had. Recalling a street preacher he had seen back in St. Louis, he began exhorting his captors with a voluminous intensity that would have put many a hellfire-and-brimstone sin-shouter to shame.

Kept it up all night, he did, and by morning, when the Blackfeet had planned on killing him, they were curious to see how long he could keep going. Too curious to kill him, which was just what Preacher intended.

He wasn't sure how many hours that ordeal had lasted, but in the end the Blackfeet let him go, impressed by his oratory. They'd had plenty of reasons to regret that decision since then, but Preacher surely didn't.

The story of how he'd escaped from certain death got around, as such stories will, and the young man who'd gone by the name Art got tagged with the moniker Preacher instead. He'd been called that for so long by now that it seemed like his given name.

The warriors who now had him pinned down behind the log wouldn't be interested in hearing any preaching. All they wanted was his hair, which was thick and dark and just starting to be flecked with silver, like his beard.

Preacher looked around, taking stock of his situation. He had his hunting knife in a sheath strapped to his right calf. He had the coffeepot, which was heavy enough to serve as a bludgeon. A couple of feet away lay a fairly thick broken branch. If it wasn't too rotten, it might make a decent club.

Those were close-quarters weapons, though. They wouldn't do him any good against bows and arrows.

He wasn't sure how many enemies lurked in the trees and brush. At least three, because he had seen arrows flying from that many locations at the same time. That proved it wasn't an actual Blackfoot war party that had attacked him, but the warriors might be scouts from a larger group. One of them might have even gone back to fetch the others already, which meant that if he was going to have a chance to fight his way out of this, it had to be soon.

To do that, he had to draw them closer, and that wasn't likely to happen unless they thought he was dead. To accomplish that goal, he would have to try something pretty risky.

But since he was likely to wind up dead anyway, what did it matter?

Moving fast, he pushed himself halfway to his feet as if he were about to make a run for it. Instantly, bowstrings *twanged* and arrows sliced through the air. Preacher twisted out of the way of a couple of them, but the third arrow raked along his side, ripping his buckskin shirt and drawing a fiery finger of pain across his flesh.

That was just what he wanted. He let out a yell and flopped gracelessly to the ground behind the log, landing on his back. The arrow was between his arm and his body where he had clamped his arm down on it. The shaft stuck straight up in the air as if the arrow had gone all the way through him.

He shuddered and twitched like his body was going through its death throes, and the arrow jumped around accordingly. The warriors hidden in the trees had to be able to see it sticking up above the log. After a moment Preacher grew still and lay there absolutely motionless.

Time dragged by. Blackfoot warriors were no fools. They would be wary of a trick.

But they would also be curious, and eager to take the scalp of the notorious mountain man who was responsible for the deaths of so many of their fellows.

The little animal noises that had fallen silent earlier now started up again. Had the Blackfeet left? Impossible, Preacher decided. Even if they had decided not to scalp him, they wouldn't go off without making sure he was dead.

In the early morning quiet, he heard his stallion moving around a few yards away. Horse wasn't happy. He snorted and snuffled and danced around skittishly, smelling the bear grease on the warriors' hair. If he had caught that scent earlier, he would have given Preacher some warning, but the lurkers had skillfully avoided getting upwind of the camp.

Dog, the big, wolflike cur who was Preacher's other longtime trail companion, was off hunting somewhere. He would be back, but maybe not in time to be of any help.

Preacher couldn't hold that against him. Dog had saved his life more times than the mountain man could count.

No, it was up to him, he thought as the sun climbed above the trees and began to shine down in his face. He closed his eyes against the glare.

More time crawled by. Preacher breathed as shallowly as possible so the arrow wouldn't move around enough for the Blackfeet to notice. What were they going to do, let him lie here all day before they came to lift his hair?

Something moved between him and the light and stayed there. Preacher hadn't heard any footsteps, but that wasn't surprising. Just like him, the Blackfeet could move mighty quiet when they wanted to.

His eyes flew open just as one of the warriors was stepping over the log, knife in hand to cut Preacher's scalp away from his head. Preacher snatched the arrow from between his arm and body, reversed it, and rammed the sharp flint head as hard as he could up into the warrior's groin.

The man screamed in agony and dropped his

knife. Preacher snatched it out of midair as it fell and rolled to the side. The other two warriors had hung back a few yards with their bows ready, just in case of a trick. They both fired, but Preacher was moving too fast for them to hit him. The arrows bracketed him.

His arm drew back and snapped forward. The knife flashed through the air and caught one of the other warriors in the throat. The blade went deep, causing blood to spurt out around it. The man gurgled and staggered as he dropped his bow to paw futilely at the wound.

The third warrior had another arrow out and was trying to nock it to his bow, but Preacher had already grabbed up the coffeepot and hurled the log. The Blackfoot threw the bow and arrow aside, knowing that Preacher was too close, and grabbed for the tomahawk at his waist.

The move came too late. Preacher swung the coffeepot and smashed it against the side of the warrior's head. Bone crunched under the brutal impact. The Indian fell and began to twitch and shudder, much as Preacher had done earlier. The death spasms were real this time, though.

Preacher dropped the pot and grabbed the warrior's tomahawk just in case either of the other Blackfeet was still alive. He quickly saw that precaution wasn't necessary. Both men had bled to death from the wounds he'd inflicted on them.

Somehow he was still alive, with nothing to show

from the encounter except a couple of scratches that didn't amount to anything.

"Horse, I reckon you're lookin' at the luckiest son of a gun on the face of the earth," he told the restive stallion.

But that luck could still run out. A strong possibility still existed that a Blackfoot war party was in the area. He needed to clear out, get up higher in the mountains, find a place where he could fort up if he had to.

If these three dead men were indeed scouts for a larger group, one thing he could count on was that as soon as the other Blackfeet discovered the corpses, they would come looking for him.

And he didn't want to be found.

Chapter Two

He had gotten his gear packed up and was tightening the cinch on Horse's saddle when Dog came bounding into the clearing beside the creek.

"Now you show up," Preacher drawled as the big cur stiffened and approached the bloody bodies to sniff at them. "Could've used a hand a little while ago."

Dog just looked at him and cocked his head a little to the side.

"Naw, I ain't mad at you," Preacher went on. "We got to pull out, though, and can't waste any time doin' it."

Less than five minutes later, Preacher was riding away from the campsite. He sent Horse into the shallow stream and followed the rocky bed with Dog splashing along beside them. The water was cold, but it stayed that way year-round because of the snowmelt from the white-capped peaks around them.

Tall pines covered the steep slopes higher up. Here in the valleys, aspen, juniper, and birch lined the creeks. Wildflowers bloomed in some of the meadows. Birds flitted from branch to branch in the trees. Preacher saw a moose raise its antlered head at the other end of a long, grassy park.

There was nothing in the world he liked better than being in these mountains, which was why he always returned to them when life took him to other places for a while. They were the only real home he had ever known. Even when he'd been a kid, living on his folks' farm back East, he hadn't felt like he'd belonged there. He had left as soon as he could, setting out to see the elephant, as the old-timers said.

He had seen the elephant, all right. Seen it and then some.

A smaller creek flowed into the stream he'd been following. He turned Horse and sent the stallion walking upstream. Within a few hundred yards, the creek bed began to rise and soon became too rocky and steep for Horse to keep going in the water. Preacher rode out onto the bank.

He dismounted and let all three of them rest for a few minutes. Then, holding Horse's reins, he led the stallion up the slope with the waters of the creek dancing and bubbling down alongside them. Dog bounded ahead to lead the way through the brush.

An hour of walking lifted them a long way above

the valley where Preacher had encountered the Blackfeet. The view was spectacular from the spot where Preacher paused to rest again. Mountains and valleys fell away all around them. He could see so far the distance became hazy even to his eagle-keen eyes.

He didn't spend a lot of time taking in the scenery, though. Instead he searched the landscape below them for any sign of pursuit.

At first it appeared there wasn't any, but then he spotted a flash of motion and color. Might have been a bird, might have been a face painted for war, he told himself. He concentrated on the area. A few moments later, sunlight winked on something metal in the same area.

A rifle barrel or a knife, Preacher thought. Definitely not a bird.

"Let's go," he said quietly to Horse and Dog. "They're down there lookin' for us."

He used the trees for cover as much as possible. The creek reached a spot where it had carved a narrow canyon into the rock. That canyon formed a pass of sorts on the side of the mountain. It looked wide enough for Preacher to get through it with the stallion. They had to cross a short stretch of open, rocky ground to reach it. He worried about being spotted while they were doing that, but the canyon was the best route away from the war party that he could see.

A hundred yards in, it grew even narrower. If it came to a dead end at a waterfall, he and his friends might be trapped in here, Preacher mused.

But if that turned out to be the case, the Blackfeet could only come at him one or two at a time in the cramped confines of this canyon. He would have his pistols and his rifle ready, and he would take them on until he ran out of powder and shot, and then he would meet them with knife and tomahawk. They would kill him in the end, but they would pay a hell of a price to do so.

Then, after a mile or so of the rock walls pressing in so close that they scraped on Horse's flanks and the sky was just a thin ribbon of blue overhead, the canyon opened out again into several valleys that branched off through the mountains. To Preacher's left was a small pool where water trickling down an almost sheer cliff gathered before forming the creek he'd been following.

This was a good place to stop for a while. He hunkered on his haunches next to the pool and made a late lunch on jerky and pemmican he took from a pouch tied to his saddle.

High above his head, a couple of eagles rode the wind currents, swooping and gliding in apparent joy at being free and living in such a place. Preacher knew how they felt.

After he had eaten and rested, he found a game trail that curled around the shoulder of the mountain and followed it to a bench where some pronghorn antelope grazed. They bounded away at the sight of him. If he hadn't been trying to dodge those Blackfeet, he might have stalked and killed one of the antelope and had fresh meat for a while, but under the circumstances he wasn't just about to risk a shot.

On the far side of the bench, at the base of a granite cliff, he found several giant slabs of rock that had sheared off and slid down over the centuries. They leaned against the cliff so that they formed a cave-like area. It was big enough for him and his two companions. He might even be able to have a small fire for warmth once the sun went down. At this altitude the nights got pretty chilly no matter what season it was.

The sun was low by the time he unsaddled Horse. It had been a long day, starting early with that fight with the Blackfeet, and he had pushed himself and his friends pretty hard.

He built the fire right up against the leaning rock so that its face would reflect the heat. After it burned down, its embers ought to keep them fairly warm the whole night, he hoped.

After another skimpy meal, he spread his bedroll and crawled into his blankets. All four pistols and his rifle were close beside him. He hoped he wouldn't need them. He had put a lot of distance between himself and the three dead warriors, and he had used every trick he knew to cover his tracks. All he could do now was hope that it had been enough.

He didn't fall asleep right away. It was very dark behind the rocks, but some starlight filtered in around them. Dog lay against him on the side away from the guns. He felt the big cur's steady breathing.

If not for the worry about the Blackfeet, it would have been a mighty peaceful night.

His thoughts strayed back over the past few months. Preacher and three of his friends had spent the winter with a German trader named Horst Gruenwald, who was better known in the mountains as Blind Pete, even though he wasn't blind.

Pete's trading post had been burned down by some of Preacher's enemies—now deceased—so it only seemed fair that Preacher help him rebuild it. That was what he had done, with assistance from Audie, Nighthawk, and Lorenzo. The diminutive Audie and the taciturn Nighthawk were old friends who had shared many a camp with Preacher. The black man Lorenzo had come west from St. Louis with Preacher after helping him settle a score back there. They were all boon companions, as the storybooks might have phrased it.

But once the weather had turned nicer, Audie and Nighthawk had set out to do some trapping on their own, and Lorenzo had decided to remain at the trading post with Pete, who was glad to have the help.

"My rheumatism's gettin' worse, and I ain't gettin' any younger," Lorenzo had explained to Preacher. "I don't think I'm in any shape to go trampin' around all over these mountains with you, Preacher, much as I might like to."

"Well, that's fine, Lorenzo," he'd said. "I'll miss your company, but I understand."

"You can come by here any time you want to,

whilst you're traipsin' around gatherin' up them beaver pelts."

"Yah," Pete had put in. "You are always most welcome here, Preacher."

Preacher had smiled and told them he would see them again, and then he'd set out, alone except for Dog and Horse, not sure exactly where he was going but knowing that he had to shake the dust off his feet and rattle his hocks. He never stayed in any one place for too long, and for Preacher, alone had never meant lonely.

Sometime while he was remembering the winter he had spent with his friends, he dozed off.

He slept soundly until Dog stiffened against him and a soft growl came from deep within the big cur's throat.

The gray light inside the shelter of the rocks meant that dawn was approaching. He listened and heard voices. The guttural sound told him they were Blackfeet.

He pushed the blankets aside, then rolled over onto his belly and picked up the rifle. A few feet away, a tiny crack between the rocks would allow him to look out onto the bench. He crawled over to it and put his eye to the gap.

His field of vision was narrow, but he was able to see several warriors on horseback riding through the newly green grass about seventy yards away. Preacher spoke the Blackfoot language fluently, so he had no trouble understanding them as they talked to each other. At this distance he couldn't pick up all the words, but he garnered the gist of the conversation.

They were looking for him, of course, but they hadn't actually followed his trail up here. Their war chief—Red Knife, Preacher thought the name was—had his warriors scattered all to hell and gone searching for the man who had killed the three scouts beside the creek.

Preacher had heard of Red Knife, although he'd never run into the man before. The stories said that the Blackfoot war chief had a special hatred of white men and killed them anywhere, anytime he could.

A couple of the passing riders glanced toward the rocks where Preacher, Horse, and Dog were hidden, but they looked away again without showing any interest. From where they were, they couldn't tell this little pocket was behind the massive stone slabs.

They rode on to the far end of the bench, turned around, and circled back. Preacher couldn't see them the whole way, but he tracked their movements by the sound of their voices. From time to time Dog growled, and Preacher put a hand on his thick fur and whispered, "Easy, old son, easy."

By the time the sun peeked over the horizon, the Indians were gone. Preacher figured they would join up with Red Knife and the rest of the war party and report that their quarry wasn't to be found in this direction. That was a good break for him, he thought. They would all move on and look elsewhere for him, and eventually they would give up the search.

"We're gonna squat right here for a day or two and give those heathens time to leave this part of the country," Preacher told his animal companions. "Then we'll work our way north and find some good trappin' country."

That sounded like a fine plan to him, and it probably would have been, too, if he hadn't seen the dust cloud a couple of days later as he was getting ready to leave this hideout among the boulders.

But there it was, too small to be caused by a buffalo stampede and moving too steadily for that as well, but big enough he could tell that it came from a large group of horses or some other animals. He was curious, since that was his nature, but more than that, he knew that if he could spot the dust cloud, so could somebody else, namely Red Knife . . . if the Blackfoot war party was still around.

So he saddled up and headed east out of the mountains, down onto the plains.